JAMES CRUMLEY'S
DANCING BEAR

"If you like your detective fiction tough and tenacious you will love James Crumley. . . . No one does it better."
— THE HOUSTON CHRONICLE

"Crumley works with fever on the brow, and the most lyrical and true English sentences I've seen lately. *Dancing Bear* is a wonder of compression, truth and wisdom."
— BARRY HANNAH

"Top-notch . . . an imaginative narrative sense, chaotic and even manic, but violently dramatic . . . excitingly new."
— THE LOS ANGELES TIMES
BOOK REVIEW

"A clear triumph."
— THE CLEVELAND PLAIN
DEALER

"*Dancing Bear* is a powerful novel by a writer of extraordinary power who mixes humor with blood, environmental issues with cocaine jangles and post-coital blues, the Dancing Bear Wilderness Area of Montana with peppermint schnapps and hopelessness."
— THE EL PASO HERALD POST

"Extremely well-written."
— THE NEW YORK TIMES
BOOK REVIEW

ALSO AVAILABLE IN VINTAGE CONTEMPORARIES

Dancing Bear

Dancing Bear

James Crumley

Vintage Contemporaries

VINTAGE BOOKS · A DIVISION OF RANDOM HOUSE · NEW YORK

First Vintage Books Edition, September 1984
Copyright © 1983 by James Crumley
All rights reserved under International and Pan-American
Copyright Conventions. Published in the United States by
Random House, Inc., New York, and simultaneously in
Canada by Random House of Canada Limited, Toronto.
Originally published by Random House, Inc. in 1983.
Library of Congress Cataloging in Publication Data
Crumley, James, 1939-
Dancing bear.
I. Title.
[PS3553.R78D3 1984]   813'.54   84-40008
ISBN 0-394-72576-X (pbk.)
Manufactured in the United States of America
Front page photo copyright © 1984 by Lee Nye

For the Dump Family Singers

— Orris, Nelon, Young Eugene, Ma,

and Little Shorty

Dancing Bear

... and remember, my little grandchildren, in the old days there were more bears than Indian people, black bears and brown bears, cinnamon bears and the great grizzly, and we had no honey, no sweetness in the teepees, and Brother Bee was always angry, going around stinging the Indian people. The bears always found the bee trees before the Indian people, ripped them apart, ate the honeycomb, and stole the honey with their sharp claws and rough tongues. And the bees were always angry, because the bears, poor souls, did not know about the sacred smoke to make the bees feel friendly, and the bears did not know about the songs of thanksgiving so the bees would forgive them, but worst of all, the bears suffered from greed and they always took all the honey, left none for the bees. The bears knew about honey but not about bees, so the Indian people had no sweetness in the teepees.

Then one day, little grandchildren, a young man of peace, Chil-a-ma-cho, He Who Dreams Awake, came upon a ruined bee tree. Even though there was no honey left for him to take and even though the bees were very angry, he smoked his pipe with the bees and sang the songs of thanksgiving for all the good things of the earth. And when the bees smelled the sacred smoke and heard the songs, they settled down and went about their business. In return, the Grandmother Bee gave Chil-a-ma-cho a vision.

When he woke from the dream, he blessed the Grandmother Bee for her wisdom, then followed the tracks of Brother Bear across the mountains to the edge of a chokecherry thicket by the meadows where once we dug the camas root, singing the songs of thanksgiving and the songs of sadness as he went along. In the thicket he found Brother Bear sleeping, his breath still sweet with honeycomb, and Chil-a-ma-cho prayed to the spirit of Brother Bear for forgiveness, then plunged his lance into the bear's throat. Once again, as we always should, little grandchildren, Chil-a-ma-cho prayed for forgiveness for killing one of Mother Earth's precious beasts. Then he skinned the hide from Brother Bear, ate the liver and the heart dipped in gall, scraped the fat from the hide, saved it, then worked the skin for three days and three nights with the brains until it was as soft as a deerskin shirt. For another three days and three nights, he purified himself with fire and fasting and bathing away his man smell. Then he rubbed his skin with the fat of Brother Bear and put the hide on his shoulders.

When the moon rose high over the meadows, little grandchildren, Chil-a-ma-cho walked on all fours into the open, grunting and snuffling, speaking the bear language the Grandmother Bee had given him. When the other bears around came to greet their new brother, Chil-a-ma-cho began to dance the steps the Grandmother Bee had given him. The first night the other bears thought their new brother must have come from someplace beyond the mountains where the bears were crazy, so they went back into the lodge-pole pine to watch. The second night a few danced with him to be polite, as we must be to our brothers from beyond the mountains, and on the third night they all joined in, danced and danced in the sacred circle, danced until all the bears dropped.

The next day as the bears slept, Chil-a-ma-cho led the Benniwah as they followed the bees, the bees whose legs were hairy with pollen, led them to the bee trees and the honey. The People were happy, in a hurry for honey, but Chil-a-ma-cho made them make the friendly smoke, made them leave half the honey for the bees, made them sing the songs of forgiveness. The bees forgave the Benniwah, and stopped going around stinging everybody.

After that we had sweetness in our lodges—except for Chil-a-ma-cho, who gave himself to the dancing and the bears and never ate honey, and it is for his memory that the Benniwah forsake honey during the days of the Bear Dance before we harvest the honey with the sacred smoke and sing the songs of forgiveness for sweetness in the lodges.

Of course, as you well know, little grandchildren, sometime later the white man showed up, and now there are not too many Indian people and even fewer bears, and even Brother Bee, bless his spirit, lives in a little square house and works for the white man. There has not been much sweetness in this world, or the next, since then, not much dancing either. Even He Who Dreams Awake, Chil-a-ma-cho, sleeps.

—A BENNIWAH TALE

Chapter 1

We had been blessed with a long, easy fall for western Montana. The two light snowfalls had melted before noon, and in November we had three weeks of Indian Summer so warm and seductive that even we natives seemed to forget about winter. But in the canyon of Hell Roaring Creek, where I live, when the morning breezes stirred off the stone-cold water and into the golden, dying rustle of the cottonwoods and creek willows, you could smell the sear, frozen heart of winter, February, or, as the Indians sometimes called it, the Moon of the Children Weeping in the Lodges, crying in hunger.

I worked the night shift for Haliburton Security, though, and didn't see or smell much of the mornings that fall, since I spent them wrapped in a down comforter with the creek-side window open wide to the cold morning breeze, only my nose, stuffy with cigarette smoke and the sweet stench of peppermint schnapps, exposed to the wind.

On this particular November morning, though, when a rumbling clatter crossed the loose boards of my front porch and a sharp rattle at my screen door jerked me halfway out of a hangover sleep, the cold breeze in my nose told me it was nowhere near noontime, far too early in the morning for civilized behavior. In the first confused moments of waking, I thought it might be a bear rummaging in my trash cans. Then I remembered it was fall, and the bears usually came down out of the Diablo Range in the spring after a hard winter sleeping. Besides, the city of Meriwether had grown up the canyon over the years, a flood of houses and people that stretched for miles beyond my small log house nestled at the head of Milodragovitch Park, so the bears did not come down to my house anymore. Even if they chanced a journey through all the pastel plywood houses, they wouldn't find an easy meal waiting in a tin trash can, but all my garbage securely bound in a fifty-five-gallon drum with a locking lid. A meal only a grizzly could eat; and nobody had seen a silvertip on this side of the Diablos in forty or fifty years. The only danger to my garbage can came from the huge new automated trucks that picked them up; sometimes the front lift held the cans too tightly, ruptured them like rotten fruit, or banged the sides flat as the lift dumped the trash into the bed of the tasteful blue garbage trucks. Progress, they called it: garbage untouched by human hands, safe from hungry bears.

Then the pounding on my front door brought me back to the present as it clearly became the rap of knuckles falling directly on the large plastic sign that politely asked that I not be disturbed before noon. During the two years and four months I had been working for Haliburton Security, I hadn't been sleeping very well. The boredom of the work—rattling doorknobs, guarding twenty-four convenience markets, and holding the hands of lost children in shopping malls—had caused a sudden, and unseemly in a man of my years, affection for cocaine. I slept through the mornings, true, but badly, lightly. I had taken the bell out of my telephone and put the sign on the front door, but it seemed nothing helped.

The pounding went on, a dull echo bound within the thick log walls, booming inside my head. I hadn't been asleep long enough to have a hangover; I was still half drunk. I feared I knew whose fist tolled for me. Sometimes my next-door neighbor came over in the mornings after her husband had left for work. Usually she wanted a toot or two, then some sordid business in my bedroom. She was young and athletic and not bad-looking for a mean, skinny girl, and I might have enjoyed her visits a bit more if I hadn't known that her husband worked two jobs just to keep her outfitted in a rainbow's hue of ski clothes and lift tickets and to keep up the payments on her new white Corvette. Ignorance might not be bliss, but too often knowledge took the fun out of some parts of life.

As I rolled out of bed and struggled into my jeans I tried to think of some way to put her off, but I had run out of exotic venereal diseases and disabling prostate disorders. Resigned to my fate, I stumbled to the door. But when I opened it, a postman in a summer uniform holding a clipboard stood on my porch, his hairy fist raised for another resounding knock. He looked as bad as I felt and as if he didn't care if he hit me or the door.

"Can't you read?" I groaned, jerking a thumb at my sign.

"Of course," he grunted, "but she said it would be all right." Then he nodded to where my next-door neighbor was standing in her driveway, dressed in a heavy sweater and a down vest while she serenely washed the dew and pulp mill smog off her beloved automobile. She smirked wisely, an eyetooth glistening in the curl of her thin upper lip.

"Special Delivery Certified Mail," the postman announced with chattering teeth. "Sign here," he said, then prodded me with the cold metal ring atop his clipboard.

"Ouch," I said, then looked at him.

He stared at me out of two painfully bloodshot eyes sunk into a swarthy, unshaven face. His short-sleeved shirt and short pants fit him like a dirty sack. Even his shoes looked too large, and when he danced as the cold breeze licked his legs, his shoes didn't move.

"Sign here," he said again.

"Who's it from?" I asked. Back in the old days when I worked as a private investigator out of my own office and when I made enough money to afford the string of ex-wives I had somehow accumulated, I learned the hard way not to sign for mail I didn't want. "Well, who's it from?"

"What the hell difference does it make?" he answered, then held the clipboard to his chest. "Just sign the son of a bitch before I freeze to death."

"No way," I said, then briefly wondered if it was against the law to impersonate a mailman to deliver a subpoena. "I'll just pick it up at the post office," I said; "maybe your supervisor will be kind enough to tell me who it's from."

"Stuff my supervisor," he said as he got me in the belly with the clipboard again. "Either sign here, man, or I'll shit-can it, and you can whistle Dixie, asshole."

"I'm a taxpayer, jerk," I said, which was partially true, "and you've got a dirty mouth for a government employee. What's your name?"

"No more shit," he muttered, dancing in a small circle, the clipboard raised, "no more fucking shit." Then he broke the clipboard over my head.

For a moment both of us were too stunned to move, then we went to the ground growling like a pair of rabid dogs, snarling and snapping, biting and scratching as we tumbled off the porch and onto the dew-damp grass, our hands at each other's throats, our teeth bared, too mad to consider technique, and if my next-door neighbor hadn't turned her hose on us, we might have hurt ourselves, but once we were wet, we were just too cold to fight.

Things took a bit to straighten out, but ten minutes later we were warm again, sitting at my breakfast bar wrapped in blankets and huddled over cups of coffee and shots of schnapps while my next-door neighbor ran the postman's uniform through her dryer. We compared wounds and laughed at ourselves, discussed the long-term tensions of marital discord. He had spent the night before drinking and fighting with his second wife, and when he passed out on the kitchen floor in his boxer shorts, his wife, in some demented vision of revenge for unnamed sins, gathered up every stitch of his clothing and threw them off the Dottle Street Bridge into the Meriwether River below. Unfortunately, the only uniform he could borrow that morning was dirty, summertime, and three sizes too large. She had done things like that before, he added sadly. Once she had cut off the left legs on all his pants, and another time she had snipped the toes out of all his socks. I had been there before, far too often. Ah, women, I thought, God love 'em. And especially my five ex-wives. But, Lord knows, don't piss them off. They can be fiendish in search of revenge. I kept my thoughts to myself, though, and when my next-door neighbor brought his uniform back, we shook hands and parted, if not friends, at least veterans of the same wars.

All's well that ends well, I thought contritely as I poured myself another shot of schnapps. The postman had a dry uniform, slightly cleaner if no better fit, his pride, and my signature; I had my mail, slightly damp; and my next-door neighbor had her morning's amusement.

I had only glanced at the envelope while we talked, just long enough to see that I didn't know who had gone to such a fuss to write to me. I picked it up again, the heavy butternut bond of envelope rich against my fingers, and stared at the return address embossed in gold script. Mrs. T. Harrison Weddington, of 14 Park Lane, Meriwether, Montana, had something to say to me. The message on the deckled-edged stationery had been written in brown ink with a spidery but firm, old-fashioned hand trained in the Palmer method.

My dear Mr. Milodragovitch, since I have been unable to reach you by telephone, either at your office or at your home, I have taken the liberty of writing you. If you find this to be an intrusion upon your personal privacy, please accept my deepest apologies in advance. However, it is imperative that we meet at your earliest convenience. I may have a case for you.

The note was signed "With kindest regards, Sarah Weddington," and included a postscript in another, more modern and casual hand with the telephone number. When I looked at the letter again, it didn't seem to make much sense. The text was clear but the words seemed strung together oddly, as if they had been written by somebody who had learned English in another country. And the name, Sarah Weddington, seemed familiar, but I didn't know why. And the phrase "a case" ... My god, even when I worked for myself, I never got cases. Whiskey came in cases; the sort of work I did came in crocks.

I hadn't had my own office in nearly five years, not since the day the trustees of my father's estate evicted me from my own building because of a small matter of six months' back rent. Actually, it wouldn't be my building until I turned fifty-two and finally came into my father's estate.

A case, I thought, then dug out my city directory, which told me nothing more than I already knew. Park Lane was a short twisting street in an old residential neighborhood, the McCravey development, just west of the campus of Mountain States College, and the houses along Park Lane were all old Victorian dowagers set on two- and three-acre lots. Just the taxes and utility bills on one of them would keep me in steaks and cocaine for a year. Even if this "case" turned out to be a crazy old woman who had lost her favorite cat, I suspected I would be well paid for my time, so I called the number.

A young woman's voice answered the telephone, said she was not Mrs. Weddington, said my call had been expected and I could see Mrs. Weddington at either eleven that morning or four that afternoon. I thought about dumping a shift at Haliburton's so I could have a nap and go at four, but I settled for eleven. No sense in losing a day's pay for a wild-goose, or -cat, chase.

"You wouldn't know what this is in regard to, would you?" I asked the young woman.

"Nope," she answered, then hung up.

Even though I had just over two hours to make the appointment, I found myself hurrying to my closet to see if I had any appropriate attire in which to call upon rich folks. But I had torn the knee out of my blue pin-stripe three-piece courtroom suit and lost one of my black boots in a scuffle on the courthouse steps a few years back after I had testified in a rather messy divorce hearing, and my last wife's cat had thrown up the remains of a garter snake on my only sport coat. Not a thing to wear, I thought, then saw myself in the dresser mirror. It wasn't going to make a bit of difference what I wore. A scrape on my forehead still bubbled watery blood and my left eye was already turning black.

After I cleaned up as best I could, showered and shaved, I went down into my basement to my mad-money cache. It had gotten thin, but I took it anyway. On the way back I patted the haunch of the cow elk I had poached with my trusty crossbow the weekend before. Meat for the winter, skinned and aging in the cool cellar light. Steaks and roasts, sausage and chili, and the memory of the elk's wide dark eye glistening in the spotlight as she leaned over the salt block. I patted her flank again, thankfully, then headed upstairs and out to my beat-up old Ford 4x4 red pickup.

Carlisle Drive skirted the eastern edge of Milodragovitch Park, sixteen wildly overgrown brushy acres that had been my backyard when I was growing up rich, then plunged out of the dark, shaded canyon into the full daylight filling the valley of the Meriwether. The air was clear, but a high hot haze made the sunshine diffuse and painful, almost like snow glare, and I fumbled in the glove box for my sunglasses, as blindly as a junkie coming out of a shooting gallery into unexpected daytime, but I couldn't find them. So I stopped to buy gas at the corner of Main, slipped into the john for two quick snorts of coke off the end of my pocketknife blade, then drove on out to the shopping mall on the south side of town, where I dropped nearly five hundred bucks on a new pair of Dan Post lizard boots and a Western-cut leather jacket. Only by the grace of God did I manage to avoid a string tie with a hunk of turquoise the size of an elk turd on it. Western clothes are all the rage these days, even back East, I understand, but when I climbed back into my pickup in the mall parking lot, I may have looked like a fashion plate, but I smelled like an old leather couch and creaked like a new saddle. Maybe these rich folk would look at my clothes and not notice my worn-out, battered face.

Meriwether was one of those old Western towns where every one of the early developers of residential neighborhoods had expressed his God-given and constitutionally guaranteed individuality by laying out his streets at cross-purposes to those of the surrounding neighborhoods. And the McCravey development was the most cantankerous of all, an absolute maze of wandering lanes, nooks and crannies, irregularly shaped lots, dead-end streets, circles, and tiny parks in the most unexpected places.

Even though I knew the neighborhood, I still missed the angled turn off Tennessee into Park Lane and had to go around to Virginia and come back to Park Lane. A few of the grand old mansions on Park had been cut up into student apartments or converted into fraternity or sorority houses, but most were owned by ancient professors at the college or survivors of the original families.

Number fourteen was the largest and most impressive of all, a grand old Victorian, sparkling with a new coat of paint in the fall sunshine, a great dame spreading her majestic wings, adrift on a small sea of mature, well-tended greenery, an eccentric old lady given over to whim and fancy: an off-center porch, a tower here, a cupola there, bay windows of rounded glass trying to balance French doors on the other side; and on the south side of the second story a huge solarium with a balcony on three sides looked as if it had been lifted bodily out of another, more modern house.

It was the old McCravey mansion, and I kicked myself for not remembering. The house had changed hands several times since the McCraveys had taken their mining and timber fortunes on to rape and pillage larger and more distant economic horizons. Whoever owned it now had restored it beautifully, expensively. I could almost feel my wallet expand, and began to consider a vacation somewhere south for the winter months.

Two towering blue spruces flanked the entrance to the brick

driveway, but I didn't want to park my pickup like a soiled dove beside the dowager queen, so I pulled up to the curb and tried to hide it behind a lilac bush. I walked back slowly along the spiked wrought-iron fence to the gate, trying to keep the leather noise down, trying to keep my new boots from eating my feet, but the silences of my pauses just made the animal squeal of the dead hides that much louder, and my little toes were already as sore as boils.

The lower story of the house seemed dark, draped behind heavy velvet, so I rested my dogs on the porch steps. Above the oak double doors, a stained-glass fanlight glowed faintly in a dull, unfinished wink. Before I could turn the brass handle of the bell, though, the front doors jerked open wide.

"So," came a voice from the gloom, "you're late. She said you'd probably be late. And now I'm late. For my graduate organic lab. Thanks a bunch." The voice paused while I wondered what sort of madness I had blundered into. "Well, don't just stand there like a knot on a log. Come on in."

Before I could step inside, a young woman stepped out on the porch to glance at the high haze. "Weather," she said calmly, meaning, as they always do in Montana, bad weather coming. She wore a pair of white painter's overalls, a cashmere turtleneck, and a chamois shirt-jacket. A small knapsack full of books dangled off her left shoulder. She stared at me through a pair of oval gold-rimmed glasses.

"I beg your pardon," I said.

"Weather," she repeated, "goddammit. And you're late. And I've missed my chem lab. But what the hell, Sarah could have used the elevator. I can make it up tonight, so come on in . . ."

As she rattled on, I followed her inside, and she shut the heavy doors with a crash that should have pulverized the stained glass of the fanlight. For a man with sore feet, I thought I managed to step aside quite deftly. She swung her daypack off onto a walnut deacon's bench, then headed down the broad hallway toward the wide stairs. The cleats of her hiking boots clattered on the polished parquet floor, and I expected to be showered with wooden tiles as I followed in her noisy wake. She rushed up the stairs, and I wondered where the elevator might be, then I wondered why she had swaddled such a nicely pert butt beneath the baggy overalls. Halfway up to the landing she realized she was talking to herself, so she stopped, turned, flipped back the tails of the chamois shirt, sighed as she hooked her thumbs into the side loops of the pants, and her young breasts rose sweetly under the thick layers of fabric. When she shook her head, her short blond hair ruffled shortly.

"Are you coming or not?" she asked sharply, then added as I hobbled up the first few steps, "New boots, huh? You guys drive me crazy, you guys in those silly goddamned boots. You might as well bind your feet like a Chinese whore—"

"Chinese princess," I interrupted.

"Huh?"

"Nothing."

"Well, as far as I'm concerned, that's the major problem with this whole goddamned state . . ."

"What's that?" I asked.

"Cowboy boots and bulldozers, that's what," she said, "goddamned romantic affectations. And I'll lay odds that you haven't been horseback ten minutes in your whole life . . ."

Although she waited on the landing for me, her mouth didn't slow down a bit. My feet hurt and I was trying to stop the cocaine sniffles, so I didn't hear much of what she said. Something about animal skins and latent homosexuality, about poor harmless iguanas slaughtered to satisfy the vanity of dudes. When I finally caught up with her at the top of the stairs, I grabbed her elbow.

"Fuck a bunch of horseback," I said. "You want to see my saddle sores?"

"Nice talk," she said, but she smiled.

The solarium was even larger than it looked from the street, filling the whole south third of the second floor. The sunlight flooded the huge room through three walls of French doors and two huge skylights; so much light so suddenly that I seemed not only blinded but somehow deafened too. White wicker furniture with gaily flowered cushions rested peacefully among a forest of large potted plants, mostly ornamental citrus trees and fan-leafed ferns. An array of Oriental throw rugs broke up some of the light as it reflected off the pale oak flooring, but most of the sunlight glanced off the floor and plunged like tiny knives into my already bleary eyes. I had done either too much coke or too little, a constant problem in my life.

Between spasmodic blinks, I watched the young woman thump across the room and out to the balcony, where an old woman leaned lightly against the rail, her face lifted into the fall sunlight. I heard their voices but not the words, and they seemed far away, as if we all stood in the brilliant salt-air haze of some Mexican Pacific beach, paralyzed by the sun and the softly pounding surf, reduced into an infinite languor, language lost in the muffled, sun-struck crash of the waves in the throbbing air. I felt like falling on the nearest couch for a long winter's siesta. The old woman raised a finger to her smiling lips, and the young woman stopped jabbering, lifted *her* hand to her mouth, but a stream of giggles slipped quicksilver through her fingers.

The old lady turned toward me, the sunlight catching her fine white hair, the polished burl of the cane in her left hand, and the stainless-steel brace on her left leg, then she came toward me out of the sun, slowly, limping, but with the grace of long-practiced motion, and when she paused just inside the French doors to set a pair of binoculars on a small table, her hand seemed to float in the air.

"No problem, Sarah," the young woman said, her hand placed lightly under the old woman's elbow, "I'll just hit the night lab, and —" Then she banged her forehead with the heel of her other hand. "Oops. Forgot the coffee. Be right back," she added, patting the old woman's elbow.

"You do drink coffee?" she asked as she stopped in front of

me. When I nodded, she looked at my face. "Jesus," she said, "some shiner." Then she darted past.

The old woman started to walk across the room. My hand rose to finger my swollen eye and the scrape on my forehead, and I had to wipe the blood off my fingers before I could take her extended hand.

"Sarah Weddington," she said in a gently hoarse voice. "Thank you for coming, Mr. Milodragovitch, on such short notice," she added with a smile, "and please forgive me for being so mysterious in my note."

"Yes, ma'am," I said. Her voice seemed oddly familiar, so I moved to the side slightly to get the sun out of my eyes.

"You don't remember me at all?" she said. "Do you, Bud?"

"No, ma'am," I admitted, "I'm sorry . . ." Then I looked at her again.

She wore a white linen suit and a raw-silk blouse that set off the sun-tanned flush of her finely boned face. Even her sensible, low-heeled shoes looked expensive and handmade. Her years, as they too often are to women, had done their cruel work to her face, but she hadn't tried to recapture her lost beauty with cosmetics but had let her face grow old with character and repose, with a serenity only highlighted by the hard touch of time. Although her blue eyes had paled, when she smiled, as she did now still holding my hand, they became clear, the limpid blue of the dawn sky rising over a mountain ridge.

"Oh, Bud," she said, grinning now, "and you had such a reckless crush on me back then."

My given name is Milton Chester Milodragovitch, III, a name chosen by my great-grandfather, Anglo-Saxon names chosen to leaven the Slavic curse of our surname. My grandfather was called Milt, my father Chet, and my mother tried and failed to call me Milton. My friends called me Milo. Only my father had called me Bud, and when he blew his head off with a shotgun when I was twelve, the name died with him.

"Seven Mile Creek," she said softly, and it all came back.

"I'll be goddamned," I whispered, and she lifted her cane, took a small step into my arms, and we hugged each other tightly, our arms wrapped around all the dead years.

My father grew up rich and useless, the scion of an old Meriwether family, interested only in fly-fishing, expensive whiskey, hunting, and any woman who wasn't my mother, which was the main reason my mother made him write his will to keep the family fortune out of my hands until I turned the ripe, and hopefully mature, age of fifty-two. She planned some useful life for me, working for a living at a job, making some small contribution to society. A life she had probably planned for my father when she met him in Boston the fall before he was asked to leave Harvard for drinking, gambling, and shooting squirrels in the Harvard Yard with a Colt .44 Dragoon pistol.

All her plans failed. My father never had a job in his life. When she said "social contribution" to him, he wrote a check and told her that was his job. Even her body betrayed her. After seven wild and painful years in Meriwether she left him, only to become morning-sick with me on the long train ride back East. I failed her too, even after her death. Except for a tour of duty in the Army during the Korean War, ten years as a Meriwether County deputy sheriff and this last terrible stint at Haliburton Security, I never held a steady job in my life.

Although I gave up fly-fishing years ago and only hunt for meat, I certainly inherited my father's taste for aimless sloth, whiskey and philandering, even without his money. And I still admired his taste in women, since Sarah Weddington was the only one of them I had ever met. Forty years ago she was the most beautiful woman I had ever seen, and the first time I saw her I fell asshole over teakettle in love.

We had been fishing up Seven Mile, my father and I, at the end of a long summer's afternoon, hard into the evening hatch and catching pan-sized cutthroat trout with each cast, when a random gust of wind or an artless back-cast lodged a 04 Royal

Coachman all the way through my right ear. My old man couldn't find his wire cutters to clip off the barb, so we trudged through the lengthening shadows of the Hardrock Peaks across a newly mown hayfield toward the nearest house, a small farm house with a collapsing barn and a concrete-block toolshed behind it. I remember Sarah coming to the front door, a grown woman as shy as a girl, apologizing because her husband was away on a long trip and hadn't left her the keys to the toolshed, then apologizing still more because she didn't even have any coffee to offer us. My father, usually as glib as an auctioneer, must have been taken by this vision, this dream woman standing before us, because he too stood as silent as a stone. Her rich blond hair fell straight to her waist, the late afternoon sunlight glowed brightly across the smooth angles and planes of her lovely face, and her lush body seemed on the point of bursting through the thin housedress she wore. She asked if she might look at the fly in my ear, and I cocked my head like a daffy pup. Her long white fingers were cool on my blushing face. Finally my father found his voice: when he mentioned that he had a thermos of coffee down by the creek, she smiled and nodded slowly, almost sadly, as if she already knew what was about to take place.

We all hurried back across the hayfield to the creek, the Royal Coachman resplendent in my ear. They had coffee, then whiskey, and the next thing I knew, my old man and this strange, lovely woman were heading back hand in hand upstream through the willows.

"Keep working that hole, Bud," my father shouted over his shoulder, laughing, "and if worst comes to worst, stick your head in the water and see if you can catch some of those little bastards on your ear."

At the time—I must have been seven or eight—I didn't think that was very funny. I sulked on a cool gravel bar, kicking rocks into the shallows, occasionally pausing to wiggle the fly riding on my ear, tugging it forward until I could just catch a glimpse of the hackles at the edge of my vision. It didn't hurt, but it tickled, and I grew enamored with the idea of wearing this gaudy decoration like a totem for the rest of my life. Or at least around the neighborhood for a few days. Until, perhaps, I felt the woman's cool fingers on my skin once more.

When Sarah and my father came back in the long mountain twilight, their arms around each other's waists, flushed and smiling, a deep, hollow ache filled me, followed by a flood of anger. I fled the creek side, leaving my fly rod and tackle box and the gunnysack of trout, plunged through the brush, snagging the fly on leaves and branches until I felt the string of warm blood eddy down my neck and across my chest, and ran breathless to where my father's Cadillac was parked beside Seven Mile Road.

"He'll be all right," I heard my father say. "He's my little buddy."

As always, on the way back, we hit a couple of bars, my father drinking, silent and darkly grave, me silent, spinning on my bar stool, refusing the money he offered for the pinball machine. Finally he reached over, ruffled my hair, smiled, and said, "You look like a pirate, Bud, or one of those goddamned Hottentots." I thought he had said "hot-to-trot" and I found that pretty funny, until I got home and showed my mother the fly in my ear and mentioned proudly that I hadn't shed a single tear. I also asked her if she didn't think I looked like one of those hot-to-trots, and she slapped the living hell out of me, Royal Coachman, bloody ear, and all. Hours later, when I finally fell asleep upstairs, I could still hear their angry voices rumbling in the huge old house.

After that, we fished Seven Mile two or three times a week during the season. Sometimes while my father worked a hole, standing thigh-deep in the cold water, his fly line stacked like a gossamer string over his head, Sarah and I sat on the bank, our feet cooling in the water, and she told me tales of men at arms and jousts, mountain glens rich with the smell of crushed heather. But never a word about her life.

Then, suddenly one summer, we no longer fished Seven Mile. In fact, my father packed his fly rod in its case and never took it out again. That fall, with an accident so carefully arranged that it took me thirty years to understand what had happened, he committed suicide late one night. I heard him tell my mother that he smelled a skunk and that he was going to get his shotgun; then as he lifted the Browning over and under out of the gun cabinet, he caught the trigger on the bolt of his elk rifle, and blew his head all over the living room.

Chapter 2

"I'm sorry, Mrs. Weddington," I said as we sat down on one of the wicker couches facing the sun, "it was so long ago, and this house . . . I'm sorry."

"Please call me Sarah," she murmured, then cradled her hands on the crook of her cane. "And please don't apologize, Bud. I meant it to be a pleasant surprise, not a shock."

"That's all right," I said. "It just took a moment to sort out all the memories."

"Pleasant ones, I trust."

"Oh, yes," I lied, "fond memories."

"I saw your advertisement in the Yellow Pages when I came back from Europe—what was it?—ten or twelve years ago. I-I can't recall exactly," she said, lifting her fingers to gently stroke her temple. "I didn't know how you would react to hearing from-from the other woman in your father's life." She smiled sadly, then forced cheer into her face. "But I suppose your father had many other women in his life."

"You're the only one I knew about."

"Thank you for that kind lie," she said. "I meant to telephone many times, Bud, but I got involved with the restoration of this old white elephant, and then I-I had this damned stroke"—she clanked her cane against her leg brace—"goddamned stroke . . . I'm sorry now that I didn't call. You look so much like your father, you know, nothing at all like that little boy with that fly dangling from his ear. Nothing at all, except for the black eye and the scrape on your forehead. You were always the most beat-up little boy I ever saw."

"I was always biting off more than I could chew and sticking my nose in somebody's business," I said. "Some people never grow up."

"But we all grow old," she said, then continued, "I never felt guilty about the affair—you understand that it was a godsend for both of us—but I always felt slightly guilty for leaving you alone that first day, bleeding and so hurt."

"Don't," I said. "I might have been a squirt but I wasn't a total dope. You guys looked great when you came back. I was pissed but I got over it."

"I could tell," she said. "I was charmed . . . by you, such a brave little boy, and your father, such a bear of a man but so sweet and even more unhappy than I was, and the coffee . . . Perhaps that was the first time in the long history of the seduction of married women—outside of the Mormon Church, that is—that a wife was ruined by a cup of tepid coffee. Goddamned Harry, every time he went off on one of his dental peregrinations, he locked up the coffee in the toolshed so I wouldn't have neighbor ladies over for coffee, as if we had any neighbors out there—"

"Dental peregrinations?" I interrupted.

"Oh," she said, "you didn't know about any of that, did you?"

"No, ma'am."

"Harry was a traveling dentist. He started out with a chair, a pedal-driven drill, and an old Reo truck. He hit all the small towns and ranches and homesteads in Montana. Did quite well for himself, the old bastard . . ." She seemed to drift away, into her own past, unshared.

"What happened?" I asked.

"Oh," she said, coming back, misunderstanding, "the old tightwad son of a bitch was changing a tire in a rainstorm over by Roundup and a cattle truck ran over him. Served him right. The old lecher always thought he'd die in the saddle. Or be gunned down by an angry husband . . . But you were asking about something else, weren't you? Forgive me, but since the-the stroke, I have a tendency to lose track of the conversation. Your father and I . . . well, your mother put a detective on him, don't you know, and she made Chet choose between you and me. She meant to take you back East . . ."

"I didn't know."

"Ironic," she said, "that you would take up this sort of work."

"Ironic," I said, then stood up and walked toward the balcony, cursing all the divorce work I had done over the years.

"I'm sorry," she said.

"No problem," I said. "It was a long time ago."

But she was still back there. ". . . then your father had that-that horrible accident. I couldn't-couldn't do anything, come to the funeral, cry, I was already cried out, send flowers, throw myself in the grave with him, nothing . . . Then Harry was killed, and suddenly I was a very wealthy young woman . . . or perhaps not so young. All those years, being locked in that tiny, cheap little house out at Seven Mile had made an old woman out of me, long before my time.

"At first I spent as much of Harry's tightly hoarded money as I could—sailed around the world, twice, wore furs and jewels, drank champagne by the gallon, I lived like a queen, or a famous courtesan—the south of France, Scotland, Spain—lived out my revenge, praying that Harry was spinning in his grave like a pinwheel.

"Then my looks began to fail, the wild nights grew so much like the night before that I couldn't tell one from another, so I came back home to Montana, came back—and please forgive an old woman's romantic affections—came back to be near the memory of the only man I ever loved . . .

"I'm sorry, Bud, to go on, to stir up foul memories."

"That's all right, Mrs. Weddington," I said. "It's always seemed as if it happened yesterday to me."

"How true that is, Bud," she whispered. "I remember that first day, the smell of the sun on the hayfield, the coffee"—she wiped her watery eyes with a brusque motion of her wrinkled hand, then she laughed—"and the smell of the fish on your father's hands." Pausing, she touched her lips with a stiff, knotty finger. "Oh, I remember what I meant to say."

"Yes, ma'am."

"Please call me Sarah, Bud."

"Yes, ma'am."

"I suppose no one calls you Bud anymore."

"No, ma'am."

"I'm sorry," she said. She seemed to falter, her hand rising again, touching her temple, her lips, then back up again, as if she could form the words with her fingers. "I know—I know I should know your given name, but I-I just can't find it in there. So many things are gone, just not there anymore . . . names, places, the faces of old friends . . . I'm truly sorry."

"Most people just call me Milo," I said.

"Milo," she said quietly, resting her head on her hands holding the cane; in a minute or two the young girl came barging into the room with a coffee pot and china cups on a silver serving tray, which she placed on the low table in front of us.

"Shall I pour, mum?" she asked in the worst parody of an English accent I had ever heard.

"Thank you very much, Gail," Mrs. Weddington said, raising her head, "but I'm sure Mr. Milodragovitch will do the honors."

"As you wish, mum," she said, then curtsied, holding out the tails of her shirt. In the doorway she stopped, saying, "If you need anything, Sarah, I'll be in the kitchen making zucchini bread, so just ring." Then she was off again, waffle-stompers pounding down the stairs.

"Such a sweet child," Mrs. Weddington said as I poured the dark, rich coffee from the silver pot into delicate china cups.

Neither a child nor all that sweet, I thought as I raised the fragile cup in my trembling hands. I couldn't tell if the sharp quivering in my blood came from a lack of sleep, drug abuse, or the flood of memories.

"Who is she?" I asked, trying to settle in the present, but Mrs. Weddington was involved with her coffee. She inhaled the warm fragrance for a long time, took a tiny sip, then set the cup back on its saucer and pushed it deliberately to the far side of the table.

"Oh, I do miss my coffee," she sighed. "I'm sorry, Bud, you were saying something . . ."

"I just wondered who that girl is."

"Gail? Oh, she's my grandniece. I cannot abide nurses or housekeepers, so Gail has lived with me since she was a freshman at college. She has been delightful company these past years, and I will miss her dearly when she finishes her master's."

"She takes care of the whole house and goes to graduate school at the same time?" I asked, impressed or amazed.

"Oh, goodness no," she said, chuckling. "One afternoon a week the two of us go out for a long leisurely lunch while a sanitation crew—'sanitation'? That can't be right, can it? Doesn't that mean 'garbage' these days?" She touched her forehead with the back of her wrist. "Housecleaning," she said, "a housecleaning crew comes in, and when we come back—slightly tipsy, I must confess, very much against my doctor's advice—the house is sparkling again. As if by magic . . . Sometimes money seems almost magical, doesn't it?"

"I'm afraid I wouldn't know," I said without thinking.

"But you must be quite well off! Your father's—"

"It's all tied up." I said, "But you were telling me about Gail."

"Gail? Oh, yes," she said, laughing. "Gail and housecleaning. The poor child might be able to clean up the world when she finishes her degree in environmental engineering, or whatever it is, but I'm afraid she'll never be a housekeeper. Never.

"Oh, but I will miss her when she goes," Mrs. Weddington added. "Most of my friends are either dead or *old,* and Gail has filled that gap. She keeps me young." Then she laughed again. "However, I fear that the little devil has become rather an evil influence in my life."

"Ma'am?" I said, afraid that I was in no shape to follow her meandering conversation.

"My politics have become embarrassingly radical," she said. "You should see some of the groups she makes me support. I know they are the sort of people the FBI watches constantly. And, much to my chagrin, I fear she has— You're not connected with the police, are you, Bud?"

"Anything but, ma'am."

"I've become something of a 'pothead,' " she said with a sweet smile.

"There are worse vices," I said, trying not to giggle.

"Quite," she admitted. "Greed, penury, the lust for power and money that makes men rape this lovely country—quite a number of far more evil vices, I am sure, but still I find myself quite embarrassed about the little bit of pot smoking that I indulge in, quite." Then she quickly put her fingers to her lips. "Oh," she whispered, "Bud, you must forgive me. I promised myself that I would not become overexcited by your visit, but it seems I have—seems I have said 'quite' nine times in the past ten seconds. Would you kindly excuse an old lady for a few moments."

"Of course," I said, standing up, not knowing what to expect. But Mrs. Weddington simply leaned her cane against the arm of the couch, folded her hands in her lap and let the heavily creased lids of her eyes fall softly shut. Within seconds her breathing grew deep and regular, and I assumed she had gone to sleep.

For a minute I stood around dumfounded, confused, like a mourner who has wandered into the wrong funeral parlor, then I picked up my cup and saucer and tiptoed in my squeaking boots outside to the balcony, set my coffee on the rail and lit a cigarette.

The balcony commanded a grand view of the old neighborhood and sat high enough so that I could see over the yellowing trees and up the valley of the Hardrock River as it flowed north into the Meriwether. On the eastern flank of the broad valley, the gently rounded humps of the Agate Range rolled south, and on the western side the mighty broken peaks of the Hardrocks, tough, hungry mountains, loomed stark over the fields and pastures of the wide, pleasant valley.

A case, I thought. I didn't mind if the old woman had only invited me for coffee and memories, didn't even mind the chunk of mad money gone to clean up my act. Already my new boots had begun to mold themselves comfortably to the knotty contours of my feet, and the leather jacket smelled sharp and clean like the interior of a new, expensive car. A fair trade, and the view a bonus. Twelve miles up the Hardrock, Seven Mile Creek still babbled merrily in my mind, brimful of pan-sized cutthroats, and the graceful loops of my father's fly line still hung in the air. Quarts of Lorelei beer still cooled in the arching curves under cut banks, and the print skirt of a lovely young woman still folded around her legs with the wind . . . Though in truth I knew that an invasion of pastel tract houses cluttered the sides of Seven Mile, that the only trout there were shit-fed stockers, and that the young woman had grown old and crippled and was taking a nap in the solarium behind me. And the kid with the Royal Coachman in his ear, Hottentot that he meant to be . . . well, God knows what became of the little fart—

"*Quite* the view," Mrs. Weddington said behind me, and when I turned she smiled to let me know she meant this "quite." She looked refreshed, not rumpled and puffy as if after an uneasy sleep, but truly rested, the angles and wrinkles of her face somehow smoothed, softened, filled with peace. "A beautiful view," she added, "but too often I find myself closing my eyes in hope of seeing the land as it once was back when we knew it."

"I think I still have a crush on you, Mrs. Weddington," I said.

"Sarah, please," she ordered. "And thank you for that charming lie. I take it that you are your father's son about women."

"Worse, maybe. I've got enough ex-wives to start a basketball team."

"Something in the blood," she said softly. "I hope there were no children."

"Just one," I said. "He looks like his mother. He doesn't even have the name. When my wife remarried, her new husband adopted the boy, gave him his name."

"Does he live here?"

"No, ma'am, he's a junior at Washington State," I said and added conversationally, "Did you have a nice nap?" Enough of my sordid past, I thought, enough.

"Not a nap," she said, "but a few moments of meditation— Gail taught me—and at my age much more relaxing than sleep. I have grown to hate sleep of late, which means, I suppose, that I fear death, which is unseemly in a woman of my years. I let Harry take so much of my life, though, that sometimes it seems as if my life has just begun and now that it is almost over." She leaned against the rail, easing the weight off her braced leg.

"Would you like to sit down?"

"Not for a bit, thank you. The sun feels so good." Then she said, "I realize we haven't discussed our business yet, but if you would indulge the ramblings of an old woman with only half a brain left, I feel that you have a right to know why your father was so important to me."

"Of course," I said. "I'll listen as long as you want to talk."

"Thank you, Bud," she said. "I hope you are not just being polite." She paused, and I could see her face visibly clench with effort. "My father had a small ranch," she began, "down along the Missouri on the edge of the Breaks, one of those hard-luck little outfits where the man spends every waking hour trying to stay ahead of the bank notes falling due like some curse each year, and the children grow up as wild and skittish as jack rabbits, and the woman . . . ah, the woman looks as if she has spent her entire life in a coal mine, or in a root cellar gnawing on seed potatoes and withered apples.

30

"The only time I ever saw my mother smile was when she was reading Sir Walter Scott aloud to my sisters and me. Every winter she seemed to grow smaller and smaller through the cold months, then she would regain her stature in the spring. One spring, though, she kept getting smaller and smaller until she finally disappeared . . . into a spring blizzard without a coat.

"The summer I turned sixteen I ran away with the first man who promised to take me as far away from that damn endless horizon as I could get. Or at least the first one who did not arrive on horseback. I had had a bellyful of men on horseback—gawky cowboys, all elbows and Adam's apples, shy when sober, mean when drunk, and they only talked to cattle, horses and each other, never to their women. So when old Harry Weddington rolled up in that Reo with his torture chair in the back . . . well, as they say, the rest is history.

"Everybody in eastern Montana assumed that Harry had seduced me—he had that sort of reputation, had been in that sort of trouble before, shot at by irate husbands and angry fathers, even had a piece of his heel shot off by a rancher over by Sidney—but the truth of the matter is that I did all the seduction that morning.

"Harry talked to me," she said, somehow still amazed after all the years, "he talked to me, and his hands were soft and gentle, his voice low and sweet, crooning . . . I remember the day perfectly, even remember the dress I was wearing, but have not the slightest notion what he said. Probably just his usual spiel to a frightened young girl in his chair. Whatever he said, though, it reached me. When he tried to take his fingers out of my mouth, I bit down, hard, and held on for dear life. Poor old Harry, he thought he was dead for sure, but then he realized what I wanted and thought all his lecherous dreams had come true.

"Of course," she said with a bitter grin, "once he had me, he didn't want me anymore, not as much, but we were already married—at my insistence—but he wanted to make sure that no other man had me, so he kept me locked away like some medieval princess out at Seven Mile . . .

"And if you hadn't caught that fly in your ear"—she paused, then patted my hand once softly—"well, I hope you got over it," she finished, then sighed as if *she* hadn't. "Thank you for your indulgence," she added. "I hope I haven't presumed too heavily on a rather ancient and tenuous connection."

"Don't be silly," I said, sniffling, hoping it was the coke.

"Old women have little purpose in this world," she said, "so they usually become either mean or silly. I prefer silly." She giggled, oddly, and the strength and composure seemed to melt off her face in the warm sunshine. Her hands began to skitter about, moving from the rail to her cane to her face as if she had lost something. "And I fear you will think me even sillier when I-I tell you why I wanted to engage your-your services. It will-will take a moment to explain, you see, a moment . . . every neighborhood needs—every neighborhood has one—needs-needs one, every neighborhood has a busy-busy-busy . . ." Then her right hand flew toward her trembling lips, catching the edge of my saucer, flipped it and the cup over, the bone china glistening as it fell, tumbling in slow motion to the brick walk below, where they shattered in a glittering splash of sharp fragments.

". . . Body," she muttered to herself, "body, goddammit, *body,* busybody, busybody." Her aching fingers pried at her temple, pleading with the throbbing veins as soundless tears poured down her cheeks.

"Sarah," I said, taking her arm, "would you like to sit down?"

"Please," she murmured, "thank you."

As I led her back to the couch her arm quivered beneath my hand, a frail and pitiful anger trickling through her body. This time she slept. I found an afghan and folded it around her legs, watched her until she fell into the regular sputtering breath of a sleep near death, then I took her cold cup of coffee out on the balcony, where I smoked and stared blindly back up the Hardrock Valley. I would have given anything for a good stiff drink.

In July of 1952 my outfit was making its third assault up the ruined slopes of Old Baldy, the one west of Ch'orwon, when a two-hundred-and-forty-pound Hawaiian staff sergeant from G Company of the 23rd jumped into the shell hole where I had taken cover. He broke three of my ribs and my collarbone, and my left wrist so badly that it had to be pinned. He probably saved my life. In the nine days of fighting over Old Baldy, my outfit took eighty percent casualties.

Six weeks later, when I was at the Oakland Depot waiting for my medical leave to begin, the chaplain came by my bunk to tell me my mother had just died. It wasn't much of a surprise, since she had been in and out of hospitals for years, at first with imagined complaints but later with liver and stomach complications as a result of her secret drinking. Then the chaplain switched to his Dr. Kildare voice and gave me the kicker: she had hanged herself with a silk stocking at a fat farm in Arizona.

I spent my leave at the Mark Hopkins, smoking cigarettes and staring through the foggy afternoons at the Bay as if I could see the great ocean rolling beyond. Somewhere out there, the war, where I would not go again. Somewhere behind me, back East, my mother's grave, which I never saw. After my discharge I went to Mexico for the first time, lost myself in a sea of mescal until I felt like an agave grub floating in the clear, fiery liquid.

Standing on Sarah's balcony, I wanted to fall back into the bottle one last time, bottom-out in some open sewer, but when I went to work for Colonel Haliburton, I had promised him that I would quit trying to kill myself with a whiskey bottle. So I drank schnapps, which I hated, and stayed fairly sober, but right then I longed for an ocean of whiskey, one last chance with self-destruction.

Twenty minutes later Sarah woke and excused herself shyly, then limped slowly toward the upstairs hallway. When she came back, she had combed her hair and freshened her light make-up, but the cosmetic changes weren't even skin-deep. She looked tired, afraid, sick unto death, but she forced a game smile, a sly wink, even a small lilt into the dark huskiness of her voice.

"I know you noticed the binoculars when you came in," she

said, "and I assume you didn't think I was engaged in bird-watching."

"No, ma'am."

"Because of my view of the neighborhood, because of my loneliness, perhaps because of my addled mind—whatever, I have taken to watching my neighbors. It is an ugly habit, true, but I keep what I learn to myself." She paused. "And I am willing to pay your usual daily rate plus liberal expenses and a substantial bonus . . ."

"To do what?" I asked, wondering if I had missed something.

"To satisfy an old woman's curiosity," she answered, "nothing more than that. Nothing illegal, I assure you, nothing complex or dangerous."

"How?" I said, surprised that I felt a small pang of loss at the promise of nothing illegal, complex, or dangerous.

"Come with me," she said as she raised herself slowly from the couch. I took her arm and followed her outside to the balcony. "See that small park?" She pointed south-southeast to a wedge of green between Park and Virginia. "Every Thursday afternoon for the past six weeks, two cars park there, a man in one, a young woman in the other—he looks to be in his forties and rather scruffy, and I would guess she is in her late twenties, an attractive young woman—and they sit in her car for an hour or so, talking, it seems." Then Sarah turned to me. "I would very much like to know who they are, what they talk about, why they meet like this. Could you do that for me?" When I didn't answer immediately, she added, "Or more to the point: Will you?"

"Well . . . ah, I don't know, I've—"

"What these people do is probably none of my business," she said as she led me back into the solarium, "but I can afford to indulge my curiosity." She opened the drawer of the small table where the binoculars sat, took out a long white envelope, and set it on the table. "This envelope contains five thousand dollars in cash, an assortment of my credit cards, which have been cleared for your use, and the license-plate number of the man's car—a

Washington plate—the young woman arrives in a different automobile each time, rented, I assume. Are you interested?"

"I don't know what to say, ma'am. This is a little weird, you know."

"I'm sorry, my dear boy," she said, smiling, "but rich old women are eccentric, not weird."

"Of course."

"Take a few days to think about it, if you like," she said, putting the envelope back in the drawer and closing it slowly. "If you would just let me know by Thursday morning what you decide. If you decide against it, perhaps you can recommend one of your colleagues."

"I'll let you know."

"And one last favor?"

"Yes, ma'am."

"See that huge globe in the far corner?"

"Yes, ma'am."

"It is, in fact, a liquor cabinet," she said, smiling again, "and inside you will find a large brandy snifter and a bottle of cognac. Would you please bring me three fingers and the joint sitting beside the snifter."

Although it wasn't much past noon, I felt like joining the old woman, but the day had been so crazy already, I knew I wouldn't stop.

After I settled her in a lounge chair with her drink and the lit joint, she thanked me, and added, "Please think about it seriously, Bud, but whatever you decide, please visit again, whenever you like."

I promised both things, then kissed her soft old cheek and said goodbye.

Downstairs, I wandered toward the rear of the house until I found the large kitchen, where Gail was leaning against the counter, a textbook in one hand, a batter-coated beater in the other. I watched the tip of her pink tongue slide slowly up one of the blades.

"Lose your way, cowboy?" she asked without looking up.

"I need a broom and a dustpan," I said. "There seems to be a broken cup and saucer on the sidewalk."

"Clumsy jerk," she muttered.

"What time do you get out of lab tonight?" I asked.

"About ten. Why?"

"Want to meet someplace for a drink about eleven?"

"You married?" she asked.

"Not now."

"You as old as you look?"

"Not nearly."

"You going to wear normal clothes?"

"What's normal?"

"Okay, why the hell not," she said, then smiled. "I'll be at the Deuce about eleven. You know where that is?" Her smile grew wicked. The Deuce of Spades was a mountain-hippie, biker, deadbeat hangout, complete with watered drinks, bluegrass stomping, and aging freaks. Also my cocaine dealer, Raoul, spent most of his free time there.

"Sure," I said, "it's a date."

"It's a drink," she said. "I'll let you know when it's a date."

"Okay."

"And that's the broom closet," she said with a motion of her thumb.

When I came back inside to empty the dustpan, Gail asked me how Sarah was feeling.

"Tired," I said. "Those hikes down memory lane ain't always easy. But when I left, she had drink and smoke and sunshine."

"She is one beautiful old lady," Gail said.

"You should have seen her back when."

"I've seen pictures," she said. "Do you look anything like your father?"

"Some."

"Are you anything like him?"

"A lot poorer."

"That's probably to your advantage," she conceded. "Is that your cowboy Cadillac hidden out front behind the lilacs?"

"You got it."

"How many miles do you get to the gallon?"

"No idea, love," I said. "When it gets empty, I give some Arab a twenty-dollar bill and he gives me half a tank of gas."

Gail gave me a sharp frown that should have cut me to the quick, or at least shamed me into a Volkswagen diesel Rabbit.

Outside, when I paused to unlock the door of my pickup, I glanced northwest and saw the high, telltale horsetail haze drifting swiftly south. Gail had been right: weather. The first serious wave of winter forming for an assault on the Meriwether Valley. Even in the sunshine I shivered and thought of Mexico. This winter, for damned certain sure, I would go. Even if I had to finally sell the last and only thing I owned in my name, my grandfather's three thousand acres of timber up in the Diablos, land he had stolen from the Benniwah Indians—a legal theft, but an outright theft nonetheless. I had had three recent offers: one from a rich kid from Oregon who wanted to horse-log the timber; one from an automobile-parts company in Detroit that wanted to turn it into a corporate hunting lodge; and one from the government, which wanted to include the land in the proposed Dancing Bear Wilderness Area.

The kid struck me as a smart-ass and he tried to impress me with a suitcase full of cash, the people from Detroit seemed bored by the whole deal, and the government . . . well, to hell with them. Wilderness areas were good ideas, but I still like chain saws and snowmobiles and four-wheel-drive vehicles too much to have them outlawed on my own ground in my own lifetime. As it was now, they had blocked my access to the land, so that I had to drive seventy miles out of my way—up to the Benniwah Reservation in the foothills of the Cathedrals, then across the old C, C&K Railroad sections, up past the abandoned mine to Camas Meadows—seventy miles, just to poach an elk on my own land.

Maybe Gail was right, and bulldozer and cowboy boot mentality had ruined Montana. Or maybe the Indians were right, and the land belonged to itself. Whatever, this particular piece of rough, sidehill timber and open meadow belonged to me. Maybe, I thought as I climbed in my pickup, trying to ignore the cold front coming, maybe I would do Sarah Weddington's crazy job, grab her money and take the sort of Mexican vacation my father would have loved.

Chapter 3

The swiftly moving Arctic front hit Meriwether in midafternoon with thundering gusts of wind that swept the street clean of all those people still dressed in light clothes who believed in Indian Summers that lasted forever. Then a stiff, cold rain began to fall, sliding down the wind. By the time I headed across town to pick up a car at the Haliburton offices, the temperature had dropped into the thirties and the raindrops hit my windshield in slushy pellets.

As I swung left off Railroad onto Dottle, I noticed one of Haliburton's armored trucks parked at an odd angle in the lot in front of Hamburger Heaven. The driver, leaning out his door, his revolver dangling from his hand, shouted at the passing traffic, occasionally lifting the pistol and aiming it at the cars. During the few moments it took me to drive down the short block of Dottle, I saw four cars and a beer truck bolt like frightened cattle right through the red light.

The driver's eyes glowed in the ashen light, drunk or drugged or simply crazed. The man, whose name I couldn't remember, was one of Colonel Haliburton's basket cases, a Vietnam vet with a good war record and a terrible employment history. The colonel was a born do-gooder, one of those unusual career military men who also think of themselves as soldiers in God's compassionate army. He had given this guy a chance at a steady job, but things didn't seem to be working out too well.

After I parked my pickup on the other side of the armored truck, I tore my uniform coat open, loosened my collar and tie and mussed my hair, thinking that if I looked as disheveled as the driver did, he might not waste me out of hand. I had never been a master of disguise, though, and when I stepped around the back of the truck and said hello, the driver dropped out of the door into a combat stance and laid a bead right on the old trembling thorax area.

"What the fuck are you doing here, man?" he asked, his voice shaking and his knuckles white on the butt of the .38.

"Oh, shit," I said, "I don't exactly know." And I meant it.

"Just like over there, right, dad? Nobody fucking knew." I didn't have to ask where *there* might be. "Nobody knew, and you don't know shit from wild honey about it, dad, what it was like."

"I spent time on the line in Korea," I offered lamely.

"Korea?" he sneered. "The line? Well, kiss my rosy red ass." Then he lifted the revolver straight up into the gray, windy rain, pulled the trigger six times, six flat ugly splats as the hammer fell on empty chambers. He laughed wildly as he tossed his piece onto the front seat of the armored truck. "Tell the colonel to stuff his charity, right, and his goddamned empty guns. I ain't much into limited warfare, man. If I'd gone to Canada, dad, I'd have both my kidneys and all my marbles, right? Ain't it the shits." He sighed, shook his head, then stumbled off toward the nearest bar, the Deuce down on Railroad, his lank hair poking wetly from under his uniform cap.

I stood there a long time, it seemed, the cold rain seeping down my collar, then decided I wasn't going to wet my pants or collapse into a frightened puddle, so I locked up the truck, took the keys and the empty .38, then drove very carefully across town, trying not to look at the bars. Some security outfits, I had read, equipped their rent-a-cops with rubber guns for their own safety. Symbolic fire power, I thought, an idea whose time has come. The .38 that I carried at work, wrapped in its holster belt on the front seat of the pickup, was, like the driver's, empty. By choice. A few years back, when I still worked for myself, I had killed two men at close range, and although I couldn't bear to throw away all that lovely, lethal machinery I had collected over the years, I did throw all my live rounds into the Meriwether River.

Haliburton's had me working relief that shift, filling in for piss-calls and dinner breaks for the first four hours, easing around the now freezing streets in my yellow Pinto with the little blue light on the roof—barbecue pits on the hoof, we called them—my door unlocked and my seat belt off. As happened every winter, most of the drivers in Meriwether seemed to have forgotten all about ice during the summer months and they drove as if the streets were bare and dry, which made my job more dangerous than philosophical discussions about war as an arm of diplomacy with armed crazy people. Dangerous, but so goddamn boring. And I felt like a clown dressed in my brown-on-brown uniform with its old-fashioned Sam Browne belt like a mule's harness across my chest.

At least the last four hours of my shift would be warm and safe, off the streets, sitting behind a sheet of one-way mirrored glass in the back room of an EZ-IN/EZ-OUT twenty-four-hour convenience market and filling station out on South Dawson. Warm because I had a small electric heater for my feet, and safe because we had video tapes of the guy we were trying to catch who had been knocking over convenience markets all over town, a tall, skinny kid in a ski mask who we knew owned a police-band radio because he only hit stores when the police were busy with fires or drunken wrecks out on the interstate, and who held the clerks at bay with what looked like a starter's pistol. In Montana, where we have more guns than people and cattle, maybe

even trees, this dude had been knocking them down with a goddamn blank pistol.

After I checked in with the Haliburton dispatcher on the company band, I settled into the little room, turned on the police
scanner and the CB radio, checked the television cameras and
the tape monitor, then made a fresh pot of coffee. Sipping that
first good cup out of the pot, I thought about Sarah, the way she
savored the smell, enjoyed her tiny sip. Most of the time, instead
of considering old age and preparing myself for some wise gentle
assault on those last years, I thought about fifty-two and my father's money. My final days might not take too long when they
came around, but I intended to enjoy them.

The CB crackled in the background. Out on the interstate
where it sliced through the northern edge of the city limits, long-
haul truckers were complaining about the slick roads, their piles,
and Smokey the Bear. On the police scanner, all the units were
too busy with a rash of fender benders and resultant fistfights to
complain. Ah, winter wonderland, I thought as I leaned back in
the swivel chair and stared through the one-way glass, down the
aisle, and out the glass front of the store. Across the street, the
blue blinking light of the Doghouse Lounge made it look like a
more romantic and mysterious place than it really was. It was a
workingman's place, and the parking lot was full of pickups with
rifles racked in the rear windows. At least they served whiskey
there, and I could think about a drink as I watched the customers
string through the store, grumbling not a bit about the thirty
percent extra they paid for *convenience*.

Two teen-aged girls on their way to the movie down the street
used the mirror side of the glass to make certain that their eyelashes were as thick and furry as tarantula legs, giggling about
some poor unsuspecting lad named Shawn they planned to surprise at the theater, then they gaggled away in a cloud of youth-
ful laughter. A bit later a lanky kid came in, swiped a can of Coke
and a package of red licorice rope, stuffing them into the game
pocket of his 60/40 parka, then spent a few minutes working on
his zits in the mirror before he left, paying for a package of gum.

I started to hit the shoplifter switch, but the clerk behind the counter had his nose in a motorcycle magazine, and I decided this shoplifter was Shawn of the giggles and already in more trouble than he could handle, so I let him walk. In the days before juveniles had legal rights, a shoplifting bust could be worked out between the parents and the store manager. But legal rights meant paperwork, which in turn meant records, and no governmental body of any size, shape, or function had ever found a way to dispose of records. After the kid had gone, I went out front, paid for the candy and Coke, and made sure that the clerk rang up the sale instead of skimming it.

About nine-thirty, with an hour left on my shift, a seven-car pile-up blocked the Dawson Street bridge, and an "every available unit" call went out on the police band. Fifteen minutes later out on the Interstate, a semi load of frozen turkeys locked its trailer brakes, skidded on the iced pavement, and jackknifed into the median, spreading toms and hens like small boulders all over the landscape.

Meriwether lived off lumber, and with interest rates up and housing starts down, two mills had closed their saws forever the previous summer, and the pulp mill had been on half shifts for three months. So Meriwether was chock-full of surly unemployed folks facing a Thanksgiving with little to be thankful for and a Christmas even more grim. When news of the turkey wreck swept through town by CB radio and telephone, a lot of unhappy people piled into their four-wheel-drive rigs and headed for the highway, muttering "Thanksgiving" under their collective breaths, "Christmas." I cheered them on. They might as well have the turkeys because the USDA would show up the next day, condemn the meat, and consign it to the dump.

As riots go, it didn't sound like a big one, but large enough to involve three sheriff's deputies and two highway patrolmen. No fatalities, either, just two broken legs when a drunk on a snowmobile ran down a housewife in the median, and a minor concussion when her husband knocked the drunk off the snowmobile with a well-aimed twelve-pound hen.

Unfortunately, I wasn't paying attention to business. When I stopped laughing long enough to glance up, a tall skinny kid in a ski mask held a small pistol behind a loaf of white bread while the frightened clerk shoveled bills and change into a paper bag between frightened looks cast my way. I wasn't ready; the rusty snap on my holster took forever to open and I couldn't have loaded my piece if I had wanted to. I hit the silent alarm, even though the police units were all busy, slipped out the door, hid behind the upright Coke cooler. When the bandit turned away from the cashier, I leapt out into the aisle to do my bit for law and order and the American way of life.

"Police!" I shouted. "Freeze!"

Well, it works on television. But this guy jumped three feet in the air and got off two rounds at me before his bandit shoes hit the tile floor. Starter's pistol, my ass; the video tapes had lied. I dove back behind the cooler, then bellied over to peek under the potato-chip rack just as the kid hit the front door. He didn't make it out, though. Two fiery muzzle flashes flamed out of the Doghouse parking lot, followed by the roar of high-velocity hunting rifles. The kid spun wildly, scattering folding money and change as he fell into a rack of motor oil and antifreeze beside the door. A whole shelf of onion-and-sour-cream-flavored potato chips exploded over my head, and a rack of Coke cans crashed through the glass doors and fell on my back, hissing like angry snakes.

Two more muzzle flashes came out of the parking lot. The rounds popped through the plate glass, spraying fragments like grenade shrapnel, ripped out whole shelves of dry and canned goods, snipped through the glass doors of the beer cooler behind me, releasing a sea of foam.

"Had enough in there?" somebody shouted from across the street.

I, for one, certainly had, but I was curled too tightly into a damp ball to answer. The bandit, though, grunted "Fuck you, white-eyes," then let off a useless round into the ceiling. The rifles answered with a four-round volley, and the whole interior of the store seemed to explode. Even a row of fluorescent lights on the twelve-foot ceiling disintegrated, the shards of tubes drifting like snow through the dust.

"Enough now?" the voice shouted again, laughing.

"Enough!" I screamed, then started to throw my piece out into the aisle until I remembered I was supposed to be one of the good guys. I stood up, praying the bastards could see my uniform under the soggy coat of chips. Behind me I could hear rivers of cold beer rushing and a punctured aerosol can wheezing in a slow circle. Out front, two men darted across the street like some dream of combat infantrymen under attack. When they didn't shoot, I stuffed my empty revolver back into the wet holster, then went up front to separate the dead from the dying.

Somehow the clerk hadn't been hit. When he saw me, he leapt from his hiding place beneath the counter, vaulted over it, and ran out the door into the freezing rain without a jacket. I knew the kid in the ski mask had been hit, knew it was going to be bad, with the way hunting rounds mushroomed and fragmented on impact and killed with hydrostatic shock. He looked dead, too, where he lay in a pool of antifreeze, oil, and blood. But when I tried to pry the cheap .22 revolver out of his hand, he had live resistance in his fingers.

Two guys wearing down vests over flannel shirts, their scoped elk rifles at port arms, charged through the front door. I asked for their help as I tried to ease the kid out of the muck, but they were too busy admiring their handiwork. When I asked a second time, louder, the nearest one said "Fuck him" and nudged the bandit's arm with a heavy hunting boot.

"Hey, that's right," I said, standing up, "we're the good guys and we don't have to mess with shit like this." When I tried for a good-old-boy grin, it felt as if my face cracked. "Damn good shooting," I said. "What the hell you guys using?" I reached for the nearest one's rifle. He let me have it rather absent-mindedly as he stared wide-eyed around the ruined store. When I hit his buddy in the forehead with the rifle butt, he still didn't seem too concerned. He had enough sense left to shake his head at me once, but maybe he didn't shake it hard enough. I took him out, too, then dragged them outside and cuffed one's wrist to the other's through the front-door handle. Up close, there seemed to be some family resemblance between them, except that one's forehead hung over his eyes and the other's nose was three inches wide and flapjack-thick. Then I quickly unloaded their rifles and made junk out of them against the curb.

When I got the bandit out of the slippery mess to a fairly clean part of the floor, I slid off the ski mask, and a long string of bubbly froth looped out of his mouth. He was just a kid, maybe twenty, with the dark coppery skin and flat round face of a Benniwah. When I cut off his shirt and jacket, I saw that he had the small delicate chest of a malnourished child. The round had taken him just below the right collarbone. Because the bullet must have been wobbling after passing through the plate glass, it caused an unusually large entrance wound, and the exit wound through his shoulder blade was as large as the bottom of a beer can. The round must have clipped the top of his lung, too, because both wounds were sucking air. Finally I found enough gauze pads on the shelf to pack them, and I bound them tightly with tape.

By then the inevitable crowd had begun to gather from the bar and the theater and the vehicles parked along the street to see the real blood, the real dying. While I was working on the kid they had stayed back, staring through the ruined windows, and they shied from my glances as if they had seen a caged animal they were afraid to recognize. As usually happens, too, some had come to help. One man held the crowd at bay, another took a flashlight and waved passing cars past the store, and a stout young woman wearing glasses and a full-length leather coat pushed through the crowd. She slipped out of her coat, under which she wore a long pink wool dress. "I'm a nurse," she said calmly as she came through the door and draped her coat over the kid. "Are you okay?" she asked as she patted my cheek.

"A little shaky," I said, "but the kid's hurt bad."

We knelt beside him and noticed that his breath turned sour and shallow, rattling, bloody spittle snaking out of his mouth.

She took his pulse, and it seemed I could feel his blood flow dwindle to a thread under her fingers.

"We're losing him," she said quietly, staring at me over the narrow, bottomless gulf.

She got on his chest, and I propped his chin back, checked to see if he had swallowed his tongue, then pinched his pug nose and started the mouth-to-mouth. Sometimes we can breathe for each other, muscle the heart. Somehow we kept him going ten, maybe fifteen minutes until the EMS technicians arrived with the ambulance. He seemed to be breathing on his own when they strapped him onto the stretcher. The nurse tossed her coat to a man she seemed to know—a husband or a date—and the two of us leaned against the counter breathing hard for ourselves, then we fell into each other's arms so hard that it knocked off her glasses, held each other like old lovers. Over her shoulder I could see her date or husband or whatever holding her bloody coat as if it were something he had found in the street.

After most of the police had come and gone, after I had stood ankle-deep in the back cooler for half an hour, breaking my schnapps vow and drinking beer after beer, then promptly throwing them up, I went out front to stand in the freezing rain with Colonel Haliburton and the chief of police, Jamison, my old buddy, asshole buddy from childhood, Korea, adopted father of my son. The three of us stood outside, even beyond the roof overhang, as if somebody had died inside the store, and watched three Haliburton uniformed guards set up sawhorse and rope barricades around the lot. The young couple who managed the store, dressed in matching maroon bathrobes and white flannel pajamas covered with tiny red and green reindeer, huddled in the dim, smoky light just inside the front door. Occasionally one or the other would break into a tiptoe trot through the mess to pick up a can of dog food or a box of breakfast cereal off the floor, place it carefully on the shelf, then gently straighten the row.

"They might as well have used hand grenades," the colonel said softly, shaking his head.

"Fucking assholes," I muttered.

The colonel lifted his flat cap off his balding head and frowned into the darkness, away from me. In spite of all his years in the Army, profanity still embarrassed him as much as it must have when he was a good little Lutheran farm boy growing up outside Grand Forks, North Dakota. He cleared his throat in disapproval, then stared even harder into the distance, as if he were watching the fresh snow on the Hardrocks. "I don't know how you do it, Milo," Jamison said sadly. "I don't know how you get into so much trouble."

"Just lucky, I guess."

He looked at me hard and for a long, silent time. We hadn't been friends since I was bounced off the sheriff's department for looking the other way from some illegal punchboards. Then he married my first ex-wife and adopted my son, which hadn't improved our affairs.

"I would like to see you in my office tomorrow morning," Jamison said bluntly, "eight A.M. sharp, Milo, not one minute later." He paused and ran his hand through his rain-wet hair. "Why did you have to break up their rifles?" he added. "Why?"

"The heat of passion," I said.

"Just be there," he said, "because I think you've bought the farm this time." Since Evelyn—my ex-wife, his wife—had recently left him to take up residence with a twenty-eight-year-old vegetarian French professor at Reed College in Portland, Jamison had trouble focusing his anger on me. "Just be there," he repeated.

"Ah-hem," the colonel said, "my lawyer will be there also." Then he walked over to comfort the young couple. I started to follow him.

"Just a minute, Milo," Jamison said. "I've been meaning to call you. Evelyn has this idea that we have to be civilized about all this shit."

"Civilized," I said. "What shit?"

"You and me and her and the boy," he sighed, "and whatever it is she lives with. She says we should all be adults about this, and she's got tickets to the Washington State–Stanford game, and she wants all to gather on neutral ground to watch the boy play."

"How's he doing?" I asked. Eric played defensive end for the WSU Cougars.

"Great," Jamison said, nearly smiling. "He's started the last three games. Kicking ass. Or so I read in the papers. I haven't been able to get away for a game this year."

"I'll think about it," I said, "even though I don't want to."

"Call me," he said, "and I'll see you in the morning." Then he stalked away in the rain, some of which had turned to sleet. The tiny white pellets gathered on the stooped shoulders of his tweed overcoat.

When I turned around, the colonel had his hands on the younger couple's arms, reassuring them all over again that his men would hang plywood sheets over the broken windows and would watch the store for the rest of the night. Then he gave them a gentle shove toward their Toyota pickup. The wife burst into tears and her husband looked as if he wanted to do the same, but he just clutched a milk carton to his chest so tightly that it leaked down the front of his robe as they walked away.

The colonel strode over to me, saying, "I want you to know that the entire legal resources of the corporation are at your disposal, Milo."

"Even if I quit?" I said.

"Even if you quit," he said, "but don't quit." The colonel had some romantic notion that because I had once worked a one-man office he had to keep me employed just in case he ever needed my old-fashioned, peculiar talents. "Don't quit."

"Sir, I can't stand any more of this monkey-suit business."

"Boredom and the bottle," the colonel said, looking at his ox-blood cordovans. His wife, it was rumored, drank. "Oh, Lord," he whispered, "there's just no call these days . . . but I did get a query from an outfit on the Coast today. They needed someone to tail a woman for a couple of days until they can get their own security people on it. I don't know the outfit, but I'll accept the job, and you can do it, then take a week or so off, with pay of course, to think about it."

"Jesus," I said, suddenly so tired that my head seemed to spin. "Sir, I just don't know—"

"Two weeks," he said, "as a favor to me."

"Only because you ask."

"Thank you," he said. "I want you to know that you handled that incident with Simmons this afternoon perfectly. I do appreciate that, Milo."

"Simmons?"

"The driver of the armored truck."

"Never can remember that kid's name," I admitted. "I just happened to be passing by, sir, and I really didn't do anything."

"Which was perfect," he said, then added to nobody in particular, "I've got to get that boy some help, somehow." Then he turned back to me, extended a hand. "I do thank you, though."

"Anytime," I said, shook his hand, then loaned him my handkerchief so he could wipe the sticky Coke slime off his hand.

"I'll leave the woman's name and address with the dispatcher," he said, "and you can pick it up after your, ah, chat with Jamison . . . You don't mind if I ask about the trouble between the two of you?"

"A long story," I said. "History."

"I see," he said, then waved aimlessly as he marched off toward his gray Mercedes, a staunch, stocky, erect figure of a man, a good soldier to the end. The colonel had retired to Meriwether and started a small security service so he could afford his fishing trips, but he was too good at the business. It kept expanding. First into alarm systems, then into armored transport, then into branch offices all over the Mountain West. I knew for a fact that he hadn't wet a fishing line in over two years.

When he started the engine of his Mercedes, the diesel clattered loudly. I wondered what sort of man tried to keep aging detectives out of the bars, to provide jobs for half-crazed Vietnam vets, and drove a thirty-five-thousand-dollar automobile that sounded like a truck, wondered, as always, what to think about the colonel. Usually, professional military men and successful businessmen gave me a pain in the ass, but I liked the colonel. I didn't even mind that he had stolen my handkerchief.

When I walked around to the rear of the store to pick up the Pinto, the cold beer in my shoes felt like frozen slush, and most of the glass had been blown out of the little tin car by errant rounds. Only a railroad embankment behind the store had saved the two vigilantes from spreading misery and mayhem throughout the neighborhood. I wiped the shards of safety glass off the front seat, as best I could in the darkness, then drove across town to pick up my truck, the sleet funneling into my face through the broken windshield.

By the time I had showered the soda syrup and chips out of my hair and off my back, changed clothes, and indulged myself in a short toot, I felt as old as I was ever going to get. Even though I was already an hour late for my meeting with Gail, I heaved myself off my couch, eased the pickup over the icy streets down to the Deuce, where a bluegrass band fretted through its last set. She was nowhere to be found in the crowded bar or among the dancers stomping on the floor. Even Raoul, my dealer, had gone home. I saw a biker gang I knew, but we didn't exchange greetings, and the armored-truck driver, whose name I had forgotten again, still in his Haliburton uniform, sleeping at a table in the shadows beside the back door. I gave up and walked across the street to Arnie's, a bar for serious drinkers, where nobody either cared or noticed if your hands trembled so badly that it took both of them to get a shot of schnapps to your mouth.

I saw my postman there, though, also still in the baggy sack of his borrowed uniform, but he had a fat lip I hadn't given him, so I had one shot, then went home to my little log house in the canyon.

Since the colonel's lawyer—a sharp young dude dressed in Western clothes and wearing, fastened to his string tie, what looked to be the piece of turquoise the size of an elk turd that I hadn't bought—and I were both on time the next morning, the police took my statement politely and with a minimum amount of fuss and bother. Jamison didn't even show up.

When I got out to the Haliburton offices, the colonel hadn't come in either, so I picked up the name and address from the dispatcher. A wildly impressive name, Cassandra Bogardus, but a rather shabby address over on the north side beyond the tracks, 1414 Gold. None of the women I knew on the north side could afford the sort of trouble that called for a two-hundred-a-day tail. I didn't really care, though, because I was so glad to be out of uniform. Two days of this, I thought, then I can do Sarah Weddington's crazy number and head south.

I signed for a white Chevy van without checking the fake magnetic signs on the doors, transferred my surveillance gear to the van from my pickup, and headed for the north side of town. By ten o'clock that morning I was on station half a block down Gold from the Bogardus house.

The freezing rain and sleet had, as the weatherman had predicted, changed to snow, and the temperature had stabilized in the low twenties. Weather, as Gail had said. But it didn't bother me; I had all the comforts of home. A snowmobile suit and down booties kept me snug and warm as I lounged in the plastic web of a lawn chair in the back of the van. If I leaned forward a bit, my eye nestled easily against the 25X spotting scope that hid behind the smoked glass of the rear window. On my right I had a huge thermos of coffee, on my left lunch—a bag full of homemade sandwiches, egg salad on light rye with a slice of Walla Walla white onion as thick as my finger—and if nature called, I was ready. In the corner of the van sat a Port-a-Potty like a faithful robot companion prepared for duty. I might not know why I was doing what I was doing, but I had done it enough in the old days to know how to do it in comfort.

The Bogardus house sat on a large corner lot. An untrimmed hedge and clumps of shrubbery drooped under the load of heavy wet snow. Two vehicles were parked in the driveway—a beautifully restored 1964 Mustang convertible with New Hampshire plates, and a brand-new three-quarter-ton 4x4 GMC pickup with a load of firewood in the bed and Maryland plates. Firewood, neatly split and stacked, also covered most of the side porch. In the backyard, a huge compost pile stood next to a large garden already winter-bedded and covered with straw. The small window in the front door showed no light in the gray, snowy day, and the other windows were dark behind half shutters and tie-dyed drapes. A wisp of woodsmoke trickled out of the chimney, though, curling among the large drifting flakes.

I settled in for the waiting, oddly excited to be working again. During the next two hours, while nothing happened, I decided that Sarah's job might be fun—picking up two unknown people, filling in their history, finding out what sordid little secrets drew them to their weekly rendezvous. An old Chicago cop had taught me how to tail by choosing a perfect stranger off the street and making me dog the man or woman for days on end, put them to bed at night, wake them up in the morning. I was surprised to find out how few strangers, when I watched their lives for a few days, turned out to be perfectly boring. Almost everybody, it seemed, led at least one secret life. Except me. I was the watcher, the uninvolved observer. Sometimes a boring job, but usually safe.

Or so I thought until I was halfway into my first sandwich and somebody started pounding on the side of the van. With the blackout curtain hanging behind the front seats and the smoked glass in the rear windows, I knew nobody could see inside, so I sat very still until a face peered blindly through one of the back windows. I peeked out from the other one. It was a wiry old man in house slippers, shiny black slacks, and an old-fashioned undershirt. He wore a huge mustache, yellowed with age but neatly trimmed and combed, long enough to nearly reach his defiant little chin. The hands of a much larger man dangled off his corded arms. He raised one of them and slapped the smoked glass hard enough to shake the van.

"I know you're in there, you lazy son of a bitch!" he shouted, then slapped the glass again while I ducked away.

When he grabbed the rear bumper and began rocking the van, I gave up. "I'm coming," I shouted, "I'm coming." Then, swaddled in the snowmobile suit and as clumsy as a drunken bear, I wrestled through the blackout curtain and out the passenger door.

"I called you sons a bitches yesterday afternoon," the old man said when he saw me, "yesterday goddamned afternoon. And you promised you'd be here before noon. So what the hell do you do? Show up and take a snooze right in my front yard." Then he shook a fist the size of a steer's kneebone under my nose, and tiny drifts of snow fell off his bare shoulders. As he looked at me, his eyes didn't seem to focus correctly, and I saw the pinched creases on the bridge of his nose where his glasses usually rested.

"Why me?" I muttered as I stepped backward to see what sort of sign hung on the van's door. Not Floral Delivery or Washing Machine Repair, not Knife Sharpening or Housecleaning Services—nothing safe for me—but TV REPAIR in large black letters.

"Well?" the old man said, raising his fist again.

"I don't know what you're talking about," I said. "You must have talked to the girl in the office."

"Didn't talk to no girl," he growled, "talked directly to you." Snowflakes gathered in his eyebrows and on his thin hair began to melt, but the old man ignored the icy water trickling down his wrinkled face.

"Not to me," I said, "you didn't talk to me." Then I chanced a glance at the sign. "Not to me—Clyde 'Shorty' Griffith," I read.

The old man looked at me as if I was crazy. He raised one woolly eyebrow as if to say, "What sort of damn fool has to read his name off a sign to remember it?" Then he squinted at the sign again, shifted his shoulders, and grumbled. I thought I had him until he said, "Did so." Even caught in confusion and blindness, the old man wasn't about to retreat. "Damn sure did."

"Couldn't have," I said, retreating myself. "I . . . ah, I was out with the flu." Then added with a whine, "And I wasn't taking a nap, I was having lunch."

"Whiskey flu," he said, "and a two goddamned hour whiskey lunch."

"No way," I said, but the old man had me backing up so fast that I didn't even believe myself anymore. "Not true."

"Well," he said, licking the snow water off his mustache, "you damn sure promised, Mr. Whatever-your-name-is, to have my TV fixed before one o'clock"—he tugged a large Hamilton railroad watch out of his pants, consulted it about six inches from his face—"and I've got a lady friend coming over in forty-seven minutes to watch *General Hospital,* and if my set ain't fixed by then, I'm gonna call the Better Business Bureau, maybe even the county attorney . . . you people think you can treat old folks like shit . . . well, I'm here to tell you that don't go with Abner Haynes—"

"Okay," I said, thinking I had run into enough crazy people in the past two days to last me a lifetime. If my cover hadn't already been blown, it certainly would be if I spent any more time in the street debating the issue with the old man. I needed to move the van now, anyway, so maybe if I took a few moments to run his set downtown to a repair shop, leave it, and rent a loaner, then I could race back, drop it off, and find another location quickly. I glanced at the Bogardus house. Nothing had moved. Maybe it would work, unprofessional as it was. Maybe I had been a security guard too long. "Listen, pops," I said to the old man, "I don't know nothing about this call, okay, but I'll take a quick look at your set—I can't promise to fix it here, may have to run it to the shop and pick up a loaner—"

"Don't you 'pops' me, you big ugly bastard," he grunted when he found his voice under the anger. He was giving away sixty pounds and twenty-some-odd years, but he didn't care. Either I apologized, and quickly, or he was going to take a poke at me.

"Listen," I said, "I'm sorry."

"My name is Abner Haynes," he said, his fists still clenched. "Mr. Haynes to you, by God."

"Yes, sir, Mr. Haynes," I said. "Now if I could take a look at your set?"

Abner shrugged and sighed, then led me toward his little frame house. The sidewalk in front of his yard, his walk and his porch steps had been shoveled often enough since the snow started so that they were bordered by substantial drifts, and the old man had carefully scattered rock salt on the concrete. The rose bushes by the porch had been pruned and wrapped in burlap, and even under the six inches of snow I could tell that Abner's lawn lay as smooth and level as a golf green.

When I stepped out of the cold and into Abner's living room, I broke into an immediate, showering sweat. I wiped my forehead and Abner chuckled.

"That old sawdust furnace works like a charm," he said proudly. "Smells good and don't smoke at all, and," he added, "those goddamn environmentalists with their smoky wood stoves ... Ha! Fools. Almost every house in the neighborhood had wood or sawdust furnaces when they were first built. Then all those fools who thought they was progressive, they switched to natural gas—ain't nothing natural about burning something you can't see or smell, something that's as likely to turn a man's house into kindling wood as keep it warm ..."

Abner carried on about the state of the world and the nature of progress while I looked at the wall covered with framed pictures above the television set: Abner in his gandy dancer days, young and cocky, as lean and tough as the hickory handle of his pick, as sturdy as the stack of ties he leaned against in some mountain pass, his mustache as black as India ink and as big as the switch on a cow's tail; Abner's wedding picture with him standing a head shorter than his large blond wife; Abner as brakeman, fireman, conductor ... Abner's life captured in fading yellow prints.

"... so what's with my TV?" he asked and tried to poke me in the ribs through the bulk of the snowmobile suit.

I didn't have any idea—it looked as if the bottom half of the picture had folded itself halfway back up the tube—but I knew how to make it work long enough for me to move the van and take off those goddamned signs.

"Well, what you've got there, Mr. Haynes," I said, "is an ABS forty-two-slash-eleven tube going bad on you, and I can tell you right now, sir, that I ain't got one on the truck, maybe not even one in the shop—don't get much call to work on that model these days—but I can make it work for a couple of hours, and I'll put that tube on order just as soon as I get back to the shop." Then I began to disconnect the set, wrapped the cord around it, and picked up the huge old-fashioned, misnamed "portable" color set.

"Where the hell you going with my TV?" he asked.

"Well, sir," I grunted, "I'm gonna set it out on the porch here and let that ABS tube cool off—you see, when it gets too hot, the resistance builds up and it pulls off the aim of the gun—"

"The gun?" he interrupted.

"Trust me," I said. "I'll leave it outside while I finish my lunch, then at five to one I'll carry it back inside and hook it up for you." Abner looked extremely doubtful. "Believe me, sir, it'll work," I said. "One time I watched the whole second half of a Raider-Jets game sitting in a snowstorm with a garbage bag over the top of my set—"

"A garbage bag?"

"God's truth," I said, and it was.

"Well," Abner said, tugging on the corner of his mustache, "I guess we can give it a try, but if it don't work, I know Yvonne'll sneak over to that damn Tyrone's, even though he's only got a black-and-white, to watch her soap . . ."

Abner opened the front door, still worrying, and I put the set down on the porch and headed for the van before he could find a new argument, promising to keep an eye on his TV while I finished my lunch.

Nothing had changed at the Bogardus house, and nothing happened while I waited. The whole neighborhood seemed frozen, still, except for two small children, who looked like bear cubs in their snowsuits, and a malamute pup playing in a yard down the street. At five to one I lugged the set back into Abner's

57

house and connected the antenna wires, and it worked like a charm. Once again I promised to order him a new tube, and Abner reached into his pocket and asked how much he owed me.

"On the house," I said.

"Don't need nobody's charity," he grumbled but left his hand in his pocket. "Thanks," he added, and we shook hands.

"That's some 'stache," I said on the way out, and good old Abner grinned somewhere behind it.

I was halfway back in the van when a tiny old woman with a painted face that looked as if it had been left too long in the weather minced down the sidewalk toward Abner's walk. She tried out a smile on me, an expression so coy and phony that not even a child would have fallen for it. Lord knows what a stand-up dude like Abner saw in a piece of fluff like that. Then I wondered if perhaps Abner and Sarah might want to double-date with Gail and me some night. I drove away, laughing.

My new location on the cross street didn't give me quite as good a view. I couldn't see the front door, but both vehicles were still parked in the driveway. Still more nothing with snow. If I decided to take Sarah's job, I hoped the weather would clear by Thursday. The money would be great, but it seemed a little crazy to me. And when I worked for myself, I had done some insane shit—divorces and child custody cases so obscene and degrading that only a month of whiskey could get the taste out of my mouth; repossessions of everything from combines to tropical fish; and once I had flown to Hawaii to steal back a dual champion Labrador retriever at the Honolulu airport from a Japanese businessman who had stolen it from a Texan in southern Alberta. However strange the jobs had been, though, they had a purpose, and somehow the satisfaction of an old lady's curiosity seemed a bit too eccentric for me.

It would be an easy job, sure, tagging two people who weren't thinking about somebody tailing them—if they were worried about tails, they wouldn't have met at the same place so many times—maybe too easy for a man of my talents . . .

But as I was complimenting myself, a police car pulled in behind the van, good old Abner glowering in the passenger seat. Nothing is ever simple or easy in my work. This took an hour to straighten out, an hour at the police station.

The colonel finally got Abner to stop shouting about lazy, crazy bastards who gave him a line of crap a mile long then set his TV out on the goddamned porch in the snow and call it fixed. He stopped because the colonel promised that Haliburton Security would buy him a new television set, which Mr. Milodragovitch would personally deliver the next morning. Then the colonel and Jamison both shook their heads and gave me the sort of look you give a puppy who brings back a dog turd instead of the stick. I even had to give Abner a ride back to his house. All the way, Abner kept his nose curled as if I was the dog turd.

Chapter 4

This time I parked two blocks west of Abner's house down Gold, nearly three blocks away from the Bogardus house, and I had to keep my eye on the spotting scope constantly. At three-forty, I got to log my first entry of the surveillance. A slender brunette in slacks and a blue down parka emerged from the side door of the house and began to scrape the windshield of the Mustang. As she leaned over the hood, her tight gray slacks stretched rather nicely over good strong legs and a great ass. I didn't put that in my report but I did make a note of it.

Then she climbed into the convertible, backed out of the driveway and took off like a shot east on Gold. By the time I had lumbered into the driver's seat, started the cold engine, and performed a full-bore three-hundred-and-sixty-degree spin instead of a U-turn on the icy street, the Mustang was nearly out of sight. If she hadn't caught a red light at Dawson, I might have lost her. When she bounced across the old rail bed on Main, the bump knocked the snow off the bottom of her license plate. "Live Free or Die," it said.

The Mustang led me east on Main and into the parking lot of the Riverfront Lodge, where the woman parked and locked her car and headed for the bar entrance, her buttocks jingling with muscle each time her boot heels hit the pavement. She was a pleasure to tail. I gave her a minute while I struggled out of the snowmobile suit and booties—winter exercise, changing clothes to match the temperature—and back into my new boots and a Japanese tractor "gimme cap."

Inside the plush bar, all mirrors and wood and décor abounding, I saw the woman up on a bar stool, chatting with the daytime bartender, my old friend Vonda Kay. I slid into a dark circular booth and tried to hide, but Vonda Kay spotted me. She charged over to pull me out of the booth, cursed me for not saying hello, then dragged me over to the bar to meet a new friend of hers. When she led me up to the woman, I tried to look anonymous, but when she started to introduce us, I gave up.

"Hey," she said as she tapped the lady on the arm, "I want you to meet an old friend of mine." The lady turned and smiled. "Carolyn Fitzgerald, shake hands with Milo Milodragovitch. Carolyn's new in town—with the Forest Service or some crap— and Milo's a rent-a-cop."

Carolyn Fitzgerald, whoever she might be, shook my hand warmly and asked, "And just how much does it cost to rent a cop these days?"

"One shot of schnapps," I said, then excused myself to go to the john and call the colonel.

He apologized for not giving me a description of Cassandra Bogardus, then told me to let it go for the day, to pick up the tail in the morning.

"Like flies on shit, sir, I promise."

The colonel coughed politely into the telephone, told me where to pick up Mr. Haynes's new television, then wished me luck.

Well, sometimes you get lucky. Carolyn Fitzgerald's broad, flat face was too blunt to be pretty, but she had grand, unfettered breasts bobbing and weaving beneath her soft gray sweater, and something even better, something women who own their own lives often find in their thirties, an intelligent, happy mind, a generous smile, and an honest laugh. We smoked and drank and exchanged those inevitable details of our histories. She had grown up in Burlington, Vermont, where her father and mother both taught government and economics in the local high schools, and she had a master's from Cornell in recreational management, whatever that might be, and had just finished a law degree at Georgetown, and had been hired as a legal consultant by the Friends of the Dancing Bear Wilderness Area to keep an eye on the Forest Service land swaps and purchases.

"And I've been trying to get hold of you for weeks," she said as she crushed a cigarette butt in the ashtray. "You don't seem to answer your telephone," she said, "or my letters."

"I took the bell out of my telephone," I admitted, "and I don't even open that kind of mail."

"Philistine," she said.

"With a vengeance."

"Oh, that's true, honey," Vonda Kay said from the back bar, where she was making something tasteless in the blender. "Don't believe a word he says."

"He has an honest face," Carolyn said, then touched my crooked nose with the tip of her finger.

Vonda Kay just laughed and put another strawberry into the machine. The two of us went way back, all the way to high school, and had served each other well over the years, safe harbors in our stormy domestic lives. Once we even took off at four in the morning to drive to Jackpot, Nevada, to get married, but somewhere among the cliffs of the Salmon River in Idaho we both realized that neither of our divorces was final. We hadn't seen much of each other lately, but I knew Vonda Kay wasn't mad at me. She had introduced me to Carolyn out of friendship.

When I finished blushing, I told Carolyn that I was no more honest than the next man.

"Which also means no less," she said. "Except for the old C, C&K Railroad sections and your three thousand acres, Mr. Milodragovitch, I think I've got the Dancing Bear settled from the waterworks dam up the Hell-Roaring drainage and over the Diablos' divide to the Stone River Reservation. We're having a little trouble finding out who really owns the C, C&K sections, but when we do, I've worked out a swap of their sidehill trash timber and that old mine for a nice stand of second-growth pine down on Forest Service land in Idaho. What's holding you up, sir?"

"You can call me Milo," I said, "and I'm more than a little reluctant to give up my grandfather's timber land for money, marbles, or match sticks, or even virgin ponderosa, but I wouldn't mind discussing it with you up at my place."

"What did you have in mind?" she asked, then sipped her martini, her eyes twinkling above the glass.

"Elk steaks cut off a dry cow killed this weekend," I said, "a bit of blow, if you're so inclined, and whatever."

"You don't look the type," she said.

"For whatever?"

"For cocaine," she answered. "You look like a cop."

"And you, lady, look like a hell of a lot of fun," I said, feeling a lot better already.

We settled our tab, got our change and Vonda Kay's blessing, and Carolyn followed me up the canyon to my house.

She *was* fun, too. She walked around the cellar, drinking gin on ice and occasionally hitting the lines I had chopped on the top of the freezer, pouring me the odd shot of schnapps and talking about this and that while I butchered the right hindquarter of the cow elk. She didn't act like I was insane when I pan-fried the steaks and made home fries and gravy, and she ate dinner with a good appetite, in spite of the coke.

"You're pretty classy," I told her as we took our coffee into the living room, "for a tourist broad."

"You're not too bad either," she said as she poked at the crackling apple-wood fire, "if you'd just stop playing Gary Cooper." Then she dug a fat bomber joint out of her purse, lit it, and said as she passed it to me, "Just in case."

"In case of what?" I asked, and she gave me a wicked smile.

And wicked she was, that long, firm body gleaming in the firelight, sweet shadowed hollows, smooth skin, muscle tone worthy of an Olympic swimmer. She waited for a long time as we played to speak.

"I've got one rule," she said, her voice in the darkness above me, "one rule you should know about."

"No business in bed," I suggested with a muffled voice.

"No all-nighters and damn few repeaters," she said, moaning and moving under my tongue. "That's how-how I keep my life simple. No-no baggage."

She meant it, too. Sometime after midnight she gathered her clothes and hiked toward the bathroom. When she came back, freshly showered and dressed, she knelt beside me where I lay on the carpet like a gut-shot bear, bleeding where she had raked my back and thighs and ears, bleeding even from the scrape on my forehead. I meant to roll over to hold her, but the weight of her cool hand held me to the floor.

"What do you want for your timberland?" she asked.

"My grandfather's timber," I groaned, correcting her, "my grandfather's."

"He's been dead for forty-three years," she said, pressing on my chest, "and your name is on the deed."

"What's in a name?"

"Be serious."

"Maybe I am."

"How about more money?"

"Sure," I said, "and a plaque in the middle of Camas Meadows with my grandfather's name on it."

"That's easy."

"And a suspension of the rules, too."

"The rules?"

"Sure," I said. "When you get the C, C&K sections, if you get them, give me a call . . ."

"On a telephone that doesn't ring?"

"Come by the house," I said. "I want to be one of those lucky damn few repeaters. A weekend in Seattle maybe?"

"All right," she said, but somehow it sounded more like a threat than a promise.

"And one time on my grandfather's grave."

"His grave?"

"His ashes are scattered in Camas Meadows."

"You son of a bitch," she said, laughing. "Thanks for the evening—all of it, old man—and the next time we discuss this matter, I expect you to be serious."

"Three times is about as serious as I get these days, love . . ."

She slapped me on the chest, kissed me, and left, her laughter and smell still warm in the living room, mixed with the fragrance of the apple wood, as I let the snowy darkness flow around my log house and over my eyes . . .

I woke around four, though, with a mild case of the cocaine jangles and a terminal case of the post-coital blues. The good ones always seem to get away, I thought, and second best is no way to love. Shit. As the child of two suicides, depression always hovered about me like a cloud while self-pity waited in the wings. I made myself get up and stumbled to the bathroom to take an old Serax left over from my hard-drinking days. In theory, it would ease the shakes. I went out into my backyard, anyway, to roll naked in the snow, to have a reason for the quivering inside. The front had passed, the sky cleared, and the temperature dropped into the teens. A sliver of moon tried, unsuccessfully, to compete with the stars.

After a long hot shower I wiped the bathroom mirror clear of mist and tried to talk to myself. "No all-nighters," I said, "and no damn repeaters at all. Travel light. You're forty-seven years old and you're carrying more baggage than you need . . ." Then I had to laugh. Sometimes when you try to talk to yourself there's nobody home. I knew all the signs, far too well, knew I was on the verge of something. Another marriage maybe, another failure at love with the first woman who would have me. Another life, another place, any place, any love.

Later that morning I was glad I woke up early and stayed awake. I was parked down the street from 1414 Gold before six o'clock, and at six-thirty a tall blond woman in a red velour robe stepped out of the front door, stretched backward so hard that her large, heavy breasts seemed to lift like wings, then bent gracefully from the waist like a dancer to pick up the Meriwether *Avalanche-Express*. She moved as smoothly as light wind across water, Cassandra in the morning, and when she bent, her long, straight blond hair rippled like gold off her shoulders. The spotting scope gathered the dawn light, and I could see her face, the high cheekbones of a model, the wide, firm mouth and dark eyes of a lover, the broad, unruffled forehead of a woman at peace with herself. I had tailed Carolyn Fitzgerald by mistake, and we had ended up in bed. I couldn't help hoping that tailing this woman on purpose might lead to that same bedroom. Cassandra Bogardus stretched again, then walked barefoot through the snow to the pickup, empty of firewood now, started it and left it idling, then went back into the house without even brushing the snow off her feet. Tough, too. I liked that.

Half an hour later she came back out dressed like a model for an Aspen ski advertisement, carrying a shoulder bag and a large purse, then jumped into the pickup and roared away west on Gold toward the interstate. By the time she passed the remains of the turkey-wreck debris, she was doing seventy. It looked like we were headed out of town, so I checked the glove box to be sure the company credit cards and the trip ticket were there, then I settled in two hundred yards behind her. What the hell, I could stand a bit of road time; but before I could get comfortable, she took the airport exit. Ten minutes later we were standing in the check-in line for the 7:48 flight to Salt Lake City. I heard the ticket agent check Ms. Bogardus through to Los Angeles, so I ducked out of line and called the colonel at home. He told me to stay with her and promised that backup help would meet me at LAX.

Since I didn't want her to see my face too many times, I stayed in the downstairs coffee shop until the arriving passengers from Missoula disembarked. I waited five minutes after the final call for the Salt Lake flight, then dashed upstairs to claim my seat. Once aboard the airplane, I hurried to the rear with my head down, fell into an empty seat in front of the aft bulkhead, shut my eyes, then did a fair imitation of a man sleeping.

I didn't wake up until we were halfway to Salt Lake. I went to the john and washed my face, then wandered forward to thumb through the tattered magazines in the rack. On my way back I checked out the passengers. Cassandra Bogardus wasn't aboard. Maybe she's in the john, I told myself, or maybe you've been had. Then I remembered that when I was sitting in the coffee shop watching the disembarking Missoula passengers—as you do in airports, looking for a familiar face—I had seen a tall, erect gray-haired woman in a tweed suit who had looked oddly familiar. Now I suspected I knew why. There had been enough commotion around the white van in her neighborhood the day before—Abner, the police, my aborted U-turn—that it would have been a wonder if she hadn't made my van. And she certainly had ditched me very neatly.

The colonel met my flight back from Salt Lake. He seemed tired but not too upset as I told him how the Bogardus woman had dumped my tail.

"Pretty goddamned smooth," I told him again. "I'm sorry."

"A one-man tail is tough," he said as we walked out to the parking lot. "We just didn't have enough information. That's why I didn't want to take the job in the first place, but I thought you would enjoy the work."

"I'll find the bitch," I said, "and she'll—"

"They have their own security people on it now," he interrupted. "Ms. Bogardus is no longer our concern." He coughed politely into an expensive deerskin glove. "I took the liberty of driving your pickup," he said, "and I'll take the van back to the office. Your paycheck, with the extra two weeks' pay, is in the glove box." We traded key rings. "And Mr. Haynes's new television set is in the cab. If you wouldn't mind . . ."

"Not at all."

"Go someplace warm," he said, "and enjoy yourself. We'll talk about your job when you get back."

"Thank you, sir," I said. "You ought to take off yourself, if you don't mind me saying so. How long's it been since you wet a line, sir?"

"Far too long," he said, smiling sadly, "far too long. I meant to get down to the Florida Keys for some bone fishing this year, but I don't seem to be able to find the time."

"It's a long time to next year's trout season, sir."

"A long time, yes. Did you hear what happened up at Downey Creek?"

"No, sir," I said. Downey Creek was the nearest blue-ribbon trout stream to Meriwether.

"That gold mine on the west fork," he said, "they're using some sort of acid process on the old tailings and one of their ponds broke . . . forty percent fish kill . . . Sometimes, Milo, I wonder what's happening to this country."

"Me too," I said, and the colonel patted me on the arm and said goodbye.

"By the way," he said, reaching into his pocket, "I believe this is yours." He handed me my handkerchief, washed, ironed, and neatly folded.

"Thank you," I said. "Would you do me a favor, sir?"

"What's that?"

"If you find out what this Bogardus deal is about, will you tell me?"

"If I find out, Milo," he said, then walked across the lot to the van.

As I drove back to town on the old highway, I wasn't very proud of myself. Perhaps Sarah's little job was just about my speed. Next day was Thursday. I decided to do Sarah's job, to take her money, easy as it was, put it in a pile with mine and head south for the winter. Maybe for good. Even though I had been born and raised in Meriwether, it didn't feel much like home anymore. Across town, the south hills had been gobbled up by developers, the softly rounded slopes layered with rows of ticky-tacky houses. Even with the pulp mill on half shifts and with the millions of dollars worth of scrubbers the mill had installed, the air smelled like cat piss and rotten eggs whenever the wind came out of the west, and the current rage for wood stoves was already filling the valley with a yellowish-brown haze, clotted thickly in the air like something you might cough up, and after a week of winter inversion, you would. All my favorite downtown bars were either closed or filled with children. Mahoney's had become a place to buy expensive coffee, sweet European baked goods, and overpriced glassware. The Slumgullion was still on the corner of Dottle and Zinc, but under new management, and they didn't serve brains and eggs or fried mush and fresh side pork anymore. Even all my old wino friends seemed to have disappeared.

Right, I thought, south for the winter, for all the winters. I knew a dope dealer in Tucson who always needed a new bodyguard, and an ex-con in Albuquerque who owned a used-car lot and always needed a salesman also licensed to do repossessions. *Right!*

Old Abner was like a kid at Christmas when I took his new television set out of the box. It was a Sony, and when I turned it on, he stared, entranced by the bright, sharp colors, then he broke into a jig, clapping his hands and dancing around the room in his flopping slippers. I had a vision of Abner and Yvonne transfixed for days in front of the endless soaps as a surly Tyrone lurked outside the windows.

On my way out, Abner caught me on the porch, grabbed my arm, thanked me again, and asked, "Are you really one of those private eyes?"

"I used to be," I said, trying for a mysterious air, then I split.

Back at my house I tried to call Sarah, but the line was busy. I thought about a drink but decided to get ready to leave instead, half afraid that if I didn't pack now, I would never get out of town when the time came. I stripped all my guns, cleaned and oiled them, put them all, along with my poacher's crossbow, behind the false panel in the basement. Then I finished quartering the elk, wrapped the front quarters, put them in the freezer, and took the remaining hindquarter over to my next-door neighbor. She wasn't home, so I left it on the front porch. I went back to try Sarah's number again. Still busy. I had a shot of schnapps, then packed. Before I knew it, I was through. All my worldly goods, everything I would need for an extended visit, fit into two B-4 bags, a duffle bag, and one cardboard whiskey box. Now I was ready. When I finished Sarah's job, I could throw my crap into the back of the pickup in five minutes, and five minutes later I would see Meriwether in my rear-view mirror.

No all-nighters, damn few repeaters, no baggage, traveling light.

When Gail finally answered the phone, she didn't sound very happy to hear my voice. I apologized for missing our drink.

"Fuck it," she said. "What do you want?"

"To see Sarah."

"You going to work for her?"

"Guess so."

"She's resting now. Why don't you come by about four."

I agreed, and she hung up without saying goodbye.

This time I wore my old boots and a down vest and parked my truck right in front of the old McCravey mansion. Gail stood in the driveway, her daypack full of books on top of a Honda Civic. She looked as if she had been standing there for a long time, and her face looked red and chapped, her eyes watery with the cold.

"I'm sorry I was so abrupt on the telephone," she said, "but I had just spent an hour talking long distance to my mother, and she took forty-five minutes of small talk to tell me that my father's in the hospital."

"Nothing serious, I hope."

"Lung cancer, they think."

"I'm sorry," I said. "I keep meaning to quit smoking myself."

"He didn't smoke," she said, "he worked in a shipyard on the West Coast during World War II. Goddamned asbestos. The fibers curl up in your lungs like heartworms. Goddamned government."

"That's too bad," I said lamely.

"Well, I am sorry about being so short on the phone."

"Don't worry about it."

"Maybe we can have that drink after you talk to Sarah," she said. "I read about the excitement the other night, in the paper."

"I don't read the newspaper," I admitted.

"Don't you care about what's happening in the world?"

"What's the world?"

"A fucking insane asylum," she said, then laughed bitterly and rubbed her eyes. "Let's go see Sarah."

When we got there, the gray afternoon light seemed to fill the solarium like a light fog. Sarah looked tired, and when I leaned over to kiss her cheek, her hand trembled on my arm.

"It's so nice to see you, Bud," she said. "Would you like some coffee? Or a drink?"

"No thanks."

"Gail tells me that you are going to-to do this bit of eccentric nonsense for me."

"Yes, ma'am."

"That's very kind of you," she said, then reached into the pocket of her dark-blue dressing gown and withdrew the envelope and handed it to me. "I've changed my mind slightly, though . . ."

"Yes, ma'am?"

"The five thousand is your fee," she said, "and we will settle the expenses later."

"That's too much, way too much."

"Hush," she said. "Don't argue with me, young man. I never let my employees disagree with me." Then she chanced a weak smile. Over by the French doors, Gail laughed her way into a coughing fit. "Except for Gail, and I fear she is a hopeless case."

"It's too much . . ."

"Hush," she said again. "And I expect you to be profligate with expenses and my credit cards." I sighed, and she took it as a sign of my agreement. "If you do not mind my asking, Bud, how do you plan to do it?"

"Well, I was going to pick up one of the cars after tomorrow's meeting," I said, "but with this much money I can afford to hire some help to tail the other one, too."

"I-I would rather you handled it alone," Sarah said quickly. "You-you can appreciate my feelings."

"Yes, ma'am, you're the boss," I said. "So tomorrow I'll—ah, there's an outdoor telephone booth on the corner of Virginia and Dottle. I'll call to give you the number."

"I don't . . . I can't . . . talk—I don't like to use the telephone," Sarah stammered.

"Will you be here, Gail?"

"Sure," she said, shrugging. "I wouldn't miss this cloak-and-dagger action for the world. But why so far away?"

"So they won't see my pickup on Virginia," I explained. "Anyway, I'll give you the number of the telephone in the booth, and you can call me to tell me which car is coming my way."

"Right," Gail said.

"And-and after that?" Sarah asked.

"I'll tail whichever one comes my way, stick on them until I find out who they are," I said, thinking about my bad luck that morning. "Then I'll figure out some way to pick up the other one later."

"Sounds real precise," Gail said under her breath.

"Trust me," I said, "it's what I do for a living." Or used to, anyway.

After a silence that seemed to last for minutes, Sarah finally said, "Thank you again, Bud."

"For this kind of money you could have them killed," I said, trying for a joke, but I didn't get any laughs.

"Now," Sarah said, standing slowly and leaning heavily on her cane, "I'm afraid you will have to excuse me. This hasn't been one of my better days. I'm afraid I must retire." Then she limped toward the door.

"I'll be back in a minute," Gail said and helped Sarah to her bedroom.

While I waited I thought about my plan, which I had made up the moment Sarah asked me what I intended to do. If I wanted to get really fancy and modern, I could rent a directional mike and a couple of contact bugs, maybe even a movie camera. But, hell, old-fashioned and cheap would work on a cream puff of a job like this . . .

"Thank you for doing this for Sarah," Gail said as she came back. "I know it sounds crazy, but this is the sort of thing that keeps her alive and kicking. How about that drink now?"

"You have any schnapps?"

"Schnapps? God, I don't think so." Gail walked over to the large globe and checked it out. "Nope. Bourbon, Scotch, gin, brandy—beer in the refrigerator downstairs."

I hadn't had many beers in the past two years, and suddenly all the work I had put into staying sober seemed a waste of time. "Damn right," I said. We went down to the kitchen, where we had a beer, then another, and one of the bomber-sized joints I had lit for Sarah the other time.

"I know I'm trying to evade my problems," Gail said after she threw the roach into the garbage disposal, "and I know I'll start thinking about my father when I'm coming down in a couple of hours, and then I'll get so goddamned mad I can't see straight, and then I'll cry . . ."

But she didn't wait for the process to work itself out. She turned and hammered her fists on the edges of the sink as she sobbed. When I touched her shoulder she spun around quickly and huddled against my chest, still crying. One thing led to another, and a few minutes later we were on the kitchen floor, tangled in our clothes, involved in a frenzied coupling that had nothing to do with love or sex or even comfort, but two frightened, befuddled animals seeking a warm place to weep.

Afterward, as she hopped around trying to fit her overalls over her hiking boots, she said, "Goddamn, it's nice to know I'm handling this like an adult. Shit."

"What's an adult?" I said, turning my back politely to look for my shirt, to keep from seeing her naked anger and grief.

"Jesus Christ," she said, "you must lead an exciting life."

"What?"

"Those scratches on your back," she said. "An exciting life."

"Or sordid," I said.

"Shit, now I've made you sad," she said. "Sorry."

"No problem."

"Want another beer?"

"No thanks," I said. "I think maybe I should go."

"Maybe you're right," she said. "How old are you?"

"Forty-seven," I said. "Why?"

"Sometimes old guys get sad afterward," she said.

"I'll be goddamned," I said.

"Why?"

"Six, maybe seven years ago, a little hippie chick said the same thing to me."

"Maybe it's true," she said as she opened another beer.

"Maybe," I said.

"Whatever," she said, "thanks for being kind to Sarah . . . and to me."

"You're welcome," I said, but I didn't feel like I had been kind, not even once in my life. "I hope your father's all right," I said, kissed her cheek, then carried myself and my life home.

Chapter 5

The next afternoon I called Gail from the phone booth at the
corner of Dottle and Virginia to make sure that she and Sarah
were set. They were, Gail on the telephone, Sarah on the balcony
with her binoculars. I had mine, too, around my neck and hidden
under my down vest, even though I couldn't see the meeting
place from my angle. I told Gail to stay on the line to keep it
open, which she did, but she wasn't interested in any chitchat.
Maybe the night before had embarrassed her, maybe she wanted
to forget it.

I kept the booth occupied by opening the paper to the Houses
for Rent section and pretending to make calls. I wondered what
sort of response I would get from landlords if I were an unemployed sawyer with three children under six, two tomcats, an un-
spayed female German shepherd, and a wife who worked as a
barmaid. I probably couldn't rent a house with a gun.

But while I was waiting I got a good look at the driver of the
little yellow Toyota Corolla as he waited to make a left turn off

Dottle onto Virginia. Lank blond hair, acne scars across a tired, bony face—a sad face rather than troublesome. As he disappeared down Virginia, I remembered Sarah telling me that they always parked on opposite sides of the street, which probably meant the woman would be coming my way. But Gail came on the line and told me the guy had made a U-turn and parked facing in my direction.

Although I couldn't see down Virginia very far, I could make out a group of young girls trying to build a snowman on the front lawn of a sorority house while a gang of young boys pelted them with snowballs. As I watched, one of the new blue automated garbage trucks with EQCS, INC. painted on its bed turned into Virginia and worked its way slowly out of sight, the arms of the loader doing its job on the fifty-five-gallon drums. It looked like some sort of prehistoric monster dreamed up by a cartoonist who had taken one too many acid trips.

Sometimes I didn't know what to think of a world where garbage had become big business, where dumps had become something called landfills, a world where some of our garbage was so terrible we had to consider burying it in salt domes or launching it into outer space—

"The woman's here," Gail said, interrupting my thoughts.

"Ask Sarah what kind of car."

"A little blue one," she answered after a moment.

"Great," I said. "License number?" In the silence I felt the old juices begin to flow. But when Gail gave me the number, she didn't sound too sure about it.

"The guy's walking over to her car," Gail said. "Now he's running back to his car, he's coming your way."

"I got him," I said, then hung up quickly and ran to the corner with my binoculars in hope for a glance at the woman's car. I had time for a glimpse of a little blue Subaru with Montana plates, Silver Bow County, Butte, and the back of the woman's head in a blue-and-white striped ski hat, then I raced back to my pickup and waited for the man in the yellow Toyota Corolla.

When he turned right on Dottle, heading north, I was waiting for him, and I tucked the pickup into the traffic five cars behind him. After he crossed the bridge, he made several left and right turns in the downtown area, and I nearly lost him, but he didn't seem to know the one-way-street grid in Meriwether, and he ended up behind me heading west on Main. I watched his blinkers, wondering how I would catch him if he turned, but we went straight out Main to the interstate entrance. He signaled for the westbound ramp, so I went east in front of him, went a quarter of a mile, then whipped an illegal U-turn across the median, spraying snowy mud and grass behind me, praying that no cops were around. Then I punched the old pickup westbound. The four-barrel carburetor on the 302 engine screamed like a tornado as it sucked down gasoline at abut six miles to the gallon, and we caught the Toyota five miles west of town.

The old Corolla was covered with rusty dents and almost all the glass was cracked but the little car went fine, and I had to keep the foot-feed almost to the firewall to keep him in sight. Both saddle tanks were full, but if the guy was on his way to Washington, I would need gas before we got there. On the interstate west of Meriwether there weren't many exits, and I knew where they were, down to the mile marker, so I could stay way behind him between exits, then catch up to watch for a turn. Twice he got off the interstate, then went across the intersection and back up the westbound ramp. He still thought he might have a tail but didn't have the slightest idea how to shake one. Mostly, I just kept heading west, ignoring his fakes, wondering what the hell was going on, wondering what the woman had said to him to make him think he was being tailed. *Flee! All is lost! My husband knows everything!* Maybe. Or *Run for your life! The killers are on the loose.* Maybe not. Who knew? Certainly not me. I just knew that if something didn't happen soon, I was going to lose him.

East of Missoula, I switched tanks. West of Missoula, he signaled for a turn onto Highway 93, then headed north toward Flathead Lake, Kalispell—the Canadian border, maybe—Sandpoint, Idaho, or the back road into Spokane, Washington. I didn't know but I had to go with him, tailed him up the black ice on Evero Hill, but when he slowed down and eased into the lot of the Evero Bar across the road, I went past like a man with Canada on my mind.

As soon as I could I turned left onto somebody's private road, dashed into a stand of pine trees with my binoculars. Although the sun had dropped behind the farthest edges of the mountains, enough light remained glowing in the clear sky so that I could see the man as he came out of the Evero Bar with a six-pack of Oly dangling from each hand. He stood in the parking lot, drinking a beer and watching the traffic. Then he climbed back into his car and headed back south toward the interstate, crossed it and pulled into a truck stop. I parked in front of Fred's Lounge, watched him until he walked into the café, sat down at the counter, and picked up a menu, then I drove like a madman toward the Missoula airport to rent another vehicle.

I wanted something that would go but ended up with one of those new General Motors front-wheel-drive cars the Arabs shamed Detroit into manufacturing, a car with all the guts of a moped.

When I got back to the truck stop, a waitress was pouring the blond guy another cup of coffee, so I drove over to Fred's, went in to buy a bottle of schnapps, a handful of jerky, and a roll of Tums. While I waited in the rental car, I had a small toot off my knife blade, a shot of schnapps, and a piece of tough dried jerky. Now I was ready. A real Western private eye again, completely outfitted.

We went back to Missoula on the old highway, then south on the 93 bypass. He drove slower now, picking his teeth and drinking a beer as we skirted Missoula in the fading light. He seemed convinced that he had lost any sort of tail, and his overconfidence gave me the break I needed to maintain a one-man tail at night. We went south on 93 to Lolo, then west up Highway 12 along Lolo Creek toward Lolo Pass and the Idaho border along the old Lewis and Clark Trail, along the Nez Percé escape route. Before we reached Lolo Hot Springs, I passed him, then pulled off on a

Forest Service road, disconnected a headlight, then picked him up and followed him one-eyed over the pass into Idaho along the Lochsa River to Clearwater Crossing where the Lochsa and the Selway merge to become the Clearwater. When he stopped at Syringa to take a leak I went past him again, reconnected the headlight, and got behind him as we wound down Highway 12 toward the Snake River and the Washington border.

At Kooskia, though, he changed direction and turned left on Idaho 13, going south, and a few miles later he turned left again on Idaho 14 up the crooked course of the South Fork of the Clearwater, which we followed sedately almost all the way to Elk City, where he pulled off into the parking lot of a small motel with a NO VACANCY sign clearly displayed. I had no choice but to go on by, turn around beyond the next curve, then go back with my lights out.

Although it was only a bit after eleven, the motel and café were dark, the little Toyota nowhere in sight. I didn't know what all these people were doing in Elk City this time of year. It wasn't on the way to anyplace. On the west side of town the paved road ended, and a dirt road led over the Bitterroot Mountains to Connor, Montana, but the first snowfall of the season had closed the road. Maybe it was elk season in Elk City, I thought, laughing as I crept around the shadowed parking lot.

Finally I hid the rental car behind a camper, then took off on foot looking for the yellow car, which I found about fifty yards up a dirt road beyond the motel, parked in front of a small cabin. I saw his shadow moving aimlessly across the window curtains. I slipped out of my boots and eased across the pine needles, the sharp rocks, and the patches of snow around to the back of the cabin, where I peeked inside through the flimsy curtains.

A can of Dinty Moore beef stew with the top cut out sat on the stove bubbling. The guy dumped the bottom third of a Tabasco bottle and two eggs into the boiling stew. Whatever sort of trouble he might be involved in, he couldn't be all bad—he cooked a lot like me. Kept house much the same way, too. Newspapers, magazines, paperback books, and dirty clothes lay in heaps all over the one-room cabin; the bed looked as if it had been slept in by a man with bad dreams; and the garbage had overflowed its can onto the dusty floor.

While he waited for the eggs to cook, he kicked his dirty clothes into one pile, then stuffed them into a plastic garbage bag. He emptied the small dresser and put his clean clothes on top of the dirty ones, glanced around the room to see what he had missed, then shuffled the rest of the trash into a corner. The smell of the beef stew slipped through the walls of the clapboard cabin, and my stomach grumbled so loudly that I had to get away from the window.

After I picked up my boots I went back to the motel and sat in the car waiting for him to leave, making my supper out of schnapps, jerky, and Tums. After half an hour, though, the Toyota still hadn't come down the track, so I went back up. The little car was still parked in front of the dark cabin, and when I leaned against the outside wall I could hear the snuffles and snores of a beery sleep, which left me looking at a long night.

I thought about it a bit, then hiked on up the dirt road to where it ended against a bulldozed hump beyond the next switchback. I walked quietly back down to my car, picked up the small traveling bag I had remembered to move from my pickup to the rental unit—winter emergency road gear, a space blanket, a bag of hard candy, matches, a toothbrush, a pint of schnapps—then crossed the highway to the river to clean up in the cold, rushing water.

An hour later I moved the car up to the dead end, where he couldn't spot it, turned it around, then took the space blanket and the pint of schnapps back down the hill until I found a hollow beneath a dead-fall ponderosa where I curled up, planning to balance the occasional shot of schnapps with the odd toot of coke, hoping to sleep a little but lightly enough so I would hear the guy when he started his car in the morning.

It had snowed up the South Fork, too, but not as much as it had over in Montana. High clouds swept overhead, flirting with the snickering slice of moon, and in the shadows of the lowing pines, the patches of snow glowed and faded and glimmered like dying phosphorescent creatures jerked from the bottom of the sea. All around me the pines creaked and sighed in the wind like mourners. I couldn't tell if I trembled from the cold or from the excitement of working again. When I smoked, I cupped the match and hid the cigarette the way I used to that long winter on the line in Korea, and although I don't remember sleeping, I remember dreaming of the war. All through the night, it seemed, shadowy figures rose from the snow and moved silently past my position, and when I woke just before dawn as the guy slammed shut the front door of the cabin, I rolled over reaching for my M-1 and was amazed in my sleepy confusion to find it wasn't there.

Sleeping in the cold on the ground was not something I did well at my age, and when I tried to stand up, my joints groaned like truck axles packed with frozen grease. Even before I got to my knees I heard his car door bang shut, the starter grinding angrily against the resistance of the cold engine, the pump of the accelerator hard against the floorboard. On my knees, I heard the muffled bang, then threw the space blanket aside and stumbled downhill through the brush.

The explosion had blown all the glass out of the small car, popped open both doors and the trunk lid, and when I got to the man, his face was covered with freckles of blood, his shirt and jacket tattered on his chest. There were smoldering bits of seat-cover fabric and clots of cotton stuffing on his naked shoulders. When I reached for him, I saw a gaping hole in the floor. His left leg was gone below the knee, his right above, and blood gushed from the nerve on his cheek, and most of his fingers were stubs, the pink, pork-chop flesh not bleeding yet. When I reached around his chest to pull him out and away from the biting stink of gasoline, he grabbed my left arm with what was left of his right hand. He could not stand to be moved. After a few seconds, while he held me so tightly with the maimed hand that I couldn't run either, he died, and his hand fell quivering from my elbow.

I wanted to run, God, I wanted to run away from the blood

and the smell of raw gasoline, but I made myself roll him over so I could empty his pockets into mine, then I grabbed the garbage bag out of the back seat, holding his goods tightly with my arms around the shredded plastic. I took a moment to glance in the open trunk, where I found a green duffle bag. I slipped the strap over my shoulder, and ran.

Okay, I panicked. I had stepped in shit and I was scared. If you don't see that sort of thing regularly, you lose your touch for dealing with it, the cynical layer that lets you see a shattered body, shake your head once, then go about your business. I tampered with evidence, obstructed justice, and ran away, leaving the dead body propped like a side of beef in the front seat. And ran.

When I started the long uphill flight to my rental car, I couldn't get enough air in my lungs, and when I got to the dead end beyond the switchback, I fell on the ground beside the driver's door, sobbing, sucking empty air, thinking, trying to remember how to survive a world at war. Think. It hadn't been a bomb connected to the ignition, or the car would have gone up when he first turned the key. Whatever it was had been under the front seat. Whoever put it there must have known I was around, must have tailed me tailing him. Think. I crawled around to the passenger door, opened it slowly, carefully, searching with bleary eyes for a wire. Nothing. Nothing under the seat on that side. Under the driver's seat, though, a simple booby trap, something I had seen explained in *Time* magazine during the Vietnam war. A grenade with the pin pulled and stuffed into a tin can to hold the handle down—a Del Monte crushed-pineapple can, a killer with a sense of humor—and a length of soft soldering wire run underneath the floor mat and tied to the clutch pedal.

My hands were shaking so badly that I thought I would never get the grenade out from under the seat without dropping the can, but I did, eventually, then I held it tightly as I crawled out the driver's door and looked for a place to put it, a safe place, but what if a kid came along, or a hunter or a bear turning over rocks looking for grubs, no safe place. I set it on the roof of the car, threw the dead man's goods in the back seat, took the grenade and the can and myself and put us behind the wheel, the grenade lodged snugly in my crotch.

I wanted to weep, and did. My balls wanted to climb back up into my body, and they tried, sweating with the effort. I started the car and tried to ease down the trail, but my foot hammered the accelerator against the floor, and the cold engine flooded and died. "Oh, Jesus God," I heard myself say, then I started the engine again, let the car coast in neutral down the hill, idling to warm it up. Even before I reached the ruined Toyota, though, I hit it again, fleeing, crazy, trying to brake, to go slow through the motel parking lot, but when I hit the highway the little car was going so fast that it lifted two wheels off the ground, which made the grenade rattle in the can, but still I jammed the throttle down, ran the gutless little bastard as hard as it would. A few seconds down the road, the gas tank of the Toyota went off behind me like a bomb, the fireball rolling through the rear-view mirror.

When I finally stopped running up and down Forest Service roads, I had no idea where I might be, but I knew I had to stop. The panic only stops when you stop running. I longed for the warm weight of my Browning 9mm automatic hanging heavy under my arm. At least I have a live grenade, I thought, laughing hysterically, riding between my legs. I shot off the road onto a logging skid trail and bounced the goddamned little car as far as it would go up it. When I got out, though, with nobody in sight as far as I could see, it still didn't help. I could feel gunsights crawling like ants across my back whichever way I turned. I reached in the back seat, hefted the duffle bag; it was heavy, it rattled, that was enough, maybe a pistol, maybe a big knife, anything . . . But I couldn't make myself wait to look there, standing by the car, so I threw it over my shoulder and ran, the can in my other hand.

When I was about seventy-five yards uphill and across fifty yards of granite scree from the car, I fell into the shadow of an outcrop, lay flat behind the lip of the shattered rocks, and decided I had run as far as I was going to. I lay my head on the duffle bag, propped the can and the grenade securely between two rocks, and waited to catch my breath. Then I unsnapped the duffle bag, dug into it, and felt better almost immediately.

Right on top were three fragmentation grenades still in their cardboard tubes. Below them, two flat packages wrapped in heavy plastic. I opened the first one and nearly shouted with joy. Not that guns kept you from running—I saw men in Korea shot in their foxholes, wrapped around their unfired weapons—but if you're done with running, a gun feels better than a woman, more comforting than your mother's breast. Although I had only seen them in movies and in magazines, I recognized the small submachine gun at once. An Ingram M-11. Not much larger than a .45 automatic pistol. Eight hundred and fifty rounds a minute. So simple a child can operate it. I dug deeper, looking for clips and ammo.

I found what I was looking for, and more. Ten loaded clips of .380 rounds, a bat-shaped suppressor. A kilo of marijuana. A bag of white powder, heroin or cocaine, I assumed. Two more grenades. The guy in the yellow Toyota might be a bad guy, but he was Santa Claus to me.

Everything except the grenades had been wrapped in the heavy black plastic, and all the packages were covered with a light pinkish-gray, dusty powder. I brushed it off my hands and the two M-11s, then turned the duffle bag inside out to see if something inside had burst, but the bag was empty. I loaded the kilo of smoking dope, its plastic wrapper still intact except for the tear I had made to look at it, and one of the M-11s back into the bag, then got ready.

I fitted the suppressor to the other Ingram, loaded it, and fired a short burst at ponderosa about thirty yards downhill and to my right. Then two more to get the feel of the kick. On the fourth burst, which emptied the clip, I chipped enough bark off the big yellow pine to convince me that I could hit a man, and the little submachine gun didn't make enough noise to frighten away the chipmunks that had come out on the scree to watch me. Then I changed clips, moved back deeper into the outcrop's shadow, stacked the grenades beside me, checked my field of fire, and waited.

After a while, I opened the baggie of white powder, tasted it. Cocaine. Maybe four or five ounces, more than I had ever seen in my life. I snorted a bit off my knife blade, and it nearly took the top of my head off. The coke must have just come off the boat, not even stepped on hard yet, maybe seventy, eighty percent pure. My admiration for the dead guy rose another few notches. He didn't look like much, he lived like a tramp, and his car was a seven-year-old wreck, but he carried good stuff in his trunk. I had another tiny snort. What the hell, I thought, if the bad guys are behind, they may have a little trouble doing in a drug-crazed, scared-shitless, middle-aged old fart like me. Especially since I had a good position, half a dozen grenades, an automatic weapon, and two hundred and seventy rounds of ammo.

But nobody was behind me—good, bad, or indifferent—and by midmorning, most of the fear washed with occasional nips of coke, I had become bored enough to be half sane again.

What in God's name had Sarah gotten me into? What *had* the woman in the blue Subaru said to the man to make him run? They hadn't been dealing weapons or drugs, not if they had met so often at the same time and same place. Never. The man was dead, the woman gone, and I had no idea who either of them might be. At least I had the license-plate number off the woman's car, and even if it was rented, I could catch up with her. And the plate number off the man's car, too, written on a slip of paper somewhere . . .

I now remembered rolling over his dead body to rifle his pockets. I checked the thinly timbered hillside and what I could see of the road, then emptied my pockets.

The leather of his wallet was wrinkled and stretched, as if it had been emptied of everything nonessential—those slips of paper with telephone numbers and names you don't remember, out-of-date insurance cards, expired credit cards, pictures that have lost their meaning. In it I found only three twenties, two tens, a five, four ones, and a two-dollar bill folded in a square with "Shit" written across it in red ink, and a Washington State commercial operator's license in the name of John P. Rideout at an address in Wilbur, Washington. Stuck to the back of the license, not with glue but from wear, was a small snapshot of a plain chubby woman with three small and indistinct children huddled at her baggy knees. The group stood in front of a small frame house on the edge of a meadow, around which loomed a dark evergreen jungle. Certainly not Wilbur, which sits on the lava-broken high desert plains of eastern Washington, but perhaps somewhere west of the Cascades.

In my other pocket I had found half a pack of Salems, and stuffed behind the cellophane, a matchbook from a bar called Nobby's in West Seattle. I used the last match out of the book to light one of my own cigarettes.

Okay, I had a place to begin, with Rideout, and a plate number for the woman. But no notions. Why had somebody blown the poor devil to bits? To rip him off? No, they left the goodies in the trunk. Maybe he ripped somebody off. And why me? And did they know who I was? Probably. All they had to do was open the glove box and read the rental agreement. But why me?

And the trembling began all over again. My cigarette slipped out of my fingers and fell inside my down vest. As I slapped at the sparks flying across my chest, I found the small bloody streaks left by his fingers. They knew me, all right. And I had to either find the bad guys to tell them I had a poorly developed sense of law and order and didn't talk even in my sleep. Or go to the law. I didn't know what kind of fall it was in Idaho to tamper with evidence and obstruct justice, I didn't even know where the Idaho State Prison was. Even turning state's evidence, probation was the best I could hope for. And what evidence? No law, not until I knew what the hell was going on. I couldn't even hang around the house and wait for the bad guys to come by for a chat, a few last words. I had to go to ground, hide as I tried to find out why Rideout had been killed, why they tried to kill me.

I wondered how many people they had working the tail—at least four, I guessed, and damn professional work at that. I thought about taking Sarah's money and the colonel's paycheck and simply running, my sense of justice superseded by my sense of survival, wondered where the bastards had picked up our tail . . .

Then I had a terrible vision of somebody watching the meeting through binoculars, like me, casing the neighborhood to be safe, seeing the old woman with her gleaming silver hair, seeing the sun low in the southern sky flash off her binoculars. Shit, I had to find a telephone, had to get that beautiful old woman out of her house for a while, someplace safe until I could find out what was going on. And I had to get rid of the goddamn live grenade, too.

Although I didn't know exactly where I had ended up, I did know that I was north of the South Fork and that if I kept heading north on the Forest Service roads, eventually I would come out on the Clearwater and back on Highway 12, which we had come over the night before. Highway 12 was the only place I could hope to find a telephone without going back to Elk City and whatever law-enforcement attention the explosion of Rideout's car had drawn. From the paved roads, national forests looked like vast impenetrable barriers, but that was strictly for show, for the tourists. In fact, all those acres of forest land were threaded by an endless maze of roads built by the Forest Service with taxpayers' money for the logging industry, access for the heavy machinery necessary to clear-cut great swaths of timber. I couldn't complain too much, though, since roads gave me a chance to get away from Elk City, from the minions of the law and the outlawed gathered there by the charred remains of John P. Rideout.

The mountain air was fresh and cold, but the road was mushy with snow melt along the sunny stretches. At least the rental car was good for something—the front-wheel drive pulled it right through the boggy places. When I finally came down off the side of the mountain to cross a creek, I stopped the car and tossed the grenade into the middle of the culvert in about two feet of running water. It seemed a safe place to dispose of the bomb. Even through the thick metal sides of the culvert and the three feet of roadbed, the explosion shook me. I stumbled about for a moment, slapping at myself, checking for wounds with an old combat habit. When I leaned over the edge of the creek to see if I had damaged the culvert, peering through the smoky mist, a great lunker of a cutthroat came floating out, belly up. I went down the bank and out into the knee-deep water, which was so cold I felt the ache all the way up to my hips, to pick up the trout. Such a fucking waste, I thought, holding the slippery length of the fish, and I felt like weeping again. "My fucking nerves are shot!" I screamed. "Shot to fucking hell!" Then I threw the fish back into the water, threw him as hard as I could. The small burst of adrenaline carried me out of the water, back to the car, down the road. But my hands were shaking on the wheel within minutes, my balls still trying to crawl away from the grenade.

Finally, in the middle of the afternoon, I reached Highway 12 and drove west to the Syringa Café, where I had a huge order of ham and eggs while I waited for a truck driver to get off the telephone. When I called Sarah's number, though, no one answered. I called the colonel, asked him to put a man on Sarah's house around the clock. He didn't ask me why or where to send the bill or what kind of trouble I was in now. He just said, "Certainly." A good soldier all the way. I headed west toward Lewiston on the Washington border, where I traded my piece of rented Detroit crap for a Datsun station wagon. The girl behind the counter started to ask me why but when she looked at my face again, she just shook her head and filled out the forms. I borrowed the key to the rest room to take a look at myself. I had only been on the job twenty-four hours and already I looked like hell, like death warmed over, like a man on the run from himself.

On the way north I tried to drive close to the speed limit, as one must when carrying the sort of load I had in the back seat, but it was a battle all the way. When I went through Pullman, where my son went to college, I had a terrible urge to give him a call, to drop by his dorm just to give him a bear hug, but it would just have confused him, so I pressed on to Spokane, then west on Highway 2 to Wilbur.

When I drove by the address on Rideout's license, the house didn't just look empty, it looked abandoned forever. I had to sleep, I thought, so I checked into a motel and called Sarah's number one last time, and Gail answered.

"Don't you people ever pick up the phone?" I asked a bit more curtly than I meant to.

"Sarah doesn't," she said, "and I've been out."

"I'm sorry," I said. "How's your father?"

"They flew him back to the Mayo Clinic this morning," she said, "for tests, more fucking tests. I wanted to be a doctor once, you know, until I found out that they don't know shit."

"Nobody does," I said. "Listen, I want you to do me a favor."

"What? I hope it doesn't take too long, Milo, because I've got two quizzes tomorrow, and I haven't cracked a book for either of them."

"Just listen a minute," I said, "please. I am in a world of trouble—"

"I told Sarah not to give you that much money," she interrupted.

"Just listen—"

"What sort of trouble?"

"Will you please just shut up for a minute!"

"Don't you be telling me to shut up, asshole," she said.

"Ah, Christ," I sighed, "whatever happened to that moment of tenderness between us?"

"You dudes in your needle-nosed boots always think you're so fucking tough," she said, "but underneath you're all just a bunch of sissy cream puffs. It went where it was supposed to, old man, the way of all flesh, ashes to ashes, dust to dust, down the toilet of life . . ." She sounded as if she was crying.

"I don't believe this conversation," I said.

"I don't either," she said and hung up.

When I called back, the line sounded permanently busy. I took a shower, tried again without luck, then lay back on the bed hoping I didn't have bad dreams . . .

. . . and I didn't. I didn't sleep enough, but spent most of the night wrapped around the submachine gun, my hands still heavy with the empty weight of the dead fish, the dead man as I rolled him over to rummage through the pockets of his life.

Chapter 6

Even though I suspected it would be wasted time, I spent the next morning working Wilbur without finding a soul who had either seen or heard of John P. Rideout, and even though I knew nobody was behind me, the back of my neck kept twitching. Everything was wrong, nothing fit, and nobody answered the telephone at Sarah's house. I called a lawyer in Butte to get him to check out the plate number on the woman's car, but his secretary told me that he was in California on vacation. I thought about the matchbook from Nobby's in Seattle. Maybe it really was a clue, and Seattle was a lot closer than Butte. I could drive over in a couple of hours, check out the bar, and with a little luck, drop the rented Datsun at the airport, and catch a night flight back to Missoula to get my pickup.

Right. So I cut across the back roads south to the interstate, across the fields of wheat stubble and sagebrush hills sliced by lava dikes. After eighteen months, the volcanic ash from Mount St. Helens still lay along the roadsides. We had even had enough ash fallout in Meriwether to close the bars for four days, which was as near to a natural disaster as I ever wanted to get.

When I picked up the interstate at Moses Lake, I tried Sarah again. Still no answer. So I called the colonel. He told me that none of his men had reported any activity, unusual or otherwise, at the Weddington house. Then he asked where I was.

"Moses Lake," I said, "heading for Seattle. But don't tell anybody if they ask."

"Why would anybody ask, Milo? Are you in some sort of trouble?"

"No, sir," I said. "Just doing a little free-lance work." My crimes were all mine, and I didn't want to make the colonel an accessory after the fact.

"Enjoying yourself?" the colonel asked pleasantly, and I had a little trouble answering him. "Still drinking schnapps?"

"My goddamned tongue tastes like fucking peppermint stick," I said, and decided to do something about it immediately. He told me to be careful and have fun, then we rang off. I went straight to the nearest market, where I bought a Styrofoam cooler, a bag of ice, and two six-packs of Rainier, then to a secondhand store to buy a trunk that locked and loaded the guns, grenades, and coke in it. Even if the Washington state patrol popped me for drinking and driving, they couldn't open the locked trunk without a warrant.

I felt pleased with myself, fairly or unfairly, as I headed west on I-90, but I still kept an eye out for the law, checking all directions before I took a drink of beer on the highway, watching my ass. And that's how I saw them watching me.

There were four of them and they were good. A four-wheel-drive Chevy pickup decked out for show, big tires, and a chrome roll-bar with quartz lamps on it. A green Ford sedan, company car stripped, with suits and shirts hanging in the back seat. A Volkswagen van. And a dude in a red Porsche 924 who thought he was the cutest one of all. These people had some money to spend, too. A four-car tail, a tap on the colonel's telephone line. Cute. I didn't seem to mind, though, it got the juices flowing. I sort of wished that I hadn't locked up the two M-11s and the grenades, but I didn't think they would try to take me out on the highway. At least not after I found a state patrol car and dogged him at fifty-seven miles an hour all the way into Seattle.

I took the boys downtown to get in line for the Bremerton ferry. I got the silenced Ingram out of the trunk, emptied my knapsack, and put the gun in it. Then I went back down the line of waiting cars, collecting a few ignition keys. They knew what was in the sack, so they went along nicely. Except for the big dude in the Porsche. First he tried to play dumb, then he acted like he wanted to get Western right in public, but I slapped him in the throat with the suppressor and he didn't have anything else to say. I even took his billfold, but it contained even less information than Rideout's had. Ninety-seven dollars in bills but nothing else.

After the ferry docked and the lanes in front of me cleared, I turned around and left the ferry traffic blocked for half a mile, headed south down the freeway to the Sea-Tac airport, where I swapped cars one more goddamn time. I wanted a Corvette, but nobody had one, so I settled for a black T-bird. I made it back to Nobby's just in time for the five o'clock rush, really pleased with myself now, pleased enough to order a Chevas on the rocks.

The bartender was too busy to talk, so I waited for business to die down, waited too long, and found myself ambushed by a two-for-one happy hour, and suddenly, miraculously, sweet gift of whiskey and fatigue, it was nearly nine o'clock, and I was drunk as a pig. I didn't care who those guys had been. In fact, I thought about looking for them, but I finally stopped the bartender and showed him Rideout's fake license. Like any good citizen, he wanted to know why. I flashed my old Meriwether county deputy sheriff's badge, but he wasn't buying any of that. So I stacked up the change from a fifty.

"Maybe I've seen him a few times with the ferryboat crowd," he said sadly, fingering the sheaf of bills. "But not in a long time."

"Which ferryboat?"

"Usually the last one. Sometimes he came in after work and stayed until the last boat. But like I say, it's been a while."

"Vashon Island or Port Orchard?"

"Who knows?"

"Ever say what he did for a living?"

"I think he was a long-haul trucker," he said, "coast-to-coast number."

"But you're not sure?" I prompted, nudging the bills closer to him with my finger.

"Not at all," he said, then leaned back and shoved the bills toward me. "Listen, buddy, you mind if I say something?" I shook my head. "You keep your money there, and use it to get a room or something, because, my friend, you look like a dead man, and you are somewhat drunk."

"You mind if I say something?" I asked, and he shook his sad, pale face, the face of a reformed drunk. "I been listening to bullshit bartender advice all my life," I said. He didn't look angry, just sadder. I dropped a ten-dollar tip on the bar and staggered out. Pretty picture. My first lungful of cold air off Puget Sound sobered me up a little bit, and I started to go back to apologize, but I had learned the hard way that drunken apologies to strangers usually just confuse them.

I got lost among the side streets of West Seattle looking for some of the Colonel's chicken, then lost again, gnawing on a drumstick, as I tried to find the ferry dock. I think I meant to show Rideout's picture to some of the boat crew, but before I had a chance, I got hassled for smoking on the car deck, then for drinking beer on the passenger deck, then severely chided when I held up disembarking traffic on Vashon because I couldn't remember which one of the six sets of keys belonged to the T-bird.

I had been on Vashon Island once before in daylight and knew there was a tavern on the short main street of the small town in the middle of the island, but in the dark, salt-misty night, I couldn't find my ass with either hand. I spent what seemed hours wandering around before I found the main street and the tavern, and I was wildly surprised to discover it was still open.

As soon as I walked in, though, I knew I had made a mistake. It was a real hometown bar. Everybody knew everybody else, and nobody wanted to talk to a weird drunken stranger who looked as if he had just escaped from the federal lockup on McNeil Island. Nobody. Especially a swarthy fellow at the end of the bar who looked like an ex-con and who reminded me of the hapless postman. As I wandered down the bar, trying to start drunken conversations, he watched me carefully out of the corner of his eye, and when I pulled up on a stool near him, he chugged his beer and scooted out the back door. Even though the Supreme Court doesn't buy it, cops can smell the bad actors. I went out right behind him.

"Hey, asshole," I said when I caught up to him in the alley, "why don't you just hold it right there."

"Shit," he groaned, "why don't you fucking guys get off my ass." And they can smell the cop stink, too. "Just leave me the hell alone," he added, but when he turned around to face me, his shoulders slumped, as tired as his voice. He had been in the joint a long time, had his ass kicked by pros. "Alone," he whined.

"How long you been out?"

"Three and a half years," he said, "and I can promise you, man, I ain't doing nothing, ever, to go back."

"Relax," I said, slapping him on the arm lightly. He flinched anyway. "Take it easy," I said, "I ain't the man no more."

"Right," he said, "sure. Let's just get it over with." He pulled up the sleeves of his flannel shirt so hard that he popped the cuff buttons, and presented me with the insides of his elbows. Somebody had been rousting the poor guy.

"That don't mean shit," I said, trying to sound like somebody in authority. "Just take a look at this picture." Even in the dim light I could see his eyes cloud and the old practiced lies forming on his mouth. "Don't jerk me around, asshole."

"Okay," he sighed, "what the hell. He told me his parole was up a long time ago."

"Can you put the right name to the face?"

"John. That's all I ever knew," he said, "but I ain't seen him in six or eight months. Not since him and his old lady split."

"She live here on the Island?"

"Maybe."

"Here?" I asked, showing him the small snapshot. He nodded. "Where is it?"

"Somewhere on the south end, toward Tahlequah," he said. "I was only there one time, and it was dark and raining, and we were—"

"—Fucked up?"

"Right," he said sadly.

"I'll find it."

"Not on a night like this," he said with bitter humor as he lifted his hands into the foggy mist.

"Don't sweat it," I said, trying to sound tough and competent. "Just tell me how to find a motel."

"A what? Oh, sure," he said, smiling around broken teeth. "Hey, you really ain't the heat, are you?"

"Maybe something worse," I said.

"It shows, man," he said, his smile growing larger, then he gave me a set of rather complicated directions to the only motel on the Island. I gave him a ten and told him to buy himself a beer, and he whistled down the alley into the murky night.

It took me a number of beers and a length of time that should have been counted in years instead of hours as I roamed the black wet roads for me to realize what the ex-con's smile had been about. No motels on the Island, no ferryboats back to the mainland, no way I could take a chance, not with all the crap in the trunk of the T-bird, on sleeping in the car beside the road or on the ferry dock, and no way I could drive around all night. Although it had been only two nights with little sleep, my body said sleep.

When in doubt, go right to the source. I remembered passing a King County police substation on my meanders, so I backtracked until I found it, then parked in the lot, put a note on my windshield explaining that I was a tourist, lost and drunk and ignorant of ferry schedules, then climbed into the back seat, where I slept far better than I had any right to.

At five-thirty a patrolman rapped on the side window until he woke me up. I climbed out to stretch and thank him. The mist had turned into a light rain that couldn't wash the fog out of the air. When I yawned, the cold damp filled my lungs, like trying to inhale wet wool. The policeman was surprisingly pleasant for that time of day, even complimented me on my good sense. I shook his hand and thanked him again.

"No problem," he said, yawning too. "Happens all the time, all the goddamned time." Then, as he walked back to his unit, he added over his shoulder, "Goddamned islands."

On the ferry back to West Seattle I stood on the bow in the cold wet wind and tossed the four sets of car keys into the dark pulsing waters of the Sound. On a bright sunny day I could have seen Mount Rainier looming like a misshapen moon on the horizon, and even through the fog and rain I thought I could feel its rocky weight. I drove back out to Sea-Tac to the large anonymous motels nearby, parked the T-bird in the lot of one, checked into another, paying cash and signing a false name. Unlike that person of the evening before, bloated with expensive Scotch and fake self-confidence, this guy wanted a few hours of untroubled sleep and no truck with the bad guys.

When the wake-up call came at noon, I was still scared, tired, hung over, and suffering that terrible morning-after, horny itch. I thought of how cool Gail's body might feel next to mine, how warm the comfort of Carolyn's heavy breasts, and the icy fire of Cassandra Bogardus' face. Nothing but hangover fantasy, though. No repeaters, Carolyn had said. The way of all flesh, down the toilet of life, said Gail. And I was still half angry at the Bogardus woman for dumping me so easily at the airport. I took a cold shower and stopped torturing myself. I had things to do.

First, I needed a new image. The bad guys were going to be looking for me with a vengeance. Professionals did not like to have their ass kicked by anybody, much less an alcoholic security guard. It took a ton of Sarah's money, but I bought a new image. A four-hundred-dollar blue pin-striped three-piece suit. Black loafers with tassels for a hundred and thirty bucks. A forty-dollar blow-dry haircut. A zircon pinky ring out of a pawnshop on 1st Avenue. Fifteen bucks.

While I waited for the alterations on the suit, I sent the colonel a hand-delivered-only telegram, telling him to have his telephones, office, and house swept for bugs. I sent Gail a telegram telling her to get Sarah out of town. Then I went over to pick up the suit. As I looked at myself in the triptych of mirrors, I thought about what the athletic young man with the wedding band had said when he finished cutting my hair. Even looking at my dirty, wrinkled Levi's, my bloodstained Woolrich shirt with pine needles still clinging to the back, he turned me around in the chair, patted the helmet of hair on my head, and said, "It's you, sir." I turned to the salesman, watching me look at myself in the mirrors, and said, "It's me." He didn't even raise an eyebrow. I went crazy and treated myself to one of those wonderful London Fog trench coats with a zip-out lining and a gray Tyrolean hat with a bright feather in the brim. "Motherfucker, it is *me*," I said to the salesman, but he just thanked me sincerely. Then I drove this new, well-dressed me out of Seattle for safety's sake, down the interstate to Renton, where I checked into a fancy motel under another cash-paying name. The new me and the old me, we did a couple of lines of that wonderful cocaine, then drove back up to West Seattle and the Vashon Island ferry to look for the former Mrs. Rideout.

Although there were no Rideouts listed on Vashon, it only took me half an hour to find the little frame house by the meadow. Even in the daylight, the low gray clouds and the drizzle made it feel like night. The three children had grown since the picture and they were dressed in matching yellow slickers that glowed in the ashen light. When I pulled into the muddy driveway, the smallest one looked at my car with the frightened eyes of a startled animal, then darted around the side of the house toward the dull, clumping sound of a splitting maul, but the largest, a pale blond boy who looked as if he lived in the rain, put his arm around his little sister and waited, his thin shoulders pulled tall and erect under the loose slicker. When I climbed out of the T-bird and walked toward him, he saluted smartly. Without thinking, I returned it, and he smiled.

"My daddy was in the Army for a long time," he said proudly.

"So was I," I said, thinking, The rockpile army.

"He was a captain," he added.

"Then I should have saluted you," I said, "because I was only a pfc."

"That's right," he said very seriously, and we exchanged salutes again, in the proper order this time.

"And what's your name, sir?"

"John Paul Rausche, Junior," he said, "and this is my sister, Sally." I shook the boy's hand, but when I offered mine to the little girl, she turned away shyly to hide her face against her big brother's shoulder. "Sally's got a cancer behind her eye," the boy explained, "and she don't like people looking at her."

"Is your mother home?" I asked. The name wasn't Rideout, but this was his father's son.

Before he could answer, though, she came around the corner of the house, the splitting maul held like a club in her raw, chapped hands. The smallest child clung to her left leg, but she walked steadily, as if she had become so accustomed to his weight that she might limp without it. Sweat drenched her red, plain face, and rain had beaded like a damp cloak across the shoulders of her buffalo plaid wool shirt.

"You kids go inside," she said, her voice as flat and hard as the slap of a piece of kindling wood against starched jeans. "Now." John, Jr., and I exchanged salutes again, but quickly, and the children disappeared into the house like sparks dropped into wet grass. "If you be looking for John, mister, he ain't here. He ain't been here in a long time, and if I got anything to say about it, he won't ever be here again."

The body hadn't been identified yet, and I wasn't about to be the one to tell her what had become of her ex-husband.

"You wouldn't know where I might find him?" I said. "I am—"

"Like I told that fella last week," she interrupted, "I ain't seen hide nor hair nor support checks for eight months and two weeks . . . three weeks now."

"I don't know where he is either," I said, making it up as I went along, "but I owed him some money and I'm on my way to California, moving out of this damned rain, and I wanted to pay him before I left."

"Ain't nobody ever owed John money," she said suspiciously. "It's always him does the owing."

"He did some work for me," I said, "but he took off before I had a chance to pay him."

"That's my Johnny," she said, some sort of perverse pride in her tone. "Elk season must've opened."

"Maybe I could give it to you," I suggested, "and you could hold it for him."

"Maybe," she said quietly as I dug out my billfold, fat with Sarah's money, and started pulling out one-hundred-dollar bills, meaning, I think, only to take a couple, maybe three, but I had to make myself stop when I got to ten. God hates a piker, I said to myself, Jesus loves the little children of the land. Then I counted ten more. When I handed her the money, her face dropped, then grew bright, not with greed, but with sheer joy. "What in the name of the Lord did John do for this much money?" she asked, stammering as she counted. "Kill somebody?"

"He hauled a couple of loads for me," I said.

"Loads?" she said.

"This is his bonus," I said. "He did a good, quick job."

"I didn't even know he was hauling again," she said, still counting.

"Who was he hauling for before?" I asked, but she wasn't listening. She brushed a damp strand of hair out of her eyes, wet her thumb, kept counting.

"Holy Jesus, Joseph, and Mary," she said when she finished.

"This other guy who was looking for John," I said, trying to get her attention, "what did he look like?"

"Like you," she answered without looking up, "except he drove a Lincoln."

"What did he want?" I asked, hopelessly, great cross-examiner that I am.

"Huh? Oh, he said John owed him money," she said, "but I just laughed in his face." Then she sprang at me, gave me a fierce hug and a wet kiss on the cheek. "Lord, thank you, mister," she said. "You know he'll never see penny one of this, don't you?"

"I like to pay my debts," I said, "and I consider this one paid in full." But she was back at the money, and I could have been talking to the wind or the soft rain or the stately, silent firs.

Driving away, I hoped Sarah would forgive me as I felt the plain woman's kiss burning on my damp face.

While I waited, parked on the ferry dock, for a ride back to the mainland, the effects of my grand gesture wore off quickly. What the hell did I have in mind? Here I was passing Sarah's money around like Christmas candy, and all the things I knew about the driver of the yellow Toyota filled me with sadness instead of knowledge, and I couldn't tell Sarah about his death without making her an accessory to my crimes. I climbed out of the T-bird and leaned against the dock rail. And what was I doing in these goddamned rich man's clothes? Maybe I thought they would make me bulletproof? Shit. I felt like ripping them off and throwing them into the cold green scummy water slapping under the dock. I settled for sailing the stupid gray hat over the gentle waves. Several gulls checked it out in the air, decided it wasn't worth eating, even though gulls will eat garbage that would gag a buzzard. While it still floated on the water, one of the gulls landed on it and seemed terribly surprised when the hat promptly sank. Jonathan Livingston Seagull Shit.

During the boat ride I sulked in the car, decided I would go back to the motel and clear my sinuses before I made any more major decisions—such as what I was going to do with all that dope. I had kept it so long after Rausche's death that not even my best friends would believe that I had kept it out of any other impulse than greed. It was great cocaine. I could keep on keeping it, maybe, but considering the sort of additive fool I had proved to be throughout my life, that much good coke in my hands would probably be the death of me. Maybe I could sell it to make up for some of Sarah's money. But I was six hundred miles from home. When I got back to the motel down in Renton I played my only card; called my dealer in Meriwether, Raoul.

Raoul tried to act like a street-wise Puerto Rican from New York, and he affected leather slouch hats, brightly colored leather jackets, and red-tinted glasses day and night, but in fact, he was the son of a Jewish fuel-oil dealer in Pittsburgh. He had even gone to Harvard for a couple of years before he split to become a cook on the Alaskan pipeline, where he had discovered the joys of dealing and of freedom in the Wild West. He knew better, knew he was on a one-way ticket to the slammer, but he had been popped once in Phoenix, lost his stash and his cash, and now he was in debt so badly to the wholesalers and the lawyers that he had to keep dealing just to stay out of jail and alive.

When I finally got him on the telephone, he wasn't very happy about it, but I promised him a sixty-forty split, and he said he would see what he could do. Twenty minutes later he called me back, told me I wouldn't believe these people, wouldn't believe how flaky they were, told me to carry a piece and to hire some armed backup if I could. Just as I had with the bartender's advice the night before, I dismissed it without thought.

As a result, two hours later in a country house on the Olympic Peninsula across the Sound from Seattle, I found myself lying flat in a dusty hallway while a skinny girl with pimples subjected me to a very thorough and not very pleasant search, and another, even more emaciated woman, who looked like a high-fashion model, held a sawed-off 12-gauge shotgun against the back of my neck. At the end of the hall a fat girl in a baggy gray sweatshirt covered with the names of famous women held two huge and slobberingly angry Rottweilers on a short leash. Lying there, convinced I had dug my grave this time, I vowed to start listening to more advice. If they didn't blow my head out from between my ears, that is.

"He's clean," Pimples said, "nothing but car keys and this." And she tossed *this,* a small packet of cocaine, down to the fat girl. She caught it and growled at the Rottweilers, who sat down at her feet, stopped drooling and started wagging their tails like dumb puppies. I stayed put, the shotgun barrels and Pimples' knee holding me on the floor. Hysterical, hushed giggles came from the mouths of unseen people and skittered like day-blind bats down the hallway.

"Shut up," the fat girl said, and the laughter stopped at once. She walked away, came back a few minutes later, and said, "Okay, bring the jerk in here."

"Does she mean me?" I asked as the bony knee and the black steel holes lifted.

"Oh, does she ever," the model answered in one of those cultured drawls that always make me think of Vassar or Smith. "Jerk."

As I hobbled stiffly down the hallway, easing around the dogs, who were bored with me now, my knees shook so badly that I nearly collapsed. One scare too many. Once during Korea, Jamison and I had spent thirty-six hours under a Chinese artillery bombardment. We had started screaming "no more" before the first five minutes had passed. That's how I felt now.

"Well, I do believe the big boy's just about to wet his pants, momma," the cultured voice murmured behind me.

"You bet your sweet ass," I whispered over my shoulder. She sneered like a brain-damaged collie, dug the shotgun into my kidney, then shoved me toward a Victorian chair, where I collapsed on the brocade in a sweat-damp puddle. She stood behind me, tapping the barrels lightly on the wood trim, and the fat girl sat down on a couch on the other side of the room.

"This is pretty good shit," she said. "Where'd you get it?"

"Does it matter?"

"If it's hot, it might matter one hell of a lot."

"It's not exactly hot," I said.

"What the hell's that mean?" she asked, smiling. Oddly enough, the smile made her plump face sweetly pretty. If she washed her hair and lost thirty pounds, she could turn heads.

"It came into my hands by accident," I said, "as part of another business deal. And nobody knows I have it."

"We do," the model said, stroking my ear with the shotgun.

"Usually I like a little more history," the fat girl said, "before I do business . . . but Raoul vouches for you, and if anything goes wrong, I'll send Lovely there to see you . . ."

"And I'll blow your fucking head off, jerk, cut off your nuts and stuff them down your throat," the model crooned.

"Lovely," I said, and the fat girl laughed.

"Where's the rest?" she asked.

"In a briefcase in the trunk of the car," I said. Not all of it, though. I had taken the liberty of buying two briefcases and had mailed one to myself with about a quarter of an ounce hidden in the handle.

The fat girl picked up the car keys off the coffee table and tossed them to Pimples where she stood at the edge of the hall. But her aim was slightly low, and one of the Rottweilers snapped them out of the air as if he were catching flies. "Orlando," the fat girl said quietly, "give." And the dog dropped the keys on the floor, curled up, and started licking his anus.

"Orlando?" I said.

"He's from Disney World," the model drawled. "Aren't you?"

The fat girl's eyes crinkled with amusement, and the strange giggles came again, creeping out of a side room, followed by a string of coughs and a cloud of marijuana smoke.

"Carry the briefcase flat and with both hands," I said to Pimples, "because there's a live grenade inside with the pin pulled."

The fat girl burst into honest laughter, but the model slapped me on the head with the shotgun. "Aren't you Mr. Smarty-pants," she said. "Let's kill the asshole, momma, and drop him in the Sound."

"He's too much fun," the fat girl said, and I tried to look charming in my sodden three-piece suit.

When Pimples brought the briefcase to me, she handled it as if it were her very own baby. I sat it on the Oriental rug, disarmed the booby trap, held the grenade in one hand and the pin in the other, then scooted the briefcase across the rug to the fat girl.

"Now we can negotiate," I said, "on semi-even terms."

Out of the corner of my eye, I saw a teen-aged boy with long hair, wearing tattered overalls but no shirt, stick his head around the edge of the doorframe. "He ain't shittin'," he whispered to somebody behind him.

"You cretins sit down and shut up," the fat girl said without looking up as she hefted the loosely wrapped black plastic bundle.

"I'll go with your weight," I said into her silence, thinking that was why she kept holding the package. But she wiped some of the pinkish gray powder on her sweat shirt and looked up at me.

"Jesus Kee-rist," she muttered, "that fucking pimp Raoul don't know shit from wild honey. He told me you were some jerk off the street, man, but you must have balls the size of a gorilla. I am truly impressed." I didn't have any idea what she was talking about, but I tried to sneer confidently and look casual at the same time. The fat girl shook her head, gathered the dusty black plastic into a wad, and tossed it to Pimples. "In the woodstove, baby," she said, "and now."

"Good idea," I said. Even if I was a jerk, Raoul, whose real name was Myron, was going to regret his mouth when next I saw him.

As she took her scales out of an inlaid Japanese box on the coffee table and weighed the cocaine, the fat girl kept glancing at me, a coy, little-girl's smile flickering about her mouth. "I make it a hair more than five and a half ounces," she said, finishing her work. "Let's all do a couple of lines," she added, taking a screen, a razor blade, and a small mirror out of the inlaid box, "and call it five and a half. Okay?"

"I never touch the stuff," I said primly. "Five and a half is fine with me."

"The way you make your living, man, I don't blame you," she said as she chopped lines.

I nodded like a man who knew what was going on, shifted my damp shorts out of the crack of my ass, and took a tighter grip on the slippery grenade.

The fat girl snorted two short lines, as did Pimples, but the model declined, saying she would wait until I had gone, downer that I was, then she tapped me lightly again with the shotgun.

"Can't you get her to stop that?" I said. "What sort of business are you running here, anyway?"

"We're sort of a family," the fat girl said, even happier than she was before. "Usually we conduct ourselves in a more professional manner, but this is a different deal. That's why we're doing it—for fun. You've got a fucking grenade, Lovely's crazy about using her shotgun—what the hell, let's enjoy."

"Let's finish our business," I said as Pimples carried the mirror into the side room, where the teen-aged voices burbled and the "Oh, wow's" and "Good shit's" twanged.

"Right," the fat girl said. "You want to dicker or you want to get down."

"Down."

"Okay, fine," she said. "It's worth eleven, but it ain't got no history, you understand. I was going to offer you six, but I figure you've got your ass covered pretty good, and I've loved meeting you, so I'll go seven, tops . . . No, seven and a half, fuck it."

"Done," I said. During this last part of the business, the model had grown bored, wandered toward the gray, rain-streaked window, the shotgun propped against the exquisite flare of her collarbone. "There's another item under the back seat," I said.

"Get it, Lovely," the fat girl said, and the model slinked out, looking even more bored. "You sure you don't want a taste?" she asked me.

"If it goes to shit," I said, "it might as well go to shit with happy noses." She laughed, shouted at Baby in the other room.

When she brought the mirror back, the fat girl brought it to me, held the mirror and the glass straw for me, and when I had finished, she kissed me on the forehead. "Thanks," I said.

"Anytime," she said. "No chance you'd put the pin back in the grenade, huh?"

"No chance."

She laughed as the model came back inside with the kilo of marijuana. She threw it to the fat girl, snarled something I didn't hear, then went back behind my chair.

"I like your style, man," the fat girl said as she sliced the black plastic wrapping off the smoke with a silver dagger, "but we don't handle pot."

"It's a gift," I said, "a bonus."

"Ah, do I ever like your style," she said, wadding up the plastic and giving it to Pimples to dispose of. "Listen, man, anytime you want to do business—buy or sell or just get purely fucked up— you call me at this number"—which she repeated several times—"and ask for, ah . . . Joan, and tell her that you're, ah . . . Leroy, and that you've got a bushel basket of fresh Dungeness crab. Leave a number, and I'll get back to you. And listen, man, now you really can put the pin back in the grenade, man, because I wouldn't jerk you around for love or money." Then she paused to laugh. "Well, maybe love. I've always got enough money, but nobody ever has enough love." Then she stood up, headed for the back of the house, still laughing.

"She eats pussy, you understand, don't you?" the model whispered in my ear. I nearly jumped out of the chair. She had moved back behind me as quietly as a snake. "But you wouldn't know about that, would you, tough guy," she said, then smacked me along the jaw line with the shotgun.

Enough is enough. She might be mean, but she didn't know not to touch the person you're covering with a gun. I dropped the pin out of my left hand, grabbed the shotgun, and shoved it toward her, pointing the barrels toward the ceiling. Shit, she had the safety on, so I jerked the gun out of her hands, and popped her lightly in the gut with my right hand heavy with the grenade.

I dropped her like a bad habit, and she fell to her knees like a nun seeking sudden forgiveness. I had forgotten about the dogs, but they just ambled over to lick the model's face. Pimples grinned at me, then walked into the side room where the teen-aged boys were whispering.

"What happened?" the fat girl said when she came back in the living room with a sheaf of bills in her hand.

"Philosophical disagreement," I said.

"Lovely *can* be a bitch, can't she?" she said, then slapped the bills against her wrinkled jeans. "You want to count it?"

"It doesn't seem necessary now, does it?"

"Way beside the point," she agreed.

"Then put it in the briefcase," I said, "and carry it to the car for me, okay?"

"Of course," she said. "You wait right there, Lovely." But Lovely didn't answer, she just lay on her side, her eyes clenched tightly shut as the two Rottweilers mouthed her gently. As she opened the five locks on the steel-core front door, the fat girl said, "Aren't you forgetting something?"

"What's that?"

"The pin."

"Fuck it," I said, "it's somewhere in the living room."

She laughed wildly all the way down the driveway, laughed as I unloaded the sawed-off, laughed even as I handed her the gun and the grenade. She tossed the shotgun into a rain puddle, and as she took the grenade from me, our hands seemed to fire in the damp air.

"Now give me a kiss," she said, brandishing the grenade. I tried, but we were laughing too hard. "And give me a call, you crazy son of a bitch."

"Maybe I'll just do that."

As I drove down the muddy road, I watched her in my rear-view mirror, watched her pitch the grenade underhanded across the road and into a deep, thickly overgrown barrow ditch. The shrapnel must have blown a tiny clear-cut in the evergreen brush. In my last glimpse of the fat girl in the rear-view mirror, she was standing over the ditch in the smoke rising in the misty rain, surveying the damage and still laughing.

I couldn't remember who said it—Freud? Margaret Mead? Phyllis Schlafly?—that no civilization could afford to send women to war because they would be too fierce.

If I had been the right sort of person, I would have some sort of remorse while I waited for the Bainbridge–Seattle ferry, would have suffered at least a modicum of moral regret, but, what the hell, if I started worrying about horrors of cocaine, who knew where I would stop worrying. Fluorocarbons out of our armpits and into the ozone? The next Ice Age? The dinky little star that made life possible going into nova? No, no, too much on my mind, too many troubles of my own. Sarah's and Gail's safety, and my own . . .

The pale, thin-faced man who had tried to look like a traveling salesman as he had tagged me from Ellensburg to Seattle leaned over the passenger deck rail watching the cars as they rumbled down the ramp onto the ferry. I turned up the collar of my trench coat, tried to look bored, and drove underneath him. I wanted a drink, and bad, but the shot of peppermint schnapps didn't cut the fear out of my mouth.

I took my time going to the motel, circling back on my trail several times, until I was sure my tail was clean, but in the motel room I shoved the two heavy easy chairs in front of the door, checked the M-11 with trembling fingers, and thought about drying out. This was no time, though, for the shakes, so I had another shot of schnapps and looked at myself in the mirror. My four-hundred-dollar suit looked as if I had worn it on a cross-country hike—dusty and damp from cuffs to collar—and my forty-dollar hairdo had a case of the terminal frizzies. Even naked after a shower, I still looked like a failure—saggy, bloated, and gray, like a stiff just fished out of Elliott Bay. I took the money out of the briefcase and spread it across the bed, but that didn't make me feel any better either. "Balls like a gorilla," the fat girl had said, meaning what I didn't know. But I had to laugh. If only she could see them now.

I fell on the bed and picked up the telephone to call the colonel, but fell immediately asleep with the dial tone buzzing in my hand. And woke four hours later, long past sundown, drenched in sweat, hundred-dollar bills pasted like leeches all over my body.

The colonel answered his home telephone before the first ring finished. I said, "Milo," and he gave me the number of a pay telephone, adding, "Ten minutes." When I called him back, he didn't even say hello, he just wanted to know who had tapped his lines. He sounded angry enough to curse, but he didn't.

"I don't know, sir," I said. "I'm sorry. And sorry, too, for involving you in my mess."

"What sort of mess?"

"I can't say."

"Why not?"

"I don't want to get you in trouble."

"Okay," he said. "Are you going to find out who tapped my lines?"

"Yes, sir," I said with more confidence than I felt.

"Then you're back on payroll as of yesterday."

"Save your money, sir."

"If you're not working for me, Milo, I've got to call the FBI about this."

"I'm working for you, sir."

"Good," he said. "And I've got some bad news for you . . ."

"Yes, sir," I said.

"After twenty-four hours with no activity at the Weddington house, Milo," he said, "I took the liberty of entering the house— we handle the alarm system—and nobody was there."

"Maybe they left town," I said, hopelessly.

"Not as far as I could tell," he said. "Both vehicles were in the garage, no signs of packing, no signs of a struggle, nothing, and when I checked with airport security, nobody remembered them taking a flight." When I finished cursing, the colonel coughed, then added, "Remember, Milo, that I have a rather large organization, if you need any help."

"Thank you, sir," I said, "but this one has to be mine."

"Good luck," he said.

"I'll check in tomorrow night, sir, same time," I said, and we rang off. Then I called the airport, made reservations on a morning flight to Butte, hoping to pick up the trail of the woman in the blue Subaru. Waiting for morning made for a long night.

Chapter 7

They sell picture postcards all over Montana bearing the legend "The Most Beautiful Sight in Montana." It is a picture of Butte in the rear-view mirror of an automobile. Butte isn't a pretty sight, coming or going. The great maw of the Berkeley Pit is eating the old town right off its mountainside, digging for copper they ship to Japan to be smelted. In many ways it is a sad city, a crumbling monument to both the successes and the failures of unbridled capitalism, seduced and abandoned first by the copper kings, then by the international conglomerates, but even as it dies, the old city still lives, filled with perhaps the best bars in a state of great bars, and rich with an ethnic mixture of Irish and Finns, of Poles and Mexicans. No true son of Montana can deny a deep fondness in his heart for the grand old whore, and a lot of people, myself included, don't think you can qualify as a native son unless you have spent at least one St. Paddy's Day in Butte.

But it is no place to be confused and depressed on a bleak and cold November afternoon. The north sides of the reddish, gray boulders up the mountainside shadow scraps of snow as dingy as a wino's sheets, the cold winds cut with a metallic edge, and the sky is the color of snot.

Only one place in Butte rented Subarus, and I didn't even have to bribe the woman behind the counter to get a look at the rental agreement for the dates in question. I suppose I shouldn't have been surprised by the name, but I was: Cassandra Bogardus.

Blind horse on a merry-go-round, back to my hometown, where not even my rich man's suit would hide me. I turned in my T-bird and rented the blue Subaru—cheap irony at half the daily rate—then went out to the mall on the Flats, looking for a new image to carry me home. A blond frizzy wig with a matching mustache, a double-knit lime-green leisure suit, Hush Puppies, an order pad, and a seventy-five-dollar twenty-pound Bible.

I made it back to Meriwether just before dusk, prime time for door-to-door salesmen, checked into the Riverfront, then drove over to the north side. Unless my hunch was completely wrong, the bad guys knew about the meetings between Cassandra Bogardus and Rausche, knew where she lived, and more than likely had somebody watching her house, and mine too, so I thought I would try to sell the Good Book, check out the neighborhood, and hope that I could find the watchers to watch them myself. I parked a block down from the Bogardus house on Gold, tucked the huge Bible under my arm, and began to ring doorbells. I chatted with a lonely old woman, survived the outrage of a drunk, got asked for my city business license by a young house-wife, and took an order for a Bible from a puffy-faced middle-aged man who looked as if he had just been released from one of the rubber rooms over at Warm Springs.

As darkness fell, bringing with it a light snowfall, I came to the Bogardus house. Since no lights showed behind the windows, I could pass it by without drawing attention to myself. I tried to look confused and Christian, dejected as I sighed and crossed over to the other side to call on Abner's house to hire some sur-veillance of my own.

Abner was not happy, to say the least, when he opened the door to a Bible salesman. He cursed and tried to slam it in my face, but I shoved my way into the living room.

"Don't swing, Mr. Haynes," I said, once I had shut the door, "it's me, Milodragovitch."

"Jesus Christ," he said, "you look like one of those homos on TV."

"You got a glass of water," I said. Even on the cold day in the light suit, sweat poured from under the wig. I tossed it and the giant book on the couch, took off the window-glass horn-rims, and sat down, trying to wipe the sweat out of my hair.

"Are you undercover?" he asked seriously, tugging furiously at the drooping ends of his mustache.

"I'm under something," I said. "How do you sleep, Mr. Haynes?"

"What?"

"How do you sleep?"

"How the hell does anybody sleep when they're sixty-seven," he grumbled, then narrowed his eyes as if he suspected I might try to sell him a dose of sweet rest.

"Working men never sleep worth a damn after they stop working," I said, "that's why retirement is such a damned hard job."

"You can say that again," he said, pulling at the straps of his undershirt in the warm room.

"How would you like to work for me?"

"Doing what?" he asked, lifting his large hands and flexing the fingers.

"See that house over there," I said, leaning over to open the drapes slightly, but the angle of the porch cut off the view, so I led him into his neat bedroom, where the side window had a clear shot. "That one there."

"Where the big blonde lives?"

"That's the one," I said. "How long has she lived there?"

"Since the Johnsons went to Alaska this summer."

"The Johnsons? Who are they?"

"He teaches wildlife biology out at the college," he said, "and she grows organic vegetables. What about it?"

"Can you see it good?" I asked, remembering his mistake with the sign on the van.

"I'm just old," he growled, "not blind." I looked at him for a moment. He shrugged, went into the living room, and came back wearing gold-rimmed spectacles. "All right," he sighed, "I can see it good."

I explained that I wanted him to keep an eye on the house for me, not on any particular schedule, just watch it and call me at the motel day or night if he saw the blond woman come in, or anybody else around the house.

"Just watch it, that's all?" he asked.

"Don't watch it all the time," I said, "just take an occasional glance at it when you're awake, maybe every fifteen or twenty minutes. That's all I ask." He looked disappointed that I hadn't asked more of him, so I added, "And I'll pay you the same thing I would pay a professional operative."

"How much would that be?" he asked, shuffling his slipper against the worn rug.

"One hundred dollars a day," I said, "a three-day minimum in advance." I couldn't tell if it was the money I counted out or the phrase "professional operative," but the old man leapt at it.

"You mind if Yvonne helps?" he asked slyly, sneaking a glance at the old oak bed.

"As long as she keeps her mouth dead-tight shut," I replied as seriously as if I were the reincarnation of J. Edgar himself, but laughing on the inside. Old Abner still had some healthy vices left in his worn, wiry frame.

"You've got my word on it," he said, reaching out his hand.

As I shook it the thought of Sarah and Gail missing hit me again, and the laughter inside died. "I mean it about Yvonne not talking," I said.

"You've got my word," he repeated.

"Day or night," I reminded him as I went back into the living room to don my shoddy disguise, "and if I'm not there, leave a message for Mr. Sloan—"

"Phony name, too," he interrupted. "Damnation, I thought this only happened on TV."

Me too, I thought. I slapped the old man's shoulder, picked up the Bible and my wig, then left. When I hit the steps—splay-footed on the foam soles, with a smile so smarmy it would have made a dog puke—I paused long enough to curse a world that teaches a man to work until he can't live without it, works him nearly to death, then shoves him out to die.

Although with the five grenades and the two submachine guns I had enough firepower to start a coup in some small Central American country, I wanted my own guns and some backup, and since I couldn't pick up my mail without getting tagged by the bad guys, some cocaine. Purely for my nerves. All three, for my failing nerve. I went back to the motel to change into something warmer and less gaudy to wear while I broke into my own house, but the telephone was ringing when I went into the room. Old Abner on the job. He said he could see what he thought to be a flashlight moving around inside the Bogardus house. I went to check it out.

I nearly missed them when they came out the back door of the Bogardus house and slipped through the snow-dark shadows of the side yard and out a gap in the hedge. Two guys in jogging suits, their hoods up and snugly tied to hide their faces. I tagged them at a distance as they circled the block once for show, then went into a small frame house east on Gold and across the street, on the same side as Abner's. I started to go up to the front door and try to get them to order a Bible, but even if I hadn't left my red-letter edition in the car, I just didn't have the nerve. Not without some help, whiskey, or cocaine. Just following them had filled me with trembling fear. I knew where they had set up the surveillance and could deal with them later, so I went after some nerve.

My next-door neighbor's driveway was empty—his rattletrap pickup had taken him to his night-bartending job, and her Corvette had carried her out on the town to boogie—so I parked there, vaulted the back fence and went into my house through the cellar door. Very quietly. I meant to take all my guns out of the house, but by the time I removed the false panel my hands were shaking so badly that I only took three handguns—the Browning 9mm, a .357 Colt Python and an S&W five-shot, hammerless Airweight .38—the shoulder holsters for them, and a box of shells for each. I strapped myself into the Browning in the cold basement air, but it looked like a thick steak under my arm beneath the thin leisure-suit coat, so I changed to the .38, trembling, then I crept up the cellar stairs, opened the door to the kitchen and slammed it hard, then went back out through the cellar door.

Outside, I dashed across the street, dove into a clump of snow-heavy creek brush and waited. The bastards had my house bugged, just as I thought. Within two minutes a light-blue van arrived and parked right in my driveway just as if it belonged there. Two men who moved like professionals went into my house, one through the front, one through the back, so quickly I knew they had already had keys cut. I wondered if they were supposed to kill me there, or take me for a ride and kill me later.

After they had checked out the empty house they came outside, stood around as casual as tourists, discussing the vagaries of electronic surveillance. In the streetlight I could see their faces—the small dark dude in the pickup and the large guy who wanted to get Western in the Porsche when I messed up their pretty four-man tail in Seattle. Huddled in the snowbank, I wished I knew what to think. Too much cocaine, though, too much fear. I didn't want to think; I wanted to run, never think again.

When they turned around and left, I ran across to the Subaru and tailed them around the park to the apartment complex at the south end. I watched them go back to their apartment, made a note of the number, then dug into my wallet for the Snowseal packet of coke. There wasn't much left by now, so I just did the last of it right off the paper. It didn't help. And stopping wouldn't help either. Maintaining the buzz, that was my only choice. Otherwise, as scared as a street punk on his first mugging, I was going to kill somebody. And soon. And probably the wrong person. I headed for the Deuce and Raoul, the dealer, the little car fishtailing across the snow-covered streets.

Raoul was amused by my disguise, when he finally recognized me, and further dismayed when I dragged him out into the alley behind the Deuce by the lapels of his leather coat. When I had him in the shadows, I jerked him back and forth so hard that his leather hat fell into a pile of frozen dog shit. He protested, and I lost it for a second, slapped off his red sunglasses, and ground the lenses into the bricks with my Hush Puppies.

"Jesus shit, Milo," he whimpered, "take it easy."

"What the fuck are you afraid of, Myron," I hissed, "some jerk off the street?"

"Okay, man, okay," he said, wiping my spittle off his face. "I made a small error in judgment, okay, man, I thought those crazy bitches would be easy on you if they thought you weren't anybody, that's all, just some guy off the street, okay. What did you want me to say—that you used to be the man, that you're an alcoholic who has occasional lapses into cocaine psychosis?"

"Right," I sighed, trying to get a handle on myself. "I'm sorry. Too much shit going down, okay. I'm sorry."

Myron took a deep breath, let it out easy, closed his eyes like a man chanting his mantra silently. "Jesus," he said, "when you did my glasses, I thought I was next . . . Are you okay?"

"Shit."

"I think you gave me whiplash," he said, but he smiled. "What can I do for you, man?"

"I brought your cut," I said as I stuffed the roll of bills into his pocket.

"Keep it," he said. "I'm out of this. All the way. I talked to the fat lady, and I'm out. I don't know what you did, don't know what's going down, but I'm out." He handed me the three thousand back.

"Keep it."

"Absolutely not."

"Okay, fuck it," I said, counting off five bills. "I need a quarter-ounce, okay?"

"You be hurting, huh?" he said softly. "Sure. But this is too much bread."

"For the glasses," I said. "The price of stupidity, okay?"

"Only for you," he said, reaching down to pick up his hat. "Thank God for cold weather and frozen dog shit. I'll catch you inside in half an hour or so." Then he paused, and added, "Maybe you ought to wait someplace else, Milo."

"Why?"

"You ain't exactly dressed for the Deuce, man."

"Fuck it."

"It's your party, man," he said, then hustled down the alley.

Inside, I tried to ease through the crowd politely, but when I went past the head hog of the local motorcycle gang, I stumbled over my Hush Puppies and jostled his beer. He was leaning against the end of the bar, daring somebody to bump into him, copping feels off passing ladies, hoping to start a fight so he and his tawdry minions could take some poor drunk dude back into the alley and put the boots to him. He looked at me as if I were some sort of subhuman species.

"What the hell, buddy," I said under the bluegrass stomp, "you never seen a Bible salesman before?" The .38 felt warm under my armpit as the blood rose. Goddammit, I thought, I knew I was going to kill the wrong person. Back off. But before I could apologize, he did. In his own way.

"Hey, dad," he said, hitching his balls, "you best take it cool and easy." Then he sauntered off toward the pisser.

Sitting at the bar, trying to nurse my shot of schnapps, which must be something like nursing hemlock, I saw the armored-truck driver, whose name I couldn't remember, at a table near the back door with three other aging mountain hippies. He had been under fire, wounded in Vietnam, and I knew he was at loose ends. Maybe he wanted to work backup for me. If I could just remember his name.

Raoul came back during my third shot of schnapps, eased up to the bar beside me and bummed a cigarette, and when he handed the pack back, I knew the quarter-ounce was inside.

"Thanks, man," he said, letting the smoke drift slowly out of his mouth. Under his breath he added, "Try to remember, Milo, that sometimes you eat the bear, but sometimes the bear eats you." It is something they say in Montana; I think it means that life has consequences. Raoul adjusted a new pair of red shades, shook his head, and went about his business.

I gunned the shot in front of me, walked toward the back door, and stopped at the table where the unemployed armored-truck driver sat. "Hey, dude," I said and tapped him on the shoulder, "remember pulling down on me in front of Hamburger Heaven the other day?" He stared at me for a long time, then nodded and smiled as if he was sorry he hadn't blown me away. "Let's talk some business," I said, "outside." Then I moved toward the door.

"In a minute," I heard him say.

But as I waited in the alley, watching the tiny crystalline flakes float in the blue light from the street lamps, the tall, slouching bulk of the biker strolled out the back door and headed toward me, walking slowly, like a man with a mission.

"Hey, man," he said as politely as anyone in his position could, "you ought not brace me like that, man, not a man like you." When I didn't say anything, he scratched his chest beneath his jacket. "I may not look it now, man, but I was brought up Pentecostal, and I've still got respect for believers, but a man like you ought not to be in a place like this. I'm lost, man, but you got a chance. Don't backslide, not like me, man; go back to the one true—"

"I'm federal heat, son," I interrupted, holding the double-knit jacket open to show him the .38, "and you best be about your own business. Now."

No matter how tough you are, you don't rise to the leadership of even a crappy small-town biker gang without a certain amount of ability to be articulate, even if only in the argot of bikers, and this guy looked as if he had never been at a loss for words in his life.

"You-you-you fucking—you pigs," he stammered, "you dudes will do anything for a bust, any-anything—"

"Forgive your enemies," I said, hoping I was quoting something, "as I forgive you, my son."

But he just muttered a string of curses as he hurried back into the bar, pushing the armored-truck driver out of the way as he tried to get into the door.

"What the hell's wrong with *him*?" he asked as he stepped over to me.

"Salvation just turned to shit in his hands one more time," I said.

"Say what?" he asked, but I didn't answer.

In fact, I didn't say anything for a long time. Or so it seemed. The small insane encounter with the biker had shaken me more than I could admit. I was tired of being half drunk, or half sober, tired of measuring out those shots of candied alcohol. The world was simply too crazy for me to handle sober. Maybe not the whole world, but at least the world where I lived—the bars and back streets, the shadows from which I watched, that world was too crazy for me to handle sober. Maybe the whole world was too crazy. Religious wars, political wars, economic wars . . . Did that world out there reflect us? Or we, that world?

I didn't much know, didn't much care. I knew I had to find out who wanted my ass, and negotiate, accommodate as much as I could and still live with myself. I had to find Sarah, if they had her, and Gail, and when I found the old woman, I had my own peace to make. That old lady and I would get happily stoned and talk about my father. And if I didn't find her, or if I found her dead, I intended to wreak havoc across the land until the guilty were punished under my hand. Even if it cost my life.

Then I realized what a coward I had been. It had been coming on me for years, the closer I got to fifty-two and my father's money. That was over now, here in this dog-shit alley, it ended, all the running, hiding, and I found myself grinning, not like a rabid animal, but like a child.

"Hey, man," the armored-truck driver asked, "are you all right?"

"I'm fine," I said, "absolutely fine. If a guy can't stand the occasional mid-life crisis, then fuck him, right?"

"Damn straight," he said. "But listen, man, I'm really sorry about the other day. I was behind a handful of downers and a pint of vodka, and my liver just won't handle it anymore, so I tend to get a little crazy—"

"What did you do in Vietman?" I interrupted.

"What'd I do?" he said. "Well, shit, man, I did what every grunt worth his C rations did, man—I killed people. What difference does it make to you?"

"Can you still handle yourself?"

"If I need to, Jack. Why?"

"I need somebody to cover my back," I said. "You want the job?"

He brushed his hair out of his face, wiped the melted snow off his forehead, then held his hands out toward me, palms down, so I could see the fingers tremble. "I can just barely wipe my ass," he said sadly.

Perhaps because we had shared that frozen moment in the gray, gusting rain or perhaps because I had finally lost my mind—whatever, I dumped a patch of cocaine on my fist and said, "Will you at least do what I say?"

He hesitated for a moment, brushed his sleeve across his wet nose and snorted off my hand. "Why?"

"Money, fun, fire power, and enough of this to keep us fairly sane," I said.

"When?"

"Now," I said, laughing, having a touch of nose myself, "right now."

"I can't remember your name, man—I know it's one of those long Polack numbers . . ."

"Russian," I said.

"But you just hired a hand."

"I can't remember your name either," I said, and we both laughed wildly in the dark alley.

"Simmons," he said, still laughing, "Bob Simmons."

"Milodragovitch," I said, and we went to work.

I left Simmons in the car, clutching the .357, while I slipped across the yard to have a look through the windows of the surveillance house on Gold. Just as I thought, it was the other two guys from Washington, the salesman and the VW van driver, sitting on folding chairs in a bare living room. A small black-and-white television screen flickered on top of a stack of radio receivers. The two guys were sitting so closely together in the chairs that it almost looked as if they were holding hands. I went back to the car and we drove down to Abner's house.

When I introduced Simmons to him, Abner wrinkled his nose as if he smelled a dead rat.

"Don't pay any attention to how he's dressed," I told him. "Simmons is undercover, too."

"Looks like he's been hid under a pile of garbage," the old man muttered.

I borrowed Abner's flashlight, his hammer, and a towel—it would be a sloppy job breaking into the Bogardus house, but since my lock picks were in the tool box of my pickup, I didn't have much choice—and told Simmons to watch the other house.

"If they come out running," I said, "you come out behind them, find some cover, and shout 'Freeze!' as loud as you can." He stuffed the .357 in his belt and wiped his hands on his dirty jeans. "Don't worry," I added, "they're probably not going to start a fire fight in the street."

"Right," he said, "right."

Abner shuffled over to a closet, drew out a Long Tom 10-gauge single-barrel shotgun. "This'll blow their shit to kingdom come," he said.

"Put that away," I said. "I didn't hire you for gunfire, Mr. Haynes."

"Make that Corporal Haynes of the AEF," he said. "And you can have your money back, son."

"Okay, but for God's sake, be careful!" I said. "That goddamned cannon will blow somebody's house down." Crazy old bastard. "Please be careful," I said again, but he just sneered. I gave up and left.

The house was a cracker box, though, so I slipped the side-door lock with Sarah's Gold American Express card and left the hammer and the towel on the stack of firewood. At least the Hush Puppies were good for something—they were quiet. I went through the house as quickly as I could and found out a great deal about the Johnsons—bounced checks and past-due credit duns, a collection of S-M magazines, some Polaroid nude studies of a dumpy dark-haired woman who was rather proud of her labia—but almost no evidence that Cassandra Bogardus had ever lived there. Just the tweed suit and the gray wig she had used to fox me at the airport. So I gave that up too.

When I got back to Abner's house, the old man asked me if I had had any luck.

"I got out alive," I said.

"Yeah, but you're a pro," the old man said proudly, "and that's not luck."

"You watch too much television, old man," I said thoughtlessly, and Abner pouted and grumbled as he put away his shotgun. He sulked for another fifteen minutes while I waited to call the colonel at the telephone booth, waited in a dead silence because Abner refused to turn on his new Sony.

When I called the colonel, he picked up the phone on the first ring, and I asked him to meet me at the office. I wanted to see who had hired Haliburton to tag Cassandra Bogardus.

On our way across town Simmons asked, as politely as a very nervous man could, what was going on.

"You just cover my back," I told him, "and don't worry about anything else."

He got a little sullen too, so I left him in the car while I went into the colonel's office.

"Milo?" he said from behind his desk. "You look terrible."

"I assume you had the building swept," I said.

"This morning," he said. "It's clean. They just bugged the telephone lines."

"Bastards," I said, and for once the colonel didn't look away when I cursed.

"I would certainly feel better if I knew what was going on," he said.

"Me too, sir."

"I don't like working in the dark."

"Me either, sir," I said.

"Well, what did you get me down here for, Milo?" he said tartly. This was my night for pissing people off.

"I need to borrow a couple of those down vests with the bulletproof lining."

"Sure," he said, tossing me his keys. "They're in the weapons locker."

"Sir, Simmons is out in the car," I said. "He's giving me some backup on this. Maybe you can talk him into coming back to work when we're done."

"Simmons?" he said. "Good man. A little confused from the war still, but a good man all the same. And a good idea, Milo. Thanks. I'll give it a shot." Then he put on his flat cap and went out.

When I heard the front door close, I used the colonel's keys to unlock his file cabinet. The Cassandra Bogardus surveillance had been instigated by a Seattle firm, Multitechtronics, Inc. I jotted down the address and telephone number, locked the files, and hurried down the hallway to pick up the vests. When I carried them out to the car, the colonel was talking very softly while Simmons stared out the windshield.

"Thank you, sir," I said as I climbed into the Subaru. "I'll be in touch." I stepped on the gas, leaving the short man standing in the snow-covered parking lot.

"What the hell was that all about?" Simmons asked.

"The colonel wants to give you another chance," I said.

"I'll be damned," he said.

"He's a good old man," I said. "A little stuffy, but he'll go to the wall with you."

"Ain't bad for an officer," Simmons said, then laughed bitterly.

"Where do you live?"

"I've got a dump over the Deuce."

"Living close to home, huh?" I said. "You want to pick up some clothes and whatnot."

"Why?"

"We've got a suite at the Riverfront," I said.

"Guess I should."

"Got a match?"

"Sure," he said.

"Then dip it into here," I said, handing him the vial of coke, "and let's fix our noses."

"You're the boss," he answered.

Although the late-evening traffic on the Franklin Street strip was light enough so that any cop cars would easily be visible, I took two or three close, searching looks to be damn sure before we did any coke. And luck was with me again. I spotted the light-blue van that had carried the two bad guys to my house earlier. They had settled in about forty yards behind us.

"Shit," I said and blew the coke off the match stick. "We shouldn't have used the same telephone booth twice."

"What?" Simmons asked.

"Do me quick," I said, "then climb over and jerk the back seat out and see if you can reach that orange knapsack in the trunk."

"What?"

"Do it!"

Simmons seemed to have some experience breaking into auto

trunks through the back seat because he did it quietly and smoothly, without much effort.

"This what you want?" he asked, handing me the knapsack.

"Right," I said and slipped the silenced M-11 out of the sack.

"Jesus," he sighed. "What the hell is that?"

"An interesting toy."

"You are into some serious shit, huh?"

"You want out?" I asked as he climbed back into the front seat.

"No way, man. No way."

"Okay. Now the vests," I said, and we struggled into them. Although I had never personally tested the Kevlar mesh vests, I had seen them stop a .357 magnum round on a dummy. "Let's go for a ride," I said.

I took them out to the interstate, not running, but not poking along either, driving like a man on business. The van stayed with me as I headed west to the Blue Creek Road exit, where I turned south up the creek. The snow seemed to be falling harder on the dark, empty stretch of road, and the wind kicked small ground-blizzard swirls through my headlights. The van had cut its headlights, but I could still catch an occasional glimmer of its parking lights in the rear-view mirror. I punched the Subaru a bit, and it pulled away smoothly across the snow-packed ruts.

When I got to the long wooden bridge across Blue Creek, which led to Moccasin Flats Road, then back to town on the old highway, I raced across the slippery planks, then another twenty yards just around the belly of a curve, where I stopped the car and told Simmons to get behind the wheel. I ran to the bridge-head and dove behind the biggest rock in the ditch. The van came on faster now, its tires crunching through the frozen snow crust as it followed our tracks onto the bridge. It seemed I could hear the men chuckling while they checked their guns.

Thinking I didn't want to just drop them in cold blood, thinking maybe I could work something out, I let the van get to the middle of the bridge before I tried to put a short burst into the left front tire. I had held too low, though, so it took a second burst to hit the rubber. The van veered sharply into the railing, bounced and slithered, but it kept coming on the flat. The guy in the passenger seat leaned out the window; a spurt of flame exploded from the end of his arm, followed by the sharp, ugly splat of a silenced revolver. I rolled to the other side of the rock, put a burst into the grill. Steam and sparks and the hiss of a ruptured gas line filled the darkness. The fan belt began to scream like a hysterical woman, and the van came to an abrupt halt.

"Listen, you guys!" I shouted. "It doesn't have to be this way!" When they didn't answer, I added, "Let me have the old lady and the girl back, I'll keep my mouth shut about Elk City and we can call it even!"

Then they answered. Three rounds ricocheted off my small boulder, rock chips and dust mixing with the snowflakes. To hell with it. I sprayed the bridge and the van to get their heads down, saw the first flickers of flame off the engine and then crawled down the ditch around the curve, jumped into the car, and told Simmons to hit it. He did, and it was the most dangerous thing we did all night. Fifty yards down the road he nearly put us into the creek.

"Jesus!" I said. "Let me drive."

"Right," he said, his voice trembling.

As we changed seats we heard a muffled roar and watched a fireball rise through the snowy night.

"Hope those boys were wearing their winter coats," I said, "because it's a long walk home."

"Shit, was that the van? On the bridge?"

"People up here have been trying to get the county to build a new one for years," I said.

Chapter 8

After we picked up Simmons' gear, we packed all the guns into
the small trunk, then called a cab, leaving the little blue Subaru
abandoned in the alley behind the Deuce with the keys in the ignition. I would report it stolen, eventually. Back at the Riverfront, the bar was closed, so Simmons and I had to make do with
the remains of my schnapps.

"I'm sorry I can't tell you what's happening," I said over the
last shots. "Some people are trying to kill me, and I'm trying to
work a deal with them without killing any of them. Anything else
I tell you would make you an accessory after the fact."

"Whatever," he said. He had been strangely silent since the
bridge. "You're the boss."

"Look, if anything happens," I said, "you're looking at a piece
of a federal firearms rap and a cocaine bust—"

"Listen," he interrupted, "I gotta tell you something . . ."

"What's that?"

"You ever kill anybody up close?" he asked. "I mean face to

face?" I nodded, but I didn't want to talk about it, even if he was going to. "Well, shit, man, I spent my sixteen weeks of the war riding an armored personnel carrier and firing fifty-caliber rounds into the fucking bush. Man, I never even saw Charlie. I was a fuck-up before the war—got into the Army because a judge in Denver gave a choice of the slammer or Uncle Sam on a little pot bust—and I got my Purple Heart when a gook rocket hit the half-track parked in front while I was sitting on the side of the APC reading a Spiderman comic, took a piece of shrapnel no bigger than a pencil eraser . . ." He paused, tugged his shirt out of his jeans, and pulled it up. "Look at this shit." The doctors had opened him up from pelvis to sternum, gutted him like a game animal, but he was pointing to a tiny blue dimple just to the right of his belly button. "So I ain't no kind of hero, man, and both times tonight, I was scared shitless, so if you want to look for some real backup, man, I'll understand . . ."

"Just shave clean in the morning," I said, "and we'll get you a haircut and a new suit. I can't have my bodyguard looking like a tramp."

He grinned and tossed off the last of the schnapps. "How do you drink this shit?"

"I'm with you there, son," I said, "and you'll do to ride the river with."

"What the hell does that mean?"

"I don't know," I admitted, "but I heard it in a Western movie one time. And another line—'Let's hit the hay.' "

I heard him laughing all the way into the other bedroom of the suite, heard him, like me, switch on the television set for the all-night company in our sleep, hoping to dream Western movies instead of our lives.

And woke the next morning to a full-blown blizzard, six inches of fresh and six more coming, hard icy winds off the Pole, and single-digit temperatures. My kind of weather, born and bred to it, and those web-footed sissies from Seattle were in trouble. I needed some clothes and winter gear out of my house, wanted a chat with Carolyn Fitzgerald about her connection with Cassandra Bogardus, but first I needed more wheels.

After I dressed in my rich man's clothes, I folded the leisure suit neatly, set it in the trash can with the snow-stained Hush Puppies on top of it, hoping the maid had a husband with no taste, then Simmons and I took a cab down to the car-rental agency, where I picked up two four-wheel-drive rigs, a Blazer for me, an American Eagle for him. I wondered if I was about to set some sort of record for rent cars, wondered if I would ever see my trusty pickup again, wondered, as we drove out to the mall, what Simmons would look like in a suit and a haircut.

As it turned out, he looked very nervous in the vested tweed, so I bought him a full-length leather overcoat, something a pimp or an actor might wear, and he felt okay again. So we went to work, Simmons tagging me around town while I looked for Carolyn Fitzgerald.

She didn't have a listed telephone number, nor, I found out for twenty dollars, an unlisted one either. When I tried calling her at the Friends of the Dancing Bear, they said she didn't come in too often, but took my message to call Mr. Sloan at the Riverfront. Thinking perhaps Vonda Kay might know where she lived, I went back to the motel bar when it opened at ten, the lady bartender told me she had called in sick.

"So she's at home?"

The bartender looked at me for a long time. Although she was dressed in ruffles and lace and made up like an actress, she had those hard bartender eyes. If it had happened, she had seen it.

"Maybe," she said.

"I'll give her a call."

"I can't give you her number," she said.

"I've got it, babe," I said, "and if I miss her at home, tell her Milo stopped by."

"Oh, you're Milo," she said, glancing about the empty room, then leaning across the bar. "Listen, she's on a tear. She called me at ten last night, drunk out of her mind, and asked me to cover her shift for a couple of days, so I don't know where she is. Your guess is as good as mine."

"Thanks," I said, then went up to the room to call Vonda Kay's favorite bars.

I caught her day-drinking at the Doghouse, and when she came to the phone, she was mumbling drunk. "Winter, winter," she kept blubbering, "I can't stand another goddamned winter alone, Ralph." Ralph was an ex-husband twice removed. When she finally understood who I was and what I wanted, she lurched out of tears and into cursing. "Why don't you want to know where *I* live, bastard, why?" Then she hung up. By the time I drove out to the Doghouse, she had left. I called some more bars without luck. Lady bartenders live a tougher life than anybody knows.

As Simmons and I went back out to our cars, I stared across the lot at the EZ-IN/EZ-OUT, but it looked permanently closed, the plywood panels, gleaming like raw meat in the gray light, looking as blank as dead faces. I thought about the two kids in their reindeer pajamas, about the Benniwah kid locked in the maximum-security cell in the hospital, about the two hunters who probably had their lawyers after my ass at this very moment.

"You okay?" Simmons asked through his open window.

"Sure."

"Where now?"

"The cop shop," I said, and he frowned. I climbed in, locked the 9mm automatic and the .38 Airweight in the glove box, stuffed the M-11 to the bottom of the knapsack beneath a dirty sweat shirt, then went to see Jamison.

"Goddamn, Milo," he said as I walked into his office, "you are looking prosperous. Come into the money?"

"Don't be a jerk," I said.

"I'm glad you stopped by," he said, smiling. Although he hadn't treated me with active disgust as often as he used to, it was odd, after all the years of enmity, to see him smile at me as if he were actually glad to see me. It made me uncomfortable, made me feel the cell doors clank shut.

"Why?"

"I wanted you to be the first to know."

"Know what?"

"I asked the colonel to let me be the one to tell you," he said.

"What?"

"He's opening a new office in Portland," he said, "and I'm going to run it . . ."

"And?"

"And Evelyn and I are getting back together."

"She dumped Captain Organic, huh?" I asked, and he nodded. "What happened?"

"I'm not quite sure," he said thoughtfully. "Hell, I was never sure why she split in the first place, but, anyway, she said she hit him in the face with a two pound T-bone and he ran away."

"She always did have a way with words," I said. "Congratulations. I guess."

"Thanks," he said, "and I've got some good news for you."

"I could use some."

"But don't tell anybody it went down this way, okay?"

"What?"

"The Blevins brothers, those upright citizens with the vigilante turn of mind who blew up the EZ-IN/EZ-OUT the other night . . ." he began, almost happy. "Well, they're not pressing charges against you, and they're not filing civil suits against you or Haliburton Security, and they're not going to Deer Lodge Prison."

"Wonderful," I said. "What about the Indian kid?"

"I suspect he will," Jamison said sadly.

"Too bad."

"You're right," he said.

"That doesn't sound like you," I said, "and I can't believe you're resigning, either."

"You know, Milo," he said, leaning back in his swivel chair and lacing his fingers behind his neck, "I can't quite believe it either. You told me years ago, you remember, that I was carrying too large a burden of morality to be a good cop, and, you know, you were right."

"Did I say that?"

"That," he said, "and I think you also asked me out into the hills for a round of fisticuffs. Several times. Maybe I would have been a better cop if I had gone with you." I didn't say anything, more than uneasy with this new Jamison. He had tried like crazy to be my friend all the years when we were growing up, while we were playing ball together at Mountain States, while we were in Korea in the same outfit. We had even gone into law enforcement—his term—together; he had joined the police department the same month I went to work for the sheriff. It had taken a long time for him to understand that I didn't much give a damn about enforcing some laws, and even longer for him to forgive me for my attitude. "So what was it you wanted?" he said after the long silence.

"A favor. Or two."

"If I can."

"I need you to run a couple of names through your computer hookup."

"Not a chance," he said nicely. "You know that."

"What do you have on that van they pulled out of Blue Creek this morning?" It hadn't made the paper yet, but the radio news was full of wild reports about bullet-ridden vans, burned bridges, and drug wars.

"It will be in tomorrow's paper," he said, fingering a sheet of computer print-out, "and on tonight's news."

"What?"

"No vehicle identification number," he said, "no engine block number until we get somebody over from Helena to do an acid test, stolen plates—you know the scenario. Why do you ask?"

"Just curious," I said.

"Goddammit, Milo," he groaned, "you draw trouble like honey draws flies."

"Or shit."

"Right," he said. "You coming to the ball game?"

"If I can."

"Try," he said. "Here's your ticket."

"Thanks." I put the ticket carefully in my wallet. "I will try."

"Buddy will be glad to see you."

"I said I'd try."

"And if you figure out a favor I can actually do," he said, "let me know."

"I will," I said, and we left it at that.

After we dropped Simmons' rental unit at the motel, and since there didn't seem to be anything else to do, we spent the rest of the day drifting with the storm around Meriwether, up and down the snow-covered streets, looking for Carolyn Fitzgerald's Mustang, looking for Vonda Kay, occasionally checking the motel for messages, without luck, rolling past the dark Bogardus house, the even darker Weddington mansion, doing cocaine and schnapps and worrying until I was half-crazy, maybe full-bore bull-goose loony.

Anyway, just after dark I parked the Blazer in my next-door neighbor's driveway, with something really insane in mind. I saw her come to the window to see who had pulled in, so I went to the front door and knocked.

"Milo," she said when she opened it, "you look beautiful. Come on in. Where have you been?"

"Maybe in a bit," I said. "Can I leave my rig in your driveway for a few minutes?"

"Of course," she said, giving me one of her wild, thin-lipped kisses, all teeth, tongue, and suction, which nearly pulled me into her house. "Oh, do come back," she said as I turned to leave, patting the Airweight under my arm. "You know how much I love it when you've got your gun on."

"Sure," I said, wishing that I didn't know how she felt about it, wishing I had lived a somewhat saner life. "Sure."

I went back to my house. Simmons and I got in through the cellar door and gathered up down parkas and sleeping bags, clothes, my .30-06 elk rifle, a Ruger .44 magnum autoloading carbine, a 12-gauge riot shotgun, my grandfather's .41-caliber derringer, two pairs of snow pacs with flannel liners. Simmons, as crazy as I was, kept stifling giggles, and when I would mouth "Bugs" at him, he had a bigger giggle to choke. It took two trips, and on the second I picked up my chain-saw case, and Simmons kept his fist stuffed in his throat until he got control of himself, then he whispered, "We've got enough arms to start a god-damned war, man, but if we're getting into Texas Chain-Saw Massacre, I'm getting out." Then he had to hold his jaws shut to keep the laughter inside.

Back in the Blazer, though, it broke out, and neither of us could stop until long after the tears had come. My next-door neighbor came out of the house to see what we were doing, but I gave her a toot off my fist and sent her back inside with empty promises.

"Where you going now, dad?" Simmons asked as I climbed out of the rig one more time.

"One last thing," I said, a short burst of laughter barking into the sideways snow.

Thinking about the grenade under my seat in Idaho, I went back inside, muttering, "Booby-trap me, bastards," all the way. I carried the crossbow upstairs to the kitchen, cocked it and ran a string off the back-door handle through a cabinet-door handle, then to the trigger, and set the bow on a kitchen chair aimed at the back door. Then I unscrewed the hunting point off the bolt, cut a hole in an old handball, and stuck it on the end. That would make the bastards think twice about messing with me again, and maybe they would want to talk when they finally realized what a sneaky bastard I was. I opened the front door, slammed it, turned on the television, rattled my old couch, then slipped quietly out through the basement.

Back in the motel parking lot I decided I had had enough time looking like somebody else, and Simmons kept tugging at his tie as if it were attached to a hangman's knot, so we went up to the suite and put on normal clothes. It felt great, especially after another toot, so we rushed down to the bar to catch the tag end of the Happy Hour.

Sometimes when hard work fails, luck succeeds. Carolyn Fitzgerald sat at the bar holding a beautiful martini. Lord, how I wanted a martini, but one would be too many and ten thousand wouldn't be enough. I perched on the stool beside her, motioned Simmons to the other side, and ordered a cup of coffee. Working-time again, and me in no condition for it.

After we exchanged trite pleasantries, and I realized that she wasn't all that pleased to see me, I said, "I need to talk to you. Privately. I've got a room upstairs. You can carry your drink up there."

"What about?" she said.

"Business."

"The last time I saw you, Milo, you were more interested in jokes than business," she said, "and from the size of your pupils, I assume you're going to be even funnier now."

"Damn right," I said and picked up her hand as if I were admiring her bevy of rings, then guided it to the place under my arm where the Airweight nestled like a snake in a skull. "Serious business."

"My God," she whispered.

"Laugh," I said, "smile, and bring your drink. My friend behind you is carrying an even bigger gun."

Her hollow laughter followed a bitter smile, but she came, and I could tell she hated every step of the way. The strap of her purse kept slipping off her trembling shoulder, and even though she held her drink with both hands, by the time we reached the door of the suite, all the gin had splashed out to run like crystalline tears over the turquoise and silver, the sapphire and ceramic of her rings.

"I'm sorry," I said, once we were locked in the room, "I'm terribly sorry, but this is damned serious."

She didn't answer but tossed her empty glass on the bed, flopped into an easy chair, and buried her face into her bejeweled hands, her long red fingernails digging into her forehead. I told

Simmons to go into the other room. He looked like I felt, like a man coming down off stone-crazy giggles into the black maw of reality. Finally Carolyn raised her head, smiled like a woman resigned to a fate worse than death, and clawed some cigarettes out of her purse.

"I didn't mean to lose it like that," she said through a streamer of smoke, "but guns scare the hell out of me. Three years ago I was raped in my apartment in D.C., at gunpoint, so I'm still a little touchy."

"I understand," I said. "I'm sorry . . . Shit, I guess no man ever understands that sort of violation. Unless he's been gang-raped in prison . . ."

"That happened to you?"

"No, no—I didn't mean that. I'm just trying to say I'm sorry, but you didn't seem inclined to talk to me, and—"

"And you're drug-crazed."

"Truth be known."

"I hope you have a good reason for this," she said, a good, tough lady gathering herself.

"Cassandra Bogardus."

"Cassie?"

"I need to see her."

"You don't need to jerk me out of the bar at gunpoint," she said, "just to see Cassie. From what I understand of her life, men get to see her just about whenever they want—never as long as they want, but just about whenever."

"Not like that," I said. "I just need to talk to her."

"Don't you all."

"Shit," I said, unfit for human conversation, thinking that perhaps Carolyn didn't know anything worth knowing.

"I've got her telephone number," she said, stubbing out the cigarette and lighting another, "and her address."

"So do I. But she's never home."

"That's not my problem."

"What is?"

"You, Milo, your gun, your friend with the crazy eyes, and wondering how you know I know Cassie."

"I was watching her house the day I met you here," I said. "I followed you here thinking you were her."

"And just why the hell were you supposed to be following her? If you don't mind my asking?"

"You know, maybe it was a real coincidence," I said, "but so many strange things have happened lately, cause and effect have gotten all confused in my mind. Truth is, lady, I don't have any idea what's going on."

"That makes two of us, buster," she said and clicked her long fingernails against the surface of the small table beside her. I felt the scars on my back itch, the flesh tremble with the old gunsight fear.

"I need to see her," I said. "People are trying to kill me, and I think she knows why." I walked over to her chair, leaned over her and took out the Airweight, set it on the table next to her hand, and backed away. "I can't hard-ass answers out of you, babe—maybe it was just one night, but it was a night—and if you know where she is, I'm asking you, please call her, tell her I need to talk to her."

"Maybe she's hiding from you," she said softly through a billow of smoke as she moved the revolver away with the backs of her fingers. "Ever think about that?"

"Maybe she's hiding from me," I said, sitting down on the bed. "Sometimes it doesn't help to know who you're hiding from. Whatever, you've got the gun, you set the meeting, I'll come alone, unarmed—you can strip-search me if you want," I added, and the idea made laughter bubble in my throat.

"Can I use your phone?"

"Sure."

"You go in the bathroom, shut the door, and turn on the shower," she said casually, and I obeyed, leaving the .38 on the table, even though I felt unbalanced without its comforting weight. It seemed that I spent an hour in the bathroom, sitting in the steamy air as the shower flowed, but it couldn't have been more than ten minutes before Carolyn knocked on the door.

"You can come out for a bit, lover boy," she said without a trace of a smile to soften her coarse features.

"Any luck?"

"She's supposed to call back in fifteen minutes."

"You want a drink while we wait?"

"A Beefeater martini on the rocks."

I went into Simmons' bedroom and asked him to go down for drinks. Back in my room, I sat down across the table from Carolyn.

"I would appreciate it if you would put that away," she said, staring at the ugly little .38. I tucked it back under my arm. "You've killed people, haven't you?"

"In Korea," I said, "when I had to. I didn't go out of my way looking for it, though. Spent ten years as a deputy sheriff without firing a serious shot. Seven years ago I shot two men who were trying to kill me."

"How does it feel?"

"Now or then?"

"Both."

"At first it makes you numb to keep you from being sick," I said, "then it makes you sick and sad, then you get over it."

"How?"

"The same way you get over anything, I guess. Time passes, you become a different person. You're thinking about the rape, aren't you?" She nodded, lit a new cigarette on the butt of the old one. "Would you have killed him?"

"No," she said flatly. "I don't want to kill anybody. Ever."

"I feel the same way." I was thinking about how careful I had been not to shoot at the guys in the van even when they were shooting at me.

"Why?"

"Enough people die in this world without my help, and I don't think I can stand it anymore."

"Interesting," she said.

"Tell me about Cassandra Bogardus."

"She's the toughest woman I've ever met," she began softly. "I think she would have killed my rapist, or died trying ... but I don't really know her that well."

"Why not?"

"We met in D.C. some years ago," she said, "then ran across each other out here a few months ago."

"What's she do for a living?"

"Clips coupons. Also works as a free-lance news photographer and magazine journalist, covers the occasional war."

"War?" I said. "She looks like a model or something."

"Don't let it fool you. She's been to at least two Middle Eastern wars and one Central American revolution."

At this point Simmons came back with a tray of drinks—two martinis for Carolyn, two *Dos X's* for himself, two shots of goddamned schnapps for me—but after he went back to his room Carolyn didn't want to talk anymore, so we smoked and drank until the ringing of the telephone broke the silence.

"Yes," she said into the receiver, then listened for several moments. "Unarmed, alone, and damn sure you aren't tailed," she repeated, glancing at me. "Can you handle that, lover boy?"

"Right," I said, which she echoed into the phone before she hung up.

"I'll meet you in the bar at ten o'clock," she said as she stood up. "And wear something warm."

"Want to finish your drinks?"

"You need them worse than I do," she said, heading for the door.

"Can you give me some small idea about what's happening?"

"Yeah," she said, her hand on the doorknob, "I'm sick and tired of this goddamned cowboy-and-Indian crap." Then she left, slamming the door behind her with a sudden and furious finality.

"Cowboy-and-Indian crap," I said to myself as Simmons came in the room.

"What happened?"

"I don't know," I said. "Maybe we should eat and try to come down a little bit."

"Eat?" he said. "Shit, man, I can just barely chew this Mexican beer."

"I know what you mean," I said. I put one finger in Carolyn's full martini, stirred the ice, sucked the gin off my knuckle. "Let's take a walk up to my place. Maybe we'll have an appetite when we get back."

"Walk?" he said. "Goddammit, Milo, there's a blizzard out there!"

"And an unsightly snowstorm in my head," I said. "Let's do it."

We laced ourselves into the Soral pacs and tucked ourselves into down parkas and shearling mittens, headed into the storm. All that talk about killing had made me want to disassemble my little joke of a booby trap.

But we were too late. Even though the snow had drifted into the tracks, we could see where they had already gone into the house, front and back doors again. At the kitchen steps the crossbow bolt stuck out of a snowbank, the handball intact on the point, and beside it, a deep wallow where someone had fallen, and gouged trenches where someone else had dragged him away through the snow. A two-foot drift like the beginning of a great sand dune had billowed against the kitchen cabinets through the open door. I shut the door quietly, and we left, trekking back through Milodragovitch Park toward the warm motel room, pausing just long enough at the apartment complex on the south end of the park to look for a light in the windows of the apartment where I had seen the two thugs go in, but the panes were as black as the wintery night.

Chapter 9

Carolyn was on time, dressed as warmly as I was, and she didn't want one for the road. Out in the parking lot I asked which car we should take, and she said to take mine. Once inside the Blazer, she checked every nook and cranny in the rig, then she searched me very carefully. True to my word, I had moved the rifles, the shotgun, and the Ingrams to the trunk of the AMC Eagle. True to my word as best I could be as scared as I was—my grandfather's .41-caliber derringer nestled inside my right mitten, tossed carelessly on the dashboard. She missed it, as I knew she would, and I felt slightly guilty that it was so easy, but I preferred guilt to death.

"Okay," she said, "now tell me how you're going to be sure that we're not followed."

"Just trust me, and watch. If there's a tail, I'll drop it. But there isn't any."

"Do it anyway, whatever it is you do," she said, "but what about those electronic things they put on cars to track them?"

"Beepers?"

"If you say so."

I drove across town to the Haliburton offices, bullied the dispatcher into giving me the key to the electronic locker, then went over the Blazer carefully. "See that dial," I explained to Carolyn. "If there's a transmitter aboard, it'll go crazy." But it didn't move. "Now the visual tail," I said when I came back from returning the equipment.

We drove up the dark corridor of Slayton Canyon to the end of the pavement, then I switched the Blazer into four-wheel drive, and headed down the dirt road to Long Mile Creek, bulling through the drifts while Carolyn tried to chew the knuckle out of her wool gloves, down the mountain road until I found the right sort of tree, an eighteen-inch-thick pine that leaned over the road toward the sidehill. I stopped just past it, got out my chain saw, checked the gas and the oil levels, and prayed it would start.

"What are you doing?" she asked, leaning out of her window.

"Roadblock," I said, tugging on the reluctant starter rope.

"This is national forest," she said. "You can't do that."

"Just shut up, will you," I said, pulling on the rope again.

The engine coughed and died in a burst of smoke, but the next time I choked it, the Poulan fired again, sputtered, then broke into smooth running. I let it warm up, then cut it off, and stepped off the side of the road into the hip-deep snow, cleared the brush around the trunk, then started it up again. It wasn't a beautiful cut, or quick, and for a second I thought I was going to drop the sucker on the Blazer, but it fell just where I wanted it blocking the road, and when the pine tree bounced, it didn't take my head off.

After I had loaded the chain saw into the back of the Blazer, I got back behind the wheel, huffing like a gut-shot bear, and turned the heater all the way up.

"Sometimes, you know," Carolyn said, then hit her cigarette, "sometimes you people out here don't seem to know what you've got in this beautiful country, because you treat it like shit."

"When I want some goddamned East Coast tourist to tell me how to live in the place where I was born and raised," I said, "I'll let you know. All right? But for now, just shut the fuck up. When you see places like Butte and the coal strip mines in eastern Montana and the goddamned clear-cuts, try to remember that we may be whores, but it's those pimps playing squash in the Yale Club in New York fucking City who are living fat on their cuts. So shut the fuck up."

"I'm sorry," she said, almost as if she meant it.

I didn't have anything left to say, nothing to do but drive, covered in frozen sweat, trembling as the last of the alcohol and cocaine washed like acid rain out of my system, feeling all the old frost-bitten parts—the tip of my nose, both cheeks, both ear lobes, my left little finger, the outside of my left foot—begin to sting and burn as if somebody held cigarettes to the spots. And I was so tired, I almost didn't care if I ever saw Cassandra Bogardus.

When we finally got down Long Mile Road to the interstate, Carolyn directed me back to town, where we changed to her Mustang, which had been parked on a side street on the south side of town. She made me climb into the back seat and cover myself with a blanket.

When she let me out, we were parked beside the end door of the new wing of the Riverfront. I was not happy.

"Too goddamned cute," I said as she unlocked the side door with a room key and led me upstairs. "Just too goddamned cute for words."

"I am sorry. Truly," she said. "But Cassie's afraid, and if she's afraid, I am scared to death."

She paused in front of a room door and gave it two taps, three taps, one, and I curled my fingers around the derringer.

"Coded knocks no less," I grumbled.

"Wait until I'm gone," she said stiffly, "then knock twice." She touched my cheek with her fingers. "I'll be in touch."

"You ain't going noplace, lover lady," I whispered into her

ear, tucking the derringer against her throat. "It was a great night, but only one night, and I don't trust you worth a shit anymore."

Her eyelids fluttered as the breath rushed out of her in a warm stream against my burning face. I thought she was going to faint, but she took a deep breath, sighed, then knocked on the door twice. When it opened, I held the small pistol to my lips to shush Cassandra Bogardus' greeting, then shoved Carolyn inside, slammed the door with my back, and motioned the two women to the floor. Then I checked out the room.

Nobody hiding anywhere, not under the bed, not even on the balcony that overlooked the black rush of the river. Wherever Cassandra Bogardus had been staying, it wasn't in this room. The dresser drawers were empty, the bathroom pristine, and a pair of stylish, dripping snow boots and a ski parka were the only objects in the closet, her large, expensive leather purse the only blot on the smooth, unruffled bedspread.

I nudged the bottoms of their feet, and the two women rose, Carolyn frightened and angry, her shallow breath coming like blasts from a blacksmith's bellows across a white-hot bed of coke, but the Bogardus woman only arched one perfect eyebrow in amusement, the corner of her perfect mouth slightly curled.

"Outside," I mouthed silently as I handed her the coat and boots and her purse. Once the three of us were in the hallway, I steered them down toward my room. Halfway there, Carolyn stopped and turned on me. "You son of a bitch," she hissed, "whose side are you on?"

"I don't even know what we're playing," I whispered.

"I'll scream my head off," she said, "then what are you going to do? Shoot me?"

"Knock you out and hope I don't break your jaw, hope your tongue isn't between your teeth, because you'll bite it off, maybe scream myself . . ."

"Tough guy," she sneered.

"Take it easy, Carolyn," the Bogardus woman said softly, her hand reaching for Carolyn's. "Can't you tell that he's as frightened as we are. Let's just do what he says. It'll be all right."

Carolyn took a long moment to decide, and I took the time to look at Cassandra Bogardus. If she had looked beautiful in the spotting scope that morning, up close and in person, she was stunning, the loveliest woman I had ever seen in real life: flawless skin made up so carefully that I couldn't see it even in the bright hallway, but make-up she could have worn under the harshest camera lights, the whitest and straightest teeth I had ever seen, jade-green eyes with flashing flicks of amber, and glowing blond hair that fell full and soft across her shoulders to curl in ardent dismay at her heavy breasts. She wore an open-weave sweater, which nearly matched her eyes, over a dull-gold turtleneck, designer jeans so tight they made me uncomfortable, and golden high-heeled sandals, which made her taller than me, with straps as delicate as spider webs.

"If you're through, lover boy," Carolyn said, "let's get on with it."

"Huh? Right, right," I said. "When we get to my room, ladies, not a sound—"

"He's afraid of electronic surveillance, darling," Cassandra said to Carolyn, "and I don't blame him a bit."

"Huh? That's right. Let's go."

Inside my room, while the two women sat at the table, I went through their purses looking for bugs and information. As far as I could tell, they were who they said they were, and not bugged, but I went through their coats and snow boots, anyway. The Bogardus woman stood up and slipped the open-weave sweater over her head, draped it over the back of the chair, then her earrings and rings clattered to the table. She slid neatly out of her shoes, tugged the turtleneck out of her jeans, and started to take it off, but she stopped just below her breasts.

I guess my mouth was open because she said, "Don't you want me to strip? And go into the bathroom with you where we can turn on the water and talk?" Before I could say it wasn't necessary, she was naked, strolling toward the bathroom, saying over her shoulder to Carolyn, whose jaw had dropped even farther open than mine, "Wait for me, darling. We'll be a bit." Then she paused by the bed, picked up a large manila envelope, went into the bathroom, and turned on the water. I took off the parka and the vest, stuffed the derringer into my hip pocket, and followed. Behind me, I heard Carolyn sigh long and hard.

For a motel, it was a large bathroom, but when I walked in, it seemed terribly crowded. She stretched her leg, arched her lovely foot, and shut the door, then she reached for my hand, ran my index finger around the inside of her mouth. "See, nothing there," she whispered, then drew it into her crotch, "and nothing there," then farther back, "or there." I swallowed something in my throat that lodged like a stake in my chest. "See, darling, I'm clean. We can talk here, safe from directional mikes, spike mikes, or those funny lasers that pick up sound vibrations off window-panes." She reached over to turn on the hot-water faucet, too, bouncing her breast solidly off my arm. "Quite safe," she said.

"You seem to know a lot about electronic surveillance," I said lamely, seemingly unable to point out that any wireman worth his fee could filter out the sound of rushing water his first pass on the tape. "Maybe too much."

"Only what I read in books," she said. She reached for my hand again, squeezing my limp fingers until I answered her touch, saying, "I'm so glad to finally meet you, Mr. Milodrago-vitch, and so sorry to have played that awful trick on you at the airport the other day. But I thought you were one of them."

"Them?"

"The people who have been watching my house and trying to follow me. Mr. Rideout warned me, but I made the mistake of thinking he was just being melodramatic. Poor chap's dead now, isn't he?"

"That's right," I said, sweating now.

"A crispy critter, poor fellow," she said sweetly, "as the boys in Nam used to say. A disgusting term, but all too accurate, I suppose."

"How did you know I knew about him?" I asked dumbly.

Since I had gone to a lot of trouble to talk to her, it seemed only right to stop looking at her breasts and ask a question, any question.

"Oh, I was watching you watching him that afternoon," she said. "I recognized you from the airport, and when I told Rideout that I thought I had been followed, he left like a shot, running back to wherever he had been hiding. I simply assumed that you were able to follow him, even though he knew you were there. He wasn't exactly the brightest sort of man, you understand. Almost repellent, too, but he didn't deserve to die that way, not burned to death." She bit her lower lip, than added, "And I hope you'll forgive me for thinking you might have something to do with his death."

"Would you put something on, please?"

"Of course," she murmured. "Forgive me." She twisted her hair into a bun and wrapped a towel around it. Almost as an afterthought, it seemed, she wound a towel about her body, then leaned against the counter, her arms crossed under her breasts. She, too, sweated now in the steam coming off the hot water running in the sink. I reached around her, careful not to brush her, and turned off the hot water. "Don't be so prissy, Mr. Milodragovitch," she said, then leaned over into the shower stall. "Oh, you've got one of those steamers," she said, turning it on. "It will feel wonderful, don't you agree, as cold as it is outside."

"Sure," I said as she moved close to unbutton my chamois shirt and gently tugged the tails out of my jeans.

"You're quite well built for an older man," she said, her long fingernails lightly scratching through the thick gray fur on my chest. Then she patted my belly and stepped back. "I like a bit of gut on men," she said, "it gives them presence." Beads of sweat began to glisten on her body, and the perfumed smell of her seemed to fill the cloudy room.

Only a fool wouldn't have known he was being played for a fool, but knowing it didn't help. I swallowed something larger, more painful, and asked finally, "What was your connection to Rideout?"

By way of answer, she picked up the limp manila envelope and slid an eight-by-ten photograph out of it. The picture had been taken at a great distance with maximum magnification of the telephoto lens, then the negative had been cropped and enlarged, so the photograph looked ghostly gray, indistinct in the steam-clouded room, I stepped over to the counter, switched on the lights around the mirror, and tried to ignore the soft tug of her fingers on the hairs of my forearm. Blurred as it was, I could make out the faces of the two men huddled over a huge supine silver-tip boar grizzly with its throat gaping open like another, larger, more awesome mouth. A 10-gauge sawed-off shotgun, a guide's weapon of last resort when leading someone after grizzlies, and a tranquilizer rifle leaned against a log behind them. The men were laughing, clearly, in the shot, John P. Rideout/Rausche and a large Indian with a braid hanging over his shoulder, a curved skinning knife held in his raised hand.

"What the hell is this?" I asked, moving away from her hand.

"Poachers," she said calmly.

"Poachers? All this shit is about poachers? That doesn't make any sense."

"Not just any poachers," she said, "but an organized gang of poachers. Do you have any idea what that hide and head are worth back East? Ten thousand dollars is my guess. Taken legally, that's a Boone and Crockett head. Can't you just see some fat-cat bastard in Chicago or Cleveland or Pittsburgh showing off that grizzly mounted in his den? Can't you? I understand that full-curl Rocky Mountain sheep ram heads go for five grand, so think what that bear must be worth."

"This can't be about poachers," I said, thinking about the goods I had lifted out of the trunk of the yellow Toyota, about the dead man's stubs clutching my arm. "No."

"Think about it. This is big business," she said, "and when you threaten their profits, they are always ready to kill."

"I've tampered with evidence, obstructed justice, over a bunch of dumb-ass poachers," I whispered.

"What?"

"Nothing," I said quickly. "Where'd you get this?"

"A little background," she said, holding up one long slim finger. "The last time I came back from Beirut, I promised myself to give up all that foolishness, gunfire and all that, dead bodies stacked like cordwood, so I came out here to take pictures of peaceful things—snowfields in the winter sun, glaciers in slow drift, elk calves at play—and I just stumbled onto this.

"I was up in Glacier Park, on the south side of Upper Quartz Lake, back in September, climbing toward the rim to take some sunset shots, when I stopped, looking back at the lake through my telephoto lens, when I saw this. I took a half-dozen shots, but this was the best after I developed and enlarged. But I knew I was on to something. Really, I mean, these two guys weren't park rangers disposing of a rogue boar or anything.

"So while they were skinning it, I hurried back down to the head of the lake, watched them load the hide and head on a raft, bring it back to the campground, then pack it on a mule they had tethered there. I tried to follow them out, but by the time I got to the trail head at Lower Quartz, the Indian and the hide were long gone, and I only caught Rideout because he was changing a flat. I followed him across the Flathead to Polebridge, then down the North Fork Road, and when he stopped for a beer in Columbia Falls, I went into the bar behind him. The rest, as they say, is history."

"How did you get him to talk?" I asked, and a warm, lovely flush rose across her chest and flamed up her neck.

"How do you think?" she said, touching herself between her breasts as if it were somebody else's body.

"I'm sorry," I said. "Listen, will you wait here a bit. I need to think and I can't—"

"—look at me," she said sadly, twisting her mouth and cocking her head, her neck bowed, it seemed, by the lovely burden of her face. "Of course."

When I went out of the warm, damp bathroom, I was surprised to see Carolyn still sitting at the table. I had, shamefully, forgotten she was there. She stubbed out a cigarette into the overflowing ashtray, then sipped at the watery remains of one of the old martinis. I couldn't say anything, I just nodded as I walked past her, opened the sliding door, and stepped out onto the balcony. "Too hot for you in there, lover boy?" I heard her say as I closed the door.

Outside, the sweat froze quickly on my face, and I knew the frostbite would be with me a long time that night. The storm still raged, cloaking the black waters of the Meriwether with frozen froth. With the first lungful of cold air, a thousand questions formed and dissolved in my mind, but the image of the woman remained clear. Like a moonstruck teen-ager, I sniffed my index finger but only smelled the cold, clear bite of the snow. I felt as if I wouldn't be able to think clearly anywhere for a long time, so I went back. Carolyn ignored me this time.

"Why Thursdays?" I asked as I barged into the bathroom. "Why that business at the airport? What's your stake in this?"

"Easy," she crooned as she finished wiping her body down with the towel, then wrapped herself back inside it. When she faced me, she said, "Shut the door. You're letting the steam out."

"How much does Carolyn know about this?" I asked, closing the door.

"Nothing," she said, mounting the counter around the sink with a single graceful motion, "nothing at all. Just that I'm in trouble, that she's a friend trying to help. Now, what were those other questions?" I repeated them. "Thursdays, because that was his day off—"

"From what?"

"He never said. And as for the airport . . . after all his warnings, I began to be careful, a little, and I saw your white van parked three different places in the neighborhood the day before, saw the police take you away, saw you follow Carolyn, called her early the next morning, heard what a wonderful man she had met, a rent-a-cop with a Russian name, so when I saw your van again the next morning I took precautions . . . the wig and the tweed suit belonged to Don Johnson, a very kinky fellow—"

"I know," I said, "I went through the house."

"—and the idea came out of a novel, and my stake in this is exactly nothing. Not after what happened to poor Mr. Rideout, darling. I'm not about to die to protect the wildlife habitat of the northern Rockies. What's your stake, Mr. Milodragovitch?"

"My life," I said. "The bastards have tried twice, they've been on my ass like warts on a toad, and"—I thought about Sarah and Gail, missing—"and there are some other considerations, but mostly I want to talk to somebody in charge, to let them know that as far as I'm concerned, I don't know shit . . . "

"Add my vote to that," she said, wiping sweat off the wings of her cheeks. "I've burned my notes, burned my tapes, and lost my memory. If you find them, tell them that, and that I've gone as far away as I can get from all this." Then she dropped both towels in the puddle at her feet. "This has given me too much pleasure to see it turned into charcoal—don't you agree?" She moved into my arms, her fingers busy at my belt buckle and the buttons of my jeans. "Just a touch, darling," she whispered as she pushed down my pants, pulled me to the counter, and into her sweet warm body. "Just a touch, because I don't have my diaphragm with me, darling." A touch like dying inside her, then she shoved me gently backward, and knelt before me.

Afterward, as she shut off the steam and turned on the shower, I tried to say something, but all my words were jammed in my throat.

"You'd like to see me again?" she said calmly. "Of course. But not here. Not until this—this mess is cleared up. And someplace warm, darling. I find I've lost my taste for winter."

"Me too," I croaked, "someplace warm. And this rabbit hole is cold but too hot. When you're someplace warm, and safe, call Goodpasture's Used Cars in Albuquerque, tell him—tell him that the fat lady called, and leave a number where I can reach you."

"The fat lady?" she asked, smiling sedately around the shower door.

"Like they say, the opera ain't over till the fat lady sings."

"How quaint," she remarked and closed the door.

Locked in a daze as Carolyn and I watched her dress, put on her clothes as if she had been born for nothing else, and dazed through the goodbyes—one bitter, one sweet—I lay back on the bed, holding the photograph of the hunters and the grizzly, but staring at the ceiling, I stayed, unbuttoned, dismayed, for a long time, nearly sleeping, thinking I dreamed, until Simmons knocked lightly on the connecting door and came in when I was unable to raise an answer.

"Boss, I think you better see this," he said as he walked over to my television, snapped it on, and found a local channel on the cable. Meriwether sometimes thought of itself as a city on the make, and the local stations had joined in the community spirit, had gotten themselves a mobile news van and a remote camera for live news events. And dead ones. In the hazy colors of the motel set, they showed live coverage of a burning house, firemen and hoses, innocent bystanders, the lot—my fucking house. Even at that, I had to have a snort of coke to bring my limp body to life, to button up, grab my parka and race Simmons down to the car. But by the time we got to my house, it was real life, not television, my house.

The police had blocked off the only road to my house, and I had sense enough not to argue with them. Simmons turned around, drove back to the apartment complex, where we parked, then plunged into the thickets of the park, heading for the dull red glow in the north, rising and falling on the wind like the northern lights.

By the time we got as close as we could, another fire truck had arrived, but they had already lost. The cedar shake roof had already fallen in on the west side, and the old logs of the walls burned like rubber tires, the thick coats of shellac funneling black smoke into the storm-tossed sky. The two large cotton-woods beside the creek had caught, then toppled under the weight of the water from the fire hoses. A blue spruce in the backyard exploded into flame and burned like a giant torch.

"It's gone, boss," Simmons said.

"It's been gone for a long time," I said.

The same year my mother donated the land to the city for a park, she had also sold the big house to the country club—they had cut it into four sections and moved it out to the golf course—and donated all the family pictures and artifacts to the county historical society, but she had missed an old safe from my grandfather's bank and a portrait of my great-grandfather dressed in a Cossack uniform, carrying a knout and wearing his Meriwether County sheriff's badge. When the trustees evicted me from my office, I donated those two bits of memorabilia to the historical society.

"Are you okay?" Simmons asked.

"Not too bad," I said. "Why?"

"You seem awfully calm for a man whose house is burning down."

"I say: Don't get mad, get even."

Back at the Eagle, I picked up the M-11 and tucked it under my parka, and Simmons followed me upstairs to the dark apartment. It took two tries to kick the door off its hinges, and even less time to check out the empty apartment. Before anybody bothered to see what the noise had been, we were on our way back to the motel. As we packed, Simmons asked, "Where now?"

"Mr. Haynes' for a minute," I said, "then I'll let you know."

Abner wasn't all that glad to see us, until I explained that somebody had just burned down my house, and then he was so angry that I felt guilty for being calm. But it made sense. Abner's house was his home. What he hadn't built himself he had worked to pay for. But my little log house had come to me because of my name, not because I had worked for it. Our investments were much different, and I understood the old man's anger and my calm, even if he didn't.

"Take it easy, Mr. Haynes," I said, but the old man kicked his living-room rug so hard that his house shoe flew across the room and crashed into the venetian blinds. "You two wait right here," I said, "until I get back."

"Where are you going?" Simmons asked.

"Reconnaissance," I said, checking the submachine gun one more time before I went out.

Every light in the surveillance house down the street was on, blazing into the storm as if a late-night party still raged. I crept around the house and a silence that seemed louder than drunken conversations and rock-'n'-roll music roared into the night. When I peeked through the living-room shades, the stack of radio equipment still sat in a pile, the black-and-white television on top, Johnny Carson looking wry as the picture rolled. One of the men seemed to be sleeping on the floor beside the equipment. The other sat at the kitchen table, facing the back door, his service revolver on the table in front of him. Occasionally, he spun it idly, as if trying to start some engine inside himself. He didn't look much like an imitation traveling salesman anymore. He had the gray, rumbled look of death in his face.

I stood on the back porch watching him and I found myself filled with a confusion so intense that it washed the need for revenge right out of me. I was almost willing to think that my house had burned down by accident. The time for gunfire had passed. It was time for talking. I waited until the man at the table had his face in his hands, not touching the revolver, then I covered him through the glass with the Ingram, and tapped the silencer on the window.

"It's open," he muttered without looking up, as if he had been waiting for me.

I reached for the doorknob and he went for the .38. I meant to give him every chance, meant to keep my trigger finger still until the last possible moment, but when he lifted the revolver, he put it in his mouth instead of pointing it at me, and blew the back of his head all over the kitchen.

If you have been unlucky enough to see something like that,

you don't want to hear about it, and if you haven't, I promise you, you don't want to know what it looks like.

I did what I had to do, numb for now, slipped out of my pacs at the back door, walked in my socks, careful not to disturb the gore. The guy in the living room wasn't asleep but dead, a dark ugly bruise over his crushed trachea. He must have ducked as he went into my back door, and caught the handball bolt right in the throat. Holding on to numbness as if my life depended on it, careful about fingerprints, I went through his wallet, writing down the information, then did the same with the dead man on the kitchen floor.

They were both retired Seattle cops, both held current Washington State driver's and PI licenses and Multitechtronics employee cards, and both had the same home addresses on Mercer Island east of Seattle, a neighborhood usually too expensive for retired cops.

Finished, still numb, I let myself out into the blizzard, the soft drumming of the snow that had muffled the sound of the shot. Thinking of any number of things I should do—let the cops know, let Abner and Simmons know, call the FBI and let them hunt for Sarah and Gail—I went back to the Blazer and drove to the nearest bar.

After my second whiskey with a beer chaser, I called Jamison at home. He was sorry about my house, which he had seen on the newsbreak, and he asked if he could help.

"Remember that favor?" I asked.

"Sure. Anything, Milo."

"Tell the reporters that you have it on good information that Milton Chester Milodragovitch III was in the house at the time it burned down."

"What?" he said, suddenly excited. "You think somebody torched it?"

"A favor," I said, then hung up.

I think I meant to go back to Abner's, but I stayed in the bar until last call. And for last call I ordered two fifths of Seagram's and a case of Rainier beer. When I checked the glove box to be sure the cocaine was still there, it was, and when I slammed the glove box shut, it sounded hollow, like cheap tin, so I drove out toward the interstate, turned west for Missoula and my pickup. But things got in the way—snowstorms, shitstorms, the dull muffled roar of a .38 or a 12-gauge or a silken noose . . .

Whatever, at ten o'clock the next morning I was parked in front of the Eastgate Liquor Store and Lounge in Missoula when Janey, the best damned daytime bartender in America, opened the bar, and I went inside like a man on his way to his own funeral.

Chapter 10

On the third morning when I sat backward on the toilet lid in the Eastgate chopping up the last of the cocaine, I heard the bathroom door open, so I stopped the click of the razor blade on the porcelain. But somebody kicked the stall door and the latch popped and whistled over my head, then the same somebody grabbed my collar and jerked me off the stool, stood me against the wall, and started slapping me. Jamison.

"Aren't you a little bit out of your jurisdiction, sir?" I said, slumped with the giggles.

Holding me up with one hand, Jamison brushed all the coke to the tile floor, and I whimpered, and then he opened the toilet lid and pulled my face toward the bowl as if it were a mirror where I might see myself, a pool where I might drown in my own image. "Look at that," he said, shoving my face closer to the bloody froth. "Janey says you been puking blood for two days."

"Damned old tattletale," I said, giggling again.

Jamison shouldered me into the wall, grabbed me by the vest, and began to bounce me off it until I heard the plaster crack behind my head. When he stopped, his fingers were working at the Kevlar mesh inside the vest. "What the hell are you doing wearing this?" he growled, but I didn't have an answer. "Why?" he asked, and bounced me again.

"I forgot."

"Forgot what?"

"I don't know, man," I said, "that's what 'forgot' means in our language." I must have thought that was funny because I started laughing again.

"What kind of trouble are you in?" he asked, and slapped me again when I didn't answer.

"I'm dead," I said, "don't you read the papers?" Then I had one of those flashes of memory that sometimes come in the worst parts of dog-shit bottom-out, a memory of reading about my death in the *Missoulian,* and telling Janey not to tell anyone I was alive. "But I'm not dead, am I?"

"It was your idea, son of a bitch," he said, tears in his eyes, "and if I wasn't an officer of the law, I think I'd kill you myself, or at least let you kill yourself."

"You ain't got it anymore," I whimpered, "and I ain't got it anymore—dead people suck."

"What are you doing here, anyway?"

"Having a taste of whiskey," I said, "and a touch of nose—or least I was until you came in—and then I was going out to the airport to get my trusty old pickup—"

"Your pickup?" he interrupted. "Shithead, your pickup is parked out front."

"Huh," I said, giggling again, "spaced that out. Wonder what I did with the Blazer ... burning down poor Sarah's credit cards ..."

"Who's Sarah?"

"Nobody you know, a better class of people than you'll ever know, you piss-ant, small-town hick copper ..."

"Milo, Milo," he said softly.

"Sorry 'bout that, chief," I said with more giggles, "lemme buy you a drink, chief."

"Sure," he said, but when he led me out of the john we went right past the bar. When I tried to resist, he put me in an arm lock as easily as he might twist a soft pretzel. "Thanks, Janey," he said, "for calling."

"Yeah, thanks, you old tattletale," I said. "Fu— oops, sorry, Jane. Onion off, okay?" Janey didn't much like the f-word, always made me say "onion" instead. That's how you can tell if you like a bartender—you appreciate their foibles no matter how twisted you are. "Onion-off, and thanks but no thanks, okay?"

"I'm sorry, Milo," she said, her eyes as soft and kind as a mother's. "I don't mind your having a good time, but if you're going to kill yourself, you can't do it in my bar, okay?"

"Prig," I said as Jamison hustled me out the door. "Where the hell you taking me, ossifer?"

"Home," he said, waving away the patrol car, which must have brought him in from the airport, "home."

"I ain't got no home," I said, "you dumb straight-arrow son of a bitch, I ain't got no home."

"My house," he said as I wept into his shoulder, "my house." Then he stuffed me into the pickup.

Surely in this vale of tears we call life, the ill, the halt, and the lame find it curious that some people with constitutions like bull calves sometimes consider their good health and strength a curse rather than a blessing. It *can* be, though. In fistfights, even beaten senseless, we don't fall down nearly soon enough; the joys of drug abuse don't seem to take their proper toll; and, sometimes, when we try to drink ourselves to death, we fail miserably. Miserably.

My mother's father, whom I only met once when he drove from Boston to Meriwether in his seventies, started drinking a quart of Jamaican rum and smoking at least ten cigars a day during the great Spanish influenza epidemic of 1917, a habit that he maintained saved his life while thousands of others died, a habit that he maintained until he died at eighty-two. My father's father drank a fifth of whiskey and smoked Prince Albert cigarettes every day from his twenties to his seventies, then he quit and lived another twenty years. God might know what it means; doctors don't. Have a good constitution and don't be miserable? I don't know either.

But after twenty-four hours on Jamison's couch and a bait of steak and eggs at a truck stop west of town where I hoped I wouldn't run into anybody I knew who would ask me why I wasn't dead, I should have been happy, but strolling out to my pickup, I realized I had to face the troubles, had to stop running, start working.

Driving through Meriwether on my way to look at the remains of my house in the daylight, I let my mind drop into idle for the slow drive. In my absence, the blizzard had blown itself out but left its heartbroken tracks behind. A gray, heavy overcast loomed dark over the afternoon as Meriwether dug itself out of the snow to face another long winter. The clotted wood-smoke smog drifted like a noxious, killer fog over the city, the mountains ranging like shaggy ghosts somewhere beyond it. The faces of the people on the streets seemed pale and empty, small animals huddled beneath fur caps and woolen scarfs or tucked into hoods. Although I knew it wasn't true—most of these people lived there because they wanted to live there, and wintertime was a cheap price to pay—it seemed that laughter had gone into hibernation for the season. Maybe just my drunken laughter, my cocaine giggles.

When I got to my house it seemed to me that the random lumps bellied up under the snow could have been anything, a battlefield, a pile of frozen corpses, the debris of a melting glacier, anything. While I was parking in front, my next-door neighbor came rushing out of her house, waving her arms and weeping.

"Milo, Milo," she shouted into my window, "you're alive!" I had forgotten I was supposed to be dead. "Come in," she said, "come in—for coffee or something—I've got some mail they delivered, and come on in. For coffee."

"Sure," I said. I didn't see how I could refuse.

Sitting at her kitchen table, sipping instant coffee, I opened my mail. Mostly bills, but a few reminded me what sort of world we live in. Three people, who evidently did not read the newspapers very carefully, wanted to build me a new home as soon as I got the insurance settlement. The city wanted to know what sort of arrangements I had made to clean up the debris, which constituted a public health hazard. Also, they had delivered the briefcase I had mailed from Seattle.

"Listen," I said to my next-door neighbor, "I've got a large favor to ask you."

"Anything," she said, "almost anything."

"You know, you introduced yourself the first day you moved into this house, and we've known each other for a year or so . . ." She smiled when I paused, and I realized that I had never really looked at her, never really even thought about her except as something that came by occasionally and did the dirty number. Behind that facile sneer of a smile dwelt a real live woman, probably massively unhappy, certainly confused, if she took up with somebody like me for casual carnal carnage. "I'm sorry," I said, "I don't have any idea what your name is."

"I know that," she said. "I realized that a long time ago and decided I sort of like it that way. Oh, and I had a wonderful cry, Milo, thinking about you dead and not even knowing my name . . . Ann-Marie."

"Thanks," I said. "Ann-Marie, I have a huge favor to ask you."

"What's that?"

"Don't tell anybody I'm not dead for a while," I said as I unwrapped the briefcase and stuffed my wonderful mail inside.

"Why?"

"That's the favor," I said, "you don't ask why."

"Whatever you say."

"Thanks."

I split the stitches on the briefcase handle, pulled out the rolled packet of cocaine, and gave her a half-gram-or-so present. She couldn't thank me enough, but I didn't have time for that.

The AMC Eagle was still parked in front of Abner's house, so buried in plowed snow that I was sure it hadn't been moved during my absence. Simmons had waited, like a good lad, but when I opened the front door and found him sitting on the couch next to Abner and Yvonne sipping tea, with his little finger cocked in the air like a dog's leg, nibbling gingersnaps, and laughing at Richard Dawson's wisecracks between the families feuding, I wondered if I should have left him there.

He even stood up, blushing, when I came into the room. "Jesus H. Christ," he said, and then, "Oh, excuse me, Mrs. O'Leary—I didn't know what to do, boss, when you didn't come back, so I just waited . . ."

"You did fine," I said. I could tell that Abner, hopping from foot to foot, wanted to introduce me to the simpering Yvonne, but I told Simmons to get packed. "Excuse me a second," I added, "I'll be right back—I promise." Then went back outside and down to the surveillance house.

Through the windows I could see that somebody had cleaned up, the rooms were empty, sparkling, the kitchen walls repainted, the floor tiles replaced, even the appliances changed. Neat, professional work. I wondered what they had done with the garbage, how they had disposed of the bodies. I pulled out the pocket notebook to look at the men's names for the first time since that night. Willis Strawn. Ernest Ramsey. I had to assume that Strawn had torched my house out of some terrible grief over the death of his partner at the hands of my dumb joke of a booby trap, and then had waited for me to take his perverse revenge. Rather than kill me, he had left me with an image of death I would carry to the grave. There was so much I didn't understand. How did he know I would find him? Maybe he had seen my tracks in the snow the night I had peeked in his window. I just didn't know. Like so many things in life, an artful guess was the best I could come up with.

Heading back to Abner's, I felt so tired that the snow seemed to suck at my pacs, to hold me frozen in a block of cold, icy ignorance. Maybe I could find some answers in Seattle amid the past lives of Strawn and Ramsey, behind the doors of something called Multitechtronics, Inc. Maybe Simmons and I could catch the afternoon flight. But as I glanced at the sky, the overcast seemed to settle lower over the valley, leaving only the bases of the mountains visible. Even if planes were taking off from the Meriwether airport today, I didn't want to fly through that rough, freezing tumble of clouds, which meant driving twelve hours or more, long hours on black ice and snowpack to Seattle.

Back at Abner's, the old man refused to take any more money, and I was too worn out to argue. Simmons and I thanked him, said our goodbyes, and headed west.

The interstate was clear traveling until we were west of Missoula, but a fresh storm began its assault outside of Alberton, horizontal snowfall skidding across the icy road. We stayed sober, clean-nosed, creeping through the blizzard, but even at that, we lost it just before midnight, spun out on the east side of Lookout Pass and into the barrow pit in about four feet of snow. It only took an hour or so of serious labor to dig out the pickup and get the chains on all four wheels, serious labor in a wind chill of forty below. Once, while we were warming up in the pickup cab, Simmons turned to me and asked through his chattering teeth, "You reckon them old folks are getting it on?"

"Abner and Yvonne?"

"Yeah."

"That's what the old goat has in mind," I said, trying to grin with a frozen face.

"You know, when you're young," he said, "you're just so damned dumb. I never thought about old folks doing it, you know, and I wondered how, ah, they go about it, you know." I couldn't tell if he was blushing or finally getting some blood back in his face.

"Are you implying that I'm old enough to know, bud?"

"No, nothing like that, boss," he said. "I just thought old men lost it, and old women . . ."

"With courage," I said, "all things are possible." And we laughed. "Now let's get that last chain on, and get out of this mess."

But even the chains didn't help. We had to get the sixteen-pound sledge and a steel stake out of the toolbox to give us an anchor for the winch. As we were pounding the stake into the frozen roadbed, Simmons stopped hammering to catch his breath.

"I hope he's banging the holy hell out of her at this very moment," he said, smiling into the wind. "I really liked that old son of a bitch, you know. I ain't never been around old folks much before—just the daytime winos in the Deuce—and them two old people are cool."

"And I'm freezing to death, son," I said. "Get on that hammer."

Before long, winter driving began to seem like an Arctic expedition—chains off on the other side of Lookout Pass, back on for Fourth of July Summit in Idaho, then off, then on again for Snoqualmie Pass, then off—and for all the good it did, we might as well have stayed in Meriwether, where I would have been warm, wrapped in dreams of Cassandra Bogardus.

When we got to the Mercer Island address I had for Strawn and Ramsey, we found a burned-out hulk beside the calm gray waters of Lake Washington dimpled with light rain.

"What are we supposed to be looking for, boss man? Burned houses?" Simmons asked, then laughed, brittle with fatigue.

"Some serious bad guys," I said, "serious." And Simmons' hand crept under his vest to touch the butt of the .357, shivering perhaps with fear or with the memory of the freezing wind and snow.

"Easy," I warned when I noticed a woman coming out of the

house next door bundled in a bright-blue rain parka and heading toward us.

"Hi," she said quietly as she walked up to us. She had one of those intelligent, perky, expensive faces you expect to find on Mercer Island, the second, younger wife of a doctor or a lawyer or a rich Indian chief. "Can I help you?" she asked politely.

"We were looking for Mr. Strawn or Mr. Ramsey," I said, "but I can see they're not home."

"Then you didn't know," she said softly. "I hope you weren't friends of theirs . . ."

"Associates," I said, and she nodded as if she knew what I meant.

"A terrible accident," she offered, "the furnace exploded, and they never had a chance . . ."

So that's how they cleaned up the garbage, brought the bodies to Seattle and blew up a house, which also meant the bad guys had enough clout to buy an arson investigator, an autopsy, and a police report. Poachers, my ass. Cassandra Bogardus was crazy.

"I was never very fond of policemen," she continued. "The sixties," she added, as if that explained everything. "But Willie and Ernie were different than you would expect . . . Excuse me, I hope you gentlemen aren't policemen."

"No, ma'am," I said, and Simmons muffled his laugh with a cough.

"They were so nice, you know, quiet and neighborly, both of them wonderful French cooks, and they had the most fantastic collection of big-band records and a stereo system that covered an entire wall, and now it's all . . . ashes." The sad little smile looked painted onto her pert, liberal face. "I'll miss them so much," she added. "My husband always claimed they were, you know, odd—ah, homosexuals. But I always maintained that they wouldn't, you know, let homosexuals be policemen—would they?"

"No, ma'am, I wouldn't think so," I said.

"Well, I wouldn't care if they were," she whispered in a rush as two large tears bloomed in her eyes.

"Yes, ma'am," I said as Simmons and I retreated toward the pickup. Driving away, we watched her standing in the driveway, her figure bent with grief as she gazed across the ashen water like a woman whose man went to sea years and years ago. A small bit of life, light, and laughter had dimmed forever in her snug suburban nest.

"You're still not going to tell me what this is all about, are you, boss?" Simmons said.

"Even if I knew, son, you're better off not knowing," I said, "but it's bad enough that if I were you, I'd get out now."

"Not a chance, boss man," he said. "They can't put you in the slammer because you're dead, or me, because I'm crazy." He sounded almost happy about it.

"Jail is the least of our worries, the least," I said, but the kid kept smiling.

Multitechtronics turned out to be an empty office over a porno shop on 1st Avenue just south of Pike Place Market, a mail drop, an answering service, defunct. I tried the painless dentist next door, but he was feeling so little pain that the only thing he could tell me was what he had drunk for lunch, and I had already smelled the bourbon and ether fumes in the hallway. I had a number of choices, checking with the owner of the building, digging out the incorporation documents, but I thought I had better have another, less personal conversation with Ms. Bogardus, so I found a hungry, lanky young lawyer named McMahon, gave him a retainer, and set him on what I assumed would be a paper maze to track down the owners of Multitechtronics, Inc.

Then we went down to Ivar's for lunch, where I had three dozen raw oysters, which disgusted Simmons so much that he couldn't even eat his chicken-salad sandwich.

On the way home that night we crashed in Ellensburg, and I dreamed not of Cassandra Bogardus, but of the fat lady cocaine dealer. Oddly enough, it wasn't a bad dream, as my dreams go, and for that I was grateful.

Back in Meriwether the next afternoon, we checked into a truck-stop motel east of town, showered the tire-chain mud and slush and cold off ourselves, and then I called Jamison at the station. His greeting seemed distant, uncomfortable.

"I guess I owe you a vote of thanks," I said.

"Milo, I don't know how you do it."

"Get twisted?"

"Survive," he said.

"It's my hardy-pioneer genes," I said, and Jamison coughed disgustedly. When my great-grandfather was sheriff of Meriwether County, he founded the family fortune on a string of opium dens, gambling hells, and cotes for soiled doves.

"I don't think I can keep you dead much longer, Milo," he said.

"A few more days," I said, "whatever you can manage."

"I'll try," he said, "but the arson investigator is pressing me. He also mentioned that although he can't find anything, he smells something hinkty about the fire."

"Well, I can promise you I didn't torch my house for the god-damned insurance money."

"I know. I've already checked that out."

"I need one more favor, Jamison."

"Lock you up for your own protection?"

"Not just yet," I said. "I need permission to visit the Benniwah kid in the hospital lockup. The one from the EZ-IN/EZ-OUT." The only people I knew up on the reservation I knew from my days as deputy sheriff, and not a single one would talk openly to me, not even the police. Maybe the kid felt as if he owed me something, maybe he would give me a hand trying to find the Indian in the photograph with Rausche and the grizzly bear. "Okay?"

"That's easy," he said. "Our Good Colonel Bleeding Heart has arranged for his lawyer to handle the defense, so you're his investigator, right."

"Right. A Mr.—ah, Grimes from Seattle. Thanks."

"And, Milo . . ."

"Yeah?"

"The game is Saturday after next."

"Right," I said and hung up. "Rich man's clothes," I told Simmons, and he sighed as if that were the worst chore of all.

On the way out to the hospital I stopped long enough to buy another Tyrolean hat and a pair of expensive sunglasses. Rich dudes can afford to wear sunglasses even in the worst snowstorms.

The Benniwah tribe was notoriously suspicious of strange white men. And with good reason. The first white trader to discover the small peaceful tribe, an Alsatian by the name of Benommen, gave them a corrupted version of his name (*they* called themselves the Chil-a-ma-cho-chio, the people of Chil-a-ma-cho) and swapped them blankets from smallpox victims of the Mandan tribe for prime beaver pelts. The survivors fled into the high valleys of the Cathedral Mountains, where most of them slowly starved to death. The remainder, although they never shed a drop of white blood, watched as their ancestral lands were slowly stripped and stolen by various government officials, including my great-grandfather of the hardy-pioneer spirit, who had paid a quarter an acre for the three thousand acres of timberland. Finally the tribe managed to secure a small reservation on the north and middle forks of the Dancing Bear River between the Cathedrals and the Diablos. What little they had left, they meant to keep. Unlike many tribes, they never sold or leased land to white men, not even to those few who married into the tribe, and when you drove across the reservation, even the children stared darkly at your pale face as if they still smoldered with racial regret for rivers of white-eye blood unshed.

For somebody who had taken a .30-06 round in the recent past, Billy Buffaloshoe looked remarkably hale and hearty sitting propped up against the pillows, staring at the green placid walls of his unhospitable cell. When the jailer on duty at the door unlocked it, Billy turned slightly, just enough to bump the elbow of his cast against the metal bed rail. His face became instantly gray, and I waited politely, staring through the heavily meshed one-way glass until he regained his naturally high, burnished color. Then I told Simmons to wait for me in the lobby, and went in.

"And who the hell are you, man?" he said when I was inside. "Another rich lawyer bearing the white man's burden? Another cop? Maybe a social worker?" I took off my glasses and hat. "Nope. You don't look social enough, man."

"Just a guy looking for a favor," I said, paused at the end of the bed, and we could hear the jailer drop the dead bolt with a clunk that seemed to shake the snow off the barred windows.

"A favor?" he said. "Wow, man, I am honored, but I ain't exactly on the uphill side of success right now. You can dig it, right, man."

"I just want you to look at a picture for me," I said, taking out the eight-by-ten of the poachers.

"And what are you going to do for *me,* man?"

"I've already done it," I said, "the night you got shot."

"The rent-a-cop," he sneered. "Jesus, man, you look good for a rent-a-cop. So you saved my life, man. Big fucking deal."

"I'll make a good witness at your trial," I said, "and at least you can beat the assault with a deadly weapon—"

"What trial, man?" he said. "I'm copping a second degree on the armed robbery, so I'm looking at Deer Lodge whatever happens."

"You don't care what I say at the pre-sentencing hearing?"

"Who listens to jerks like you, man," he said, "so you ain't got shit to trade."

"Money?"

"How much?"

"You tell me, tough guy."

"Five hundred and a television in this stinking goddamned room," he said, "and that's my first and last price."

"I can't do nothing about the entertainment, son," I said, "but the five is okay."

"You got it on you?"

"Sure," I said, "but they'll just take it away from you."

"Hey, man, *I* ain't no jerk," he said, as if I was. "I been there before. Ain't nobody gonna take it off me."

Screening the door window with my back, I counted out five bills, and handed them to him with the photograph. As he leaned over to slip the money into his crotch, he started coughing. When he worked up a bloody froth, I leaned over for the stainless-steel bowl, let him spit and catch his breath.

"You okay?" I asked. "Need a nurse or anything?"

"Fucking service in this hospital is for shit, man," he gasped, then glanced at the picture. "Don't know the white dude, man, or Brother Bear, man ... " He laughed and brought up another coughing fit, more blood. "And I don't know the other dude's name—he's not one of us, he's a breed, Assiniboin, Cree, I don't know, don't even live on the res, man, just hangs out at the bars in Stone City—ask Tante Marie."

"Tante Marie?"

"The grandmother lady, man," he said, then sighed and told me how to find her, stirred in the bed in the telling and pulled out the end of his lung drain from the bedside bottle.

"You sure you don't want me to call the nurse?"

"Not only do they have piss-poor service here, man," he gasped between shallow breaths, "but this hospital is renowned for its shitty drugs."

"Thanks for the help," I said and held out my hand.

He stared at me for a long time before he took it and gave it a brief pump, but our eyes held—his, growing dark and deep like that narrow passage to the other side, where the eternal springtime sang, where the maidens' breath always smelled sweetly of honeycomb, where the ghostly deer leaped lightly into the humming flight of the arrow. He had nearly made it this time, and his knowledge made the back of my throat taste bloody and raw. Next time, his eyes said, he would go.

The clouds had lifted and the snow stopped, but as we eased across the black ice up Wilmot Hill toward the reservation, the pickup rose into the lowering overcast, and a corn-snow squall swept out of the gray fog and lashed at the windshield. Even though I had the heater cranked all the way up, Simmons and I had been cold too long and tired, and the cold air seemed to rush into the cab on clattering hooves.

"How long's it been since you had a drink?" I asked Simmons.

"Not since you left that night," he said, tugging at his tie, "and it's really weird, you know, I don't seem to want one."

Lord, did I want one. Whiskey for warmth in the gut, for fire to burn the ugly taste of violent death out of my throat, whiskey for laughter. I thought about stopping at the Wilmot Bar for a quick one, at least one, but my old friend Jonas no longer stood behind the bar, surveying his domain like a crazed dwarf king. Like too many of the old ones, the crazy ones, he was dead. Fat Freddie, the Chicago cop; and silent Pierre, who had drunk the English language right out of his brain; Leo from Mahoney's, the recorder of our faces; and good Simon the Roamer. Dead. Me, too, according to recent reports. But maybe it was really true, I was really dead. What a wonderful joke. After death, the crossing over, we find neither heaven nor hell, not even happy hunting, but just more of the same sad, silly life we thought we left behind. Confusion and muddle, disorder and despair.

But just as I worked myelf into an alcoholic's glorious and sober self-pity, as we rolled past the shadowy outline of the Wilmot Bar, we popped out of the clouds and into the blinding winter sunlight firing black off the snowfields. I locked all four wheels of the pickup, scrambling in my pockets for the new sunglasses. When I had them on, I saw before me the snow-capped towers of the Cathedrals glistening against a sky as blue as the backside of heaven, the sort of vision that makes you forget tire chains and frostbite, makes you remember why you live in Montana until you die.

Tante Marie, Billy had told me, was the most honored woman among the Benniwah, the keeper of the tales, the teller of the sacred stories, and in a tribe where all the grandmothers, once having put away the bloody stain of womanhood, were honored for their patience, wisdom, and kindness, and entrusted with the most treasured objects of a tribe that had nearly disappeared, the children and the old stories. Tante Marie was the grandmother of grandmothers, more obeyed than a war chief, more trusted than a peace chief, and more powerful than the lawyers who advised the tribal council.

Even with all that tradition resting on her shoulders, Tante Marie didn't live in a teepee or an earthen lodge, but in a small yellow frame house up the Middle Fork of the Dancing Bear, just beyond where the South Fork Road turned south up the north side of the Diablos, a road that led into the mountains past the old C, C&K sections, the abandoned mine and over the divide to Camas Meadows and my grandfather's timberland. Fifty yards down the Middle Fork Road beyond her house set the locked gate that protected the last bit of sacred Benniwah land from the roaming gangs of white-eye hunters, fishermen, and beer drinkers.

Because it was on a school-bus route, the Middle Fork Road had been plowed that morning, and it looked as if the South Fork Road had been too, which seemed odd, but maybe the Forest Service was keeping it open for loggers. A small school bus was parked in front of her house, and past it I could see a new gate across the Middle Fork Road. When I was a kid, the old gate was an easy one, and we could either shoot the lock off or ride around it on dirt bikes, but over the years, every time I saw that gate it had become a more formidable barrier. Now it was constructed of steel pipe, fastened with a Master padlock as large as a sandwich, set in concrete and flanked by rocky berms higher than a man's head. A long-dried and frozen coyote skin had been draped over the top rail.

After I parked behind the school bus, I asked Simmons to wait in the pickup, then trudged toward the shoveled walk where the drifts were piled four feet high on either side, my rich man's shoes useless in the snow. They had had even more snow than we had down in the Meriwether, and some of the drifts reached nearly to the roof eaves.

When I paused on the front steps to try to kick the snow out of my shoes, a deep voice, happy in its seriousness, rumbled inside the small house.

". . . and that, little grandchildren," it said, "is why poor Brother Raven is cursed with his black, black feathers and his ugly caw. He traded his pollen-yellow feathers, his sky blue and his cloud white, traded even his once sweet song that filled the air with the sacred rainbow, traded his honor for one chew of the white man's tobacco, and even to this day, little grandchildren, he caws and caws but cannot spit that bitter, dishonorable taste away . . ."

Then the voice grew soft and low, the words indistinct, replaced by the shuffle and hum of children, broken now and again by respectful laughter.

When Tante Marie opened the door, she saw me but ignored me so furiously that I naturally stepped aside to watch as she gently ruffled black-haired heads before she tucked them into snow hoods and patted tiny rumps to speed them on their merry way. Although they still had wonderfully solemn looks gracing their faces, the line of small children filing out the door toward the bus carried happy smiles, bronze cheeks glazed with apple, and dark, singing eyes. The driver, an old snaggled-toothed man named Johnny Buckbrush, who knew me from my deputy sheriff days, glanced at me once, then lowered his eyes. I had known him in his days of shame.

"You're looking great, Johnny," I said, "a new man."

"Thank you, Milo," he answered, his face turned away from me as he followed the troop of happy children.

Tante Marie watched them until the bus was loaded and on its way, watched until it passed a granite outcrop beyond the South

Fork turn, then she looked at me, and said, as if it were a command, "Yes."

From the way Billy had talked about her, I expected some sort of Hollywood version of a female shaman, an ancient English actress in wrinkles and copper face, draped in buckskin and beads, but Tante Marie was a large, strong woman, wearing high heels that matched her beige sheath. Her long, heavy face, framed by a pair of horn-rimmed glasses, could have belonged to a Mexican, or an Italian, or a rich white woman with a deep-water tan.

"Yes," she said again.

"Excuse me," I said, "but I couldn't help overhearing the end of your story, ma'am—and please correct me if I'm wrong—but wasn't it the Indian people who introduced the white man to tobacco? When Columbus discovered—ah, the Indies."

"True enough," she said as if this were a question she had waited all her life to answer. "Indian people smoked—tobacco, kinnikinnick, red-cedar bark—but we smoked for ceremony, not for pleasure, for what you white people might call prayer, thanksgiving for the sun and moon, the wind and rain, the coming, and going, of life. Smoking for pleasure, for the tobacco lobby and the government subsidy, for sophistication, *is* hazardous to your health." Then she flicked a finger against my breast pocket, and the cellophane of the cigarette pack rattled like a snake.

"Yes, ma'am," I said, "you win," trying to be friendly, but the face she offered me had been carved out of something harder than stone. "Billy Buffaloshoe sent me," I explained, "for a favor."

"A favor?"

"Yes, ma'am,' I said again, tugging the rolled photograph out of my overcoat pocket. "Did you know Billy was in jail?" I added, but her face didn't even bother to answer. She knew everything. "Maybe I can help keep him out of prison."

"Ha," she snorted, "he was born for Deer Lodge."

"Maybe I can help postpone his fate," I said. "Do you know this man?" I asked, holding up the picture.

She took it and looked at it for a long time, nodded, then stepped back inside the house out of the snow glare and removed her glasses. I started to follow, but she raised that stony gaze and I moved away, nearly falling on the icy porch. While she stared at the photo and I tried to regain my balance, one of the bright-blue EQCS garbage trucks rumbled around the outcrop and turned up the South Fork Road.

"What the hell—" I started to ask.

"They have the reservation contract," she explained, and left it at that. "Which man?"

"The Indian."

"Is it about the bear?"

"Sort of," I said. Tante Marie wasn't the kind of woman I wanted to lie to. "The bear and other things."

"He's the sort," she said, nodding, "to do something like this. A jailhouse Indian, a mixed breed without honor. His real name is Charlie Two Moons, but he calls himself Charlie Miller. At this time of day you can find him—" She paused and looked at me. "Take off those glasses and that silly hat." After I complied, she said, "You're a Milodragovitch, aren't you?"

"Should I confess, ma'am, or admit it proudly?"

"It's your name," she said, "you decide."

"I am the last of the Milodragovitches," I said.

"Good," she said. "How badly do you want to find this man?"

"I'll find him," I said, "with or without your help, ma'am."

"Not if I make a telephone call," she said. "I'll trade you my help for Camas Meadows. We'll even buy it at a fair price."

"Okay."

"I love a joke, coyote tongue," she said, not laughing. "You'll do everything you can to have Billy placed on probation in my care?"

"Yes, ma'am."

"All right. At this time of day you can find Charlie Two Moons leaning on a bar down in Stone City." I must have raised a frozen eyebrow because she answered a question I didn't ask.

"Before I came home to the land," she said, "you might have found me there, too."

"Thank you."

"You've got frostbite on your face," she said, then reached up to peel a tiny sliver of black skin off the side of my cheek. "Take care of it."

"Yes, ma'am,' I said, "and I do appreciate your help."

"Don't mention it, coyote tongue," she said, then shut the door so firmly in my face that I felt as if I had been locked out of someplace very important.

Stone City sat just west of the Benniwah Reservation, the sort of small ugly town you find embedded like a tick along the borders of dry reservations or military encampments, a town forged of homesickness and grief, greed, a town of bars and pawnshops where nobody ever grew up. I found Charlie Two Moons in the fifth joint we tried, huddled over a shot of bar bourbon and a short draw of beer. He had looked large in the photograph, but in real life he was one big son of a bitch, at least six-six and grown up toward two-seventy, and there was no way even two of us was going to waltz this half-drunk and completely unhappy giant out of the bar.

"What's happening, boss man?" Simmons asked while the bartender ignored us.

"I think maybe we better have a drink," I said. "See that big dude behind me? Well, we need to have a serious conversation with him about a felony."

"How did you ever get into this business, man?"

"It was back in my hard-drinking days, bud, and I don't exactly remember," I admitted as I rapped my knuckles on the bar to get the bartender's attention.

The silence in the small bar was suddenly very intense. A group of day-drinkers at a back booth stopped laughing, the three other customers at the bar besides Charlie Two Moons halted their drinks in midair, and the bartender gave us a murderous scowl. But he came down the bar anyway, slowly.

"Can I help you gentlemen?" he said as if we were going to need more help than he could provide.

"Yes, sir," I said as if I hadn't heard the silence. "My friend and I would like shots of Black Jack and beer backs," I ordered, lifting a fifty from my wallet, "and get yourself one too, sir—hell, get everybody in the bar one . . . I just hit the poker game at the Slumgullion down in Meriwether, so let's all have a drink for luck."

"For luck," the bartender said, seeming to imply that we were going to need that too.

But after I bought a second round for the house, the silence eased, Simmons and I took a deep breath and sipped slowly at our drinks.

"You hear the one about the great North Dakota artist?" Simmons whispered in a low voice. In Montana, what the rest of the country calls "Polack jokes" we set in North Dakota.

"No," I said.

"The North Dakota Historical Society hired the most famous painter in the state," he whispered even more quietly, "to paint a giant mural depicting the Battle of Little Bighorn, and when he finished, they had this big party for the unveiling, all these fat-cat preachers and society matrons gathered to see the finest work of North Dakota's greatest painter. But when they pulled back the curtain, there was this picture of a huge goddamn fish with a halo over its head surrounded by thousands of Indian couples balling.

"Of course, all the fat-cat preachers swallowed their snuff and all the society matrons peed in their girdles and everybody went charging out of the room in a great North Dakota huff. So the president of the historical society goes over to the artist, who has been too busy admiring his work to notice the fuss, and he says to the painter, 'What in the world do you call this?' And the painter smiles and says, ' "Custer's Last Words." ' ' "Custer's Last Words"?' the president says. 'Right,' the artist says. ' "Holy mackerel, I've never seen so many fucking Indians." ' "

When Simmons finally stopped giggling into his hand, he

added, "You can understand what made me think of that, boss—'Custer's Last Words.'" Then he laughed again. Some people will laugh at anything.

"I love a joke, coyote tongue," I said, quoting Tante Marie, "but how are we going to get this big son of a bitch outside?"

"No problem," Simmons said. "He's on his way out now."

I picked up my change, and we followed his wavering gait out into the cold, windy street. As I came up behind him I slipped my Buck folding knife out of my pocket and opened it.

"Charlie Two Moons," I said, grabbing his right shoulder with my left hand, and jabbing the blade into his right armpit through the wool coat and shirt until I felt flesh. "If you jump, man, you'll never lift that arm again." When he hesitated, I gave him a bit more of the knife point, and the sharp, unexpected pain took the fight out of him. He puked without jerking forward, then spit on the sidewalk.

"Whatever you say, dude, you got the blade."

"You got a rig?" I asked. "I don't want blood and vomit all over mine."

He bobbed his head sourly, spit again, then led me down the street to a battered pickup, a 1965 Dodge Power Wagon, the best back-country rig ever to come out of Detroit City. Maybe I was too busy admiring it, but as we eased into the cab he got away from me. We engaged in a very silent, very tense struggle that ended with my blade under his ear and with the .38 snubnose he had hidden in the crack of the seat partially blocked by my left hand, but still nuzzling coldly into my left thigh. He didn't seem sick or drunk now; he seemed to fill up the whole cab.

"What we've got here, dude, is a Mexican stand-off," he finally said, his lips barely moving.

"My buddy's behind you with a .357," I pointed out. Simmons had his piece out, the barrel resting on the window ledge and shielded by his leather overcoat.

"A .357, dad, will make mush out of both of us at that range," he said.

"A Mexican stand-off," I said, the sweat freezing on my face. "I'll be crippled, Charlie, but you'll be dead."

"I don't much give a shit, man."

"Neither do I," I said, and was surprised to discover that I meant it. "If you're going to pop that cap, sucker, do it now because this conversation is over."

"Whoa, man, hold it," he said quickly as he let the revolver fall to the cluttered floorboard. I let him slide, trembling, to the far side of the seat, where he buried his face in his shaking hands, moaning, "It ain't even loaded, man, ain't even loaded." I picked it up and checked it. Empty. When I looked at him, Charlie Two Moons looked like a much smaller man.

"Afraid of doing yourself?" I guessed, and he nodded with shame.

"What do you want with me, man?" he whimpered. "I ain't done nothing to nobody. Not in a long time." I put the photograph in his lap. He took one glance and handed it back. "Bad medicine," he said quietly. "We should've never killed that grizzly. It's all gone to shit since then. I lost my job a week later, my old lady split, then I got drunk over in Butte, got the shit kicked out of me by two miners in the alley behind the M&M Bar, and they cut my braid, man, they cut my braid. Bad medicine." He sat silently for a bit, staring at his huge hands as if he couldn't believe they had failed him. "So what's going down, dad?" he said. "It's clear you're not Fish and Game or Park Service, not with that cute blade-in-the-armpit number. So what is it? The goddamned Sierra Club hiring hoods now, putting out contracts on poachers? Ducks Unlimited, maybe?" Then he laughed, the taut, bowstring squeal of a man on the edge. "Goddamned liberal phony white folks . . ."

"Who's the other guy?"

"Johnny Rausche," he said, "calls himself Rideout now. He's a brother."

"A brother?"

"Yeah, dad, we used to share the same accommodations over at Walla Walla."

"Who did you guys work for?"

"Well, I used to run a fork lift at that wholesale grocery warehouse down in Meriwether," he said, "and Johnny, he was a long-haul trucker—"

"No, not that," I interrupted. "The gang?"

"The gang?" he said, seemingly honestly amazed.

"Poachers, you know, don't jerk me . . ."

"Poachers?" he said, then loosed a fairly healthy bray of laughter. "Who the hell do you work for, man?"

"That's a damn good question," I admitted. I turned to look out the side window, fogged now with our breath, and cleared a small circle, a peephole, but all I could see was the snow rustling down the gray street, a few cars and pickups parked in front of the line of bars, some idling in the cold, banners of exhaust wind-whipped out of their tailpipes, others abandoned to the frozen drifts.

"Where's the grizzly hide?" I asked, even though I already believed him. There was no gang of poachers. Or if there was, Charlie Two Moons certainly didn't belong to it. I wondered if Rideout/Rausche had been stringing Cassandra Bogardus along just to keep her around, or if she had been blowing angel dust in my ears to, to . . . to what? To keep me around. Hell, all she had to do was blow in my ear, and I'd follow her anywhere. To keep me away? From what? Shit. "Where's the hide?"

"In the hock shop across the street," he said. He took out his billfold and found the pawn ticket. "Two hundred bucks," he said.

"Let's go take a look at it." I knew in my bones that he wasn't lying, but I wanted to see the grizzly hide, anyway, wanted to touch it, as if the coarse, thick hair held the answer to questions I hadn't even been smart enough to ask yet.

The chubby old man behind the counter smiled when the three of us came in, kept smiling even after Charlie told him he wanted to redeem his pledge, but his smile didn't blunt his hard, greedy eyes, and I could tell the old man had just been waiting for ninety days to pass so he could claim the hide for himself. But he had to live in the same town with Charlie. He didn't mutter as I counted out two hundred, didn't grumble as he led us to the fur storage vault in the back. The hide and head, wrapped in a tarp, looked like a humpbacked pig on the floor, and when Charlie and I picked it up, it felt as heavy as a slaughtered hog.

"Good God," I grunted as I followed Charlie out of the pawnshop. Simmons took my end from me and nearly fell with the weight.

"Old Ephram," Charlie said, "carries one big skin. Where's your car?"

"Over there. Why?"

"You just bought yourself a grizzly hide," he said. "Best job of mounting and tanning I've ever done, but Brother Bear is yours now, dad, and I'm damned glad to be rid of his spirit sitting on my medicine."

"But I—ah . . ."

"Don't even say thanks, dad," Charlie said as he and Simmons lowered the bundle gently into the bed of my pickup.

"Hey, how can I be sure this is the same bear that you and—"

"Sleep on it," Charlie said happily, "sing to the spirit of Brother Silvertip. You'll know." Then he hoofed back toward the bar. He stopped at the door, opened his arms wide to the clean, windy sky, and shouted, "Hey, brothers, can I buy you a drink?"

"I think I just went on the wagon," I said, much as I hated the idea.

"What now, boss?" Simmons asked as we got back in the pickup.

"I'm tired of being dead," I said. "Let's get your rent car, check out of that crappy motel and into the Riverfront, and try to live up to our clothes."

"You sure, boss?"

"Sure," I said. "Only Jesus Christ and Mark Twain ever made the evening news when it turned out that the reports of their deaths had been exaggerated."

Simmons chewed on that until we were halfway back to Meriwether, then he said, "I don't know what we're doing, boss, but I do know one thing."

"What's that?"

"This shit's crazier than the war."

Chapter 11

In spite of my leanings to be among the living again, there were too many advantages to staying among the dead, so I let Simmons check us back into the Riverfront as Mr. Rodgers and Mr. Autry. It took four trips to pack our arsenal, luggage, and the bearskin up to the room the back way. We unrolled the hide, and it nearly covered the king-size bed, but the head looked too alive dangling off the foot of the bed, so we turned it around, propped the giant head on the pillows, and let the glass eye stare blankly at a terrible painting of a romantic mountain valley, waterfalls and crags, mists and dancing fawns.

"That son of a bitch weighs a ton," Simmons sighed. "What the hell are you going to do with it?"

"Sleep under it."

He giggled nervously. "Smother under it, more likely," he said.

I gave him some money to buy gun-cleaning supplies, and while he was gone I considered the grizzly, wishing I had a drink.

I ordered half a dozen stinking shots of peppermint schnapps from room service, but when they arrived I left them sitting on the table. "I'd almost rather be sober," I said to the hide. Brother Silvertip didn't give me any answers, just raised questions in my mind, stories, memories.

A friend of mine had been on the trail crew that found the bodies of the three girls killed by a grizzly at the Granite Park campground up in Glacier back in 1967. Over a bottle of Jack Daniel's one night, he told me about the body he had found. "Nothing left but bones," he kept saying softly, "nothing but bones from hipbones to collarbones, nothing but bones." And I talked to a park ranger once who had lost his tail bone and seven inches of his colon to a grizzly sow as he scrambled up a piss-fir. He had mastered an interesting sound effect to imitate the sound of her teeth on his bones, a sound he said he heard not with his ears, but through his bones. About the closest I had ever been to Lord Grizzly, though, was on my third honeymoon. My new wife and I sat on the porch of the Granite Park Chalet in Glacier, sipping unblended Scotch and watching, at the safe distance provided by our binoculars, a sow with two cubs cavorting by the side of a small lake down the mountainside. I wanted to get closer; she didn't; that marriage didn't make it back to town.

I didn't know how many grizzlies were left—six or eight hundred, at the most—and here was the dead hide of one of the last few, draped over my bed in a goddamned motel room.

"You deserve better accommodations than this, old man," I said, then choked down one of the shots. It was a beautiful piece of work Charlie Two Moons had done, but I thought he perhaps deserved forty moons more of bad medicine. I didn't know, though, that poor Johnny deserved to fry the way he had. Maybe just beaten with a stick every day for the rest of his life. Except for the occasional poached cow elk or white-tailed doe, I hadn't hunted for years, and looking at the obscenity on my bed, I quit forever. I went into the other room, away from the hide, to use the telephone.

The woman at the Friends of the Dancing Bear Wilderness

Area took my message for Carolyn politely enough, but she had trouble with my name. "Mr. Grandfather Timberland," I repeated slowly, "it's an old Native American name." She got so effusively apologetic that it drove me into a sulk. If the hunters and the Sierra Club ever went to war, I suspected I would like to sit on the sidelines and drop 81mm mortar rounds at random on the field.

I called Sarah's number, with no luck—with no hope, really. Somehow in all the confusion, I suppose I had resigned myself to the fact that I wasn't going to find the old woman or Gail. Not by myself. So I called the colonel. Since I was afraid the lines were still tapped, I wouldn't give the receptionist my name, and she wouldn't let me talk to the colonel without a name, so I gave her Jamison's name, and she put me through. When the colonel heard my voice, he said, "It's okay, Milo. The taps are gone."

"Dying helped, sir."

"Jamison told me. Both of us are somewhat concerned, Milo, about the trouble you seem to be in. Very concerned, as a matter of fact."

"I'm in so deep, sir, that if you reached out a hand for me, you'd go down too."

"Please try to remember that I am not without resources, Milo."

"Yes, sir," I said, "that's why I called. I want to hire the firm to mount a search for Mrs. Weddington and—"

"I already have some men on it," he said, "and I thought we had located them through the young girl's mother—or rather, through her telephone records; she had nothing to say to the operative who talked to her in Minot—located them at the Hilton in Seattle, but by the time we checked, they were no longer there. An older woman and a young girl had been registered under the name of Hildebrandt. The descriptions were too vague to make a positive identification. But they had paid cash, which is in itself suspicious . . ."

"The world has gone to shit, sir—"

"I beg your pardon."

"—when cash is suspicious, sir."

"It's not the world we made, Milo, just a world we have to live in."

"Yes, sir," I said. "Thanks for taking this on yourself, Colonel Haliburton."

"Please remember that it was *my* telephones they tapped, Milo," he said tartly. "But I would like to know—"

"I'll make a tape, sir, and mail it to myself at the office, and if I turn up dead, at least you'll know as much as I do."

"Not a very pleasant thought."

"What the hell, sir, I'm getting used to being dead, and I'll check back in every afternoon, sir."

"You need any expense money, Milo?"

I told him no, thanked him again, and rang off. I sat there, running the whole number back through my mind one more time, the whole knotted string of events, as I held the receiver in my hand. The dial tone didn't have any answers either. I hung up the phone, and it rang before I could get my hand off it.

"Goddammit, I hate that," I grumbled as I jerked it back up.

"Hate what, Mr. Grandfather Timberland?" Carolyn said over the wires.

"Everything."

"I got your message," she said. "I'm glad you called, I've needed to talk to you . . ."

"Where are you?"

"At the office."

"Why don't you meet me in my room?" I said, and she said she would within the hour. I went back into my bedroom, where the bearskin and the schnapps waited.

Simmons returned shortly, and when he sat down at the table in his room to clean the guns, I asked him if he wanted a drink. Since the two drinks in Stone City still sat uneasily on his stomach, he thought not, but he did wonder, shyly, if I really had done up all the cocaine.

"All of that," I said, "but there's this." And I retrieved the packet from the briefcase and chopped two large lines of the heady shit from the trunk of poor Johnny's car. Two lines, too large, perhaps, then two more too quickly. By the time Carolyn knocked on my door, Simmons was cleaning arms in a frenzy and trying to tell me his life story at the same time. He had gotten as far as his second pre-adolescent sexual experience with his third cousin by his mother's second marriage, or second cousin by her third marriage ... But when he heard the knocking, he picked up the .357 and cocked it.

"Easy," I said, "easy."

"Maybe I'm too nervous for this shit, boss."

"Maybe," I said, "but uncock that son of a bitch, Bob, and put it back on the table." He did, carefully, and I released the breath I had been holding. "Thanks."

"Sorry."

"No sweat."

Since it was closer, I went to Simmons' hallway door, stuck my head out, and whistled at Carolyn.

"Cute," she said, "lover boy."

"Lay off the lover-boy shit, okay?" I said as I stepped out of the way to let her in.

When she saw the guns scattered around the room, she stopped dead. "Are you guys starting a war?" she asked, wide-eyed.

"Finishing one," I said, then took her arm and led her into my room.

She liked the grizzly hide and head even less than she had the arsenal. I kicked the connecting door shut with my heel, and said, "Now, before you give me your latent-homosexuality and hunting lecture, I want you to know that I didn't shoot that bear, I've never shot a bear, never intend to, and it's not even my bearskin, it's a piece of evidence, in a—ah, very important case, and before you bother to ask what it's about, let me tell you that I can't tell you ..."

She held up a finger to stop me, used it to tug down one of my lower eyelids, then walked over to the table and picked up my sunglasses, saying, as she handed them to me, "It's about a quarter gram beyond reality, Milo, so put these on before your eyes start bleeding."

"Huh? Right you are," I said. "Sorry." I threw down a shot of schnapps and a glass of water, then opened the drapes and the sliding door to the balcony for a lungful of fresh air. "Hey, it's goddamned dark, for Christ's sake." And it was. Even after I took off the sunglasses.

"Busy day, huh?" she said, then took off her full-length down coat and lit a cigarette. "Nice weather," she added, "but why don't you shut the door."

"Of course," I said. "Anything for a lady. Why don't you sit down, make yourself comfortable. Can I get you a drink? Dinner? Anything?"

"You're in a good mood, aren't you?"

"Great," I said. I shut the door and drapes, and held her chair for her at the table.

"Looking good, too," she said. "You should wear a suit more often, Milo."

"Right," I said, laughing as I took off the suit coat and draped it over a chair.

"And a shoulder holster less often."

"You got it," I said, unstrapping, and I took the Airweight into Simmons.

"Maybe I'll have that drink now, boss man," he suggested. "Either that, or clean all these goddamned guns again."

"Sure. A pitcher of martinis for us, Beefeater, and whatever you want, lad—call room service."

When I got back to Carolyn, she had already snubbed out her first cigarette and started another. "I'm glad you called," she said, tapping her long nails on the table. "I've been trying to get in touch with you."

"Me? Why? I'm supposed to get in touch with you." I hadn't forgotten why I had called Carolyn—Cassandra Bogardus—but I just couldn't seem to keep it in my snowy mind long enough to mention the name. "Why?"

"Well, you know that night we were here ..." she began

slowly. "When we left, I sat in the parking lot downstairs while I let the motor warm up, and I heard about the fire, about your house, on the car radio, so I knew you were still alive. When I—ah, we left, you were lying on the bed, depleted but alive, and I wondered about the reports of your death . . . By the way, I am truly sorry about your house, Milo, I know what it must have meant to—"

"Don't mention it."

"And I wanted to apologize for my behavior that—ah, night . . ."

"Behavior?"

"I just had a childish fit of jealousy," she said, "perhaps as much directed at Cassie as at you. She is—ah, an impressive-looking woman without her clothes."

"Impressive?"

"Yes," she said, "but it's none of my business. My business is the proposed Dancing Bear Wilderness Area. A friend of mine in D.C. has gotten a line on the owners of the old C, C&K Railroad sections—some holding company out of Luxembourg—and he thinks they will go for a land swap, since most of the timber on their sections is third growth and on sidehills too steep to log economically under currect regulations. And I've been working on your deal—"

"My deal?"

"My God, you really are out of it, aren't you!" she said. "I've arranged for a plaque to be placed in Camas Meadows and come up with private monies to supplement the price we can offer, and I've also decided that those private things we talked about can be arranged."

"Private things?"

"You know," she said, snuffing out the cigarette butt, "the weekend in Seattle, the night on your grandfather's grave . . ." Even in the fading light her dark hair glistened, and a blush rose from beneath the collar of her brown satin blouse, flushed across her neck and softened the rough planes of her face.

I leaned over, brushed her cheek with my lips, then whispered in her ear, "You listen to me, lady . . ." She tried to move away but I pulled her closer. "And listen good. I am about to go fucking insane, lady, my house has been burned down, people have been trying to kill me, and I've seen enough dead bodies in the last week or so to last a lifetime, and I'm in no mood to talk about some goddamned wilderness area. If you don't tell me where the fuck Cassandra Bogardus is, I'm going to rip this ear right off the side of your head." I took a sturdy grip on her ear with my teeth. From someplace so deep in my chest that I couldn't imagine it, a low, rumbling growl rattled.

Only Simmons saved me. He came in without knocking, the martini pitcher and two glasses in his hands.

"Oops! Sorry, boss," he said, then unloaded the drinks on the table, excused himself again, and rushed out of the room as I released Carolyn's ear, straightened up, and stopped growling. At least I couldn't hear it anymore, but I felt it down there waiting to be let out again.

"Jesus Christ," I sighed, "I'm sorry, babe." But when I put a hand on her shoulder, Carolyn bolted for the bathroom, her face in her hands.

When she came out, I sat slumped in a chair at the table, feeling as small and tired as Charlie Two Moons had looked in the cab of his pickup. I had poured a martini, but it sat untouched before me, the crystal liquid still trembling in the dim light. Carolyn switched on the hanging lamp over the table.

"I'm sorry," I said, "it's been—"

But she held up her hand to stop me. She gunned the martini I had poured and wiped the tears off her tough face. Then she stood across the table from me, saying, "Don't interrupt me, Milo, please. I do not know where Cassie is, I do not know what sort of trouble she is in, and I do not think I can stand one more second of this goddamned cowboy-and-Indian shit. It is just too crazy for me." She paused to take a deep breath. "And now will you do me a favor?"

"Anything, love."

"Will you please stand up and hold me?"

I did, standing up, then lying down in our clothes on the thick fur of Brother Silvertip, held her until she finally went to sleep. I went into Simmons' room to borrow a blanket. He was watching *Blood on the Moon* with Robert Mitchum, a movie I hadn't seen since my childhood. But I didn't have time to watch it now.

"Anything I can do, boss?" he asked.

"Watch this movie for me," I said, then used his telephone to call the young lawyer, McMahon, at his home number in Seattle. He wasn't there, so I tried his office, even though it was late. He was there, but it sounded as if a party was going on around him. He had news, but not good news. Multitechtronics, Inc., was a wholly owned subsidiary of a Hong Kong import-export firm, which in turn was owned by a Bangkok holding company. A paper maze, he explained, that only more money could solve. I promised to send more money, then went back to cover up Carolyn's sleeping body.

I poured a martini and took it out to the balcony. The moon had waxed toward fullness since last I saw it, and in its quiet glow the rushing waters of the Meriwether looked like a sheet of black ice. Maybe if I took a steam bath, sweated the confusion and poison out of my bloodstream, then slept, I would know what to do tomorrow—a three-day steam bath and a long winter's nap, maybe. Sarah, Gail, poor Johnny Rideout/Rausche with his saluting son and Sally with the cancer behind her eye, Korean nightmares in Elk City, a dawn full of guns and drugs, dead bodies and fire, that goddamned Cassandra Bogardus and her windy tale of poachers who acted like a Mafia family . . .

Maybe she had already called Goodpasture in Albuquerque to tell him where the fat lady sang, maybe she hadn't lied about that. But as I thought of the fat lady, I remembered the fat cocaine dealer on the Olympic Peninsula fingering the thick plastic wrapping, the odd pinkish-gray powder, and telling me I must have balls the size of a gorilla. And the brain of an addled chicken, lizards with feathers. She had seen the black plastic and the powder before. Maybe she knew where it came from. Whatever, at least it was a place to begin again, something to do besides watch the Meriwether run its rocky, cold course to the sea.

After Simmons and I had shed our rich duds and loaded all our goods, except the grizzly hide, into my pickup, I tried to wake Carolyn, but she had fallen so deeply asleep that she didn't even stir. I lifted her limp body off the bed as Simmons tugged the bear hide from beneath her, then I laid her back in the middle of the bed. We rolled up the skin and head in the tarp, and I got the keys to Carolyn's Mustang out of her purse.

As we struggled out the side door with the heavy bundle, a pair of drunks were coming in, faces red with whiskey and cold. One held the door for us, and the other laughed and said, "Hey, buddy. Whatcha got there? A dead body?" I guess the look I gave him wasn't exactly pleasant. "It's a joke, buddy, a joke," he added lamely.

"You're the fucking joke, jerk," I said, but he acted as if he hadn't heard.

"Easy, boss," Simmons huffed.

"Right."

As soon as we managed to fit the hide into the small trunk and slammed the lid, I started to worry about it. What if it froze and cracked? Or the cold made the hair fall out? But, like Charlie Two Moons, I was glad to be rid of bad medicine, so I shoved the worries aside and went back up to leave Carolyn a note.

Love, you were sleeping hard, and we had to split. Sorry. Hope you wake from happy dreams. Brother Silvertip is in your trunk. Keep him for me, please, and if I don't come back—well, I trust you to do something appropriate to his spirit. Sorry we didn't meet in another world. Take care.

"What now, boss?" Simmons asked when I got back to the pickup.

"Listen, son, I'm sorry I don't ever tell you what we're doing until it's too late, and I appreciate your backing me up and not asking too many questions . . ."

"Shit, I trust you, Milo."

"God knows why, Bob," I said, "but trust me now. If I can't work out this shit in Seattle this trip, I'm going to give it to the law dogs and run for Mexico—"

"I ain't never been to Mexico, boss," he interrupted, grinning.

"You son of a bitch," I said to his grin. "Let's drop your rent car at the airport and head out into the sunset, Mr. Autry."

"Mr. Rodgers," he said, and we shook on it.

We made good time on the plowed and sanded interstate, kept our noses clean, stayed sober, and made Seattle by dawn, in time to catch the first ferry to Bremerton. We had breakfast in Poulsbo, then I called the number the fat girl had given me and left the message about Leroy and the basket of crabs. She called back in five minutes, suggested we meet on neutral ground on the Port Angeles–Victoria ferry that noon, no guns, no drugs because we would have to clear Canadian customs going and American coming back. "And no funny shit with hand grenades, okay?" she said with a laugh.

It took us longer to drive to Port Angeles than I had thought it would, so I had Simmons drop me at the dock, where I left him with my pickup, all the weapons and cocaine, told him to check into the Holiday Inn and wait for my call.

"Thanks, boss," he said as I stepped out of the cab.

"Thanks?"

"For not thinking I'd run with all the goods."

"Shit," I said, "it never crossed my mind."

"So thanks," he said, grinning.

Instead of searching for the fat girl, I went up to the bow to watch the ferry back away from the dock and turn into the Juan de Fuca Strait. A light mist mixed with an occasional snowflake, which melted as soon as it touched the deck, seemed to hang in the air between the lowering clouds and the gray sea as deep, heavy swells rolled down the Strait with a power that suggested they had risen in the middle of the Pacific with the sole purpose of washing down the rocky bluffs of this narrow neck of water. The fat girl came up beside me, slipped her hand into the pocket of my parka, and nestled her fingers in mine.

"Hello," she said. Her hair had been curled, her face softly made up. Even in the electric-blue down parka she seemed slimmer somehow, and in her gold-rimmed granny glasses she might have been a schoolteacher playing hooky. "No business for a while," she said, then helped me stare at the mists as if we could see the far shore on Vancouver Island.

"I don't know your name," I said.

"You can call me Monica. I've always thought of myself as a Monica. And yours, sir?"

"Carlos."

"Have you ever been to Victoria, Carlos?"

"Only in the summertime."

"Let's have lunch at the Oak Bay Hotel."

"I've been drunk there," I said. "One of my favorite places."

"I reserved a room, just in case."

"Good idea, as long as we catch the last ferry back to Port Angeles."

"No problem. We've got all the time in the world," she whispered into the rain.

Over a slow lunch in a dining room that might have been brought over from England brick by brick, beam by beam in the hold of a clipper ship around the Horn, gazing out the wide windows into a light rain that seemed British in its damp stodginess, we got our stories straight. I had been a friend of her father's when she was growing up someplace dull, Cleveland or Pittsburgh, Des Moines or St. Paul, and she had always had a crush on me. We had happened upon each other in this English village of a city so far from home. Monica had been around a bit too much to suit herself, and I was once again between marriages, and as we walked hand in hand up the carpeted stairway we trembled like children.

We nearly missed the ferry back to the States, and stood again on the bow as the mist became snowflakes. When we could see the gray form of the Port Angeles dock, she shook her wet curly hair and said, "What did you want to know?"

"The coke you bought from me," I said, "you'd seen that powder-coated plastic before, right?" She nodded carefully. "Can I ask where?"

"If this comes back on me, man, I am not just dead," she said softly, "I am bad hurt before I get a chance to die. You understand that?"

"Monica . . ."

"Carlos," she said, "goddammit," then gave me an address on West Marginal Way in Seattle, a pat on the cheek, a damp kiss. Behind her foggy glasses, her blue eyes turned dark-gray. "Good luck."

"Thanks," I said, "but I'm not afraid anymore. For the first time since all this started."

"Maybe you should be," she said and walked back toward the warm lights of the passenger lounge. Once she was safely inside, I turned back to face the black waters, the heavy, tolling swells.

It was past midnight by the time Simmons and I drove back to Seattle, but I was determined to get to the address anyway. Even though the dank air seemed to absorb the glow from the street lights, I could make out the small sign on the chain-link gate: ENVIRONMENTAL QUALITY CONTROL SERVICES, INC.

"What the hell does that mean?" Simmons asked.

"Garbage," I said, "fucking garbage."

Chapter 12

It took McMahon, the young lawyer, all day and a large jolt of cash, but by seven o'clock that evening in his office, he was able to hand me a fairly complete file on EQCS, Inc., and its president and founder, Richard Tewels.

During WWII, Tewels had served in the European theater as a supply sergeant for a motorized transport outfit. After he mustered out at Fort Lewis, and with money he said he had won in a crap game on the troop ship back to the States but which one reporter suggested had come from a black-market operation in gasoline and tires, he bought a junkyard south of Tacoma. From there on, Tewels was an American success story.

In less than five years he owned half-a-dozen junkyards, a small trucking outfit, and three sand-and-gravel pits. When the pits were exhausted, he turned them into private landfills. In 1964, outside Chicago, where he had been raised, he bought his first garbage-truck company from a small town that could no longer afford to operate it themselves. By 1972 he owned over three hundred garbage trucks and more than twenty landfills in small towns and medium-sized cities from coast to coast, and he incorporated as EQCS, Inc. He kept growing richer and richer on garbage and junk. Along with his fortune, he also collected a number of indictments, but no convictions, for possession of stolen automobile parts and illegal dumping. At the same time, he was cited for achievement by state environmentalists from sea to shining sea.

In 1976 he sold EQCS, Inc., to an international consortium, although he remained president and a major stockholder. The consortium, based in Luxembourg, held controlling interests in casinos in the Caribbean, oil tankers, wheat farms in eastern Washington, hog farms in Iowa, and the usual range of investments. In 1980 EQCS bought a small tanker ship from one of its sister corporations and converted it into a floating furnace for the disposal of liquid toxic waste. The onboard incinerators could achieve Fahrenheit temperatures above 2500 degrees, hot enough to dispose of even the dreaded chemical polychlorinated biphenyls, PCBs. The tanker operated out of Tacoma and burned waste in international waters, four or five hundred miles out in the Pacific.

Well, the information didn't cause me to see a burst of clear, absolute light, but it did give me some notion of whom I had been dealing with, running from. Starting at the lowest end, junkyards had always been perfect covers for chop shops that dealt in stolen automobile parts. Say, for instance, that you stole a Caddy worth twenty thousand; you might be able to fence it for a third of its value, but if it was cut up into body parts, you could sell it for two or three times the original value. Or say you wanted to ship some cocaine or stolen arms or hot money across the country. Why not hide it in a barrel of PCBs, a toxic liquid so deadly that some environmental experts considered even one part per million part of water as carcinogenic? And say you had been at sea burning toxic wastes on board your own ship. What sort of customs agent would crawl around in the holds of your tanker searching for cocaine?

Here I thought I had been playing gunfire games with something as nice as a large drug ring, and it turns out that I am playing hardball with a multinational corporation with a gross profit larger than two thirds of the countries in the world. Suddenly I felt even worse than I could deal with. When the father of a friend of mine found out he was dying of cancer, he went to see all his old friends and greeted them with, "Boys, you're looking at a dead man." Well, I couldn't beat them, and running would be a waste of time, but at least for Sarah's sake, I could go out in a small match flare of glory, maybe make the bastards flinch.

Or so I thought, dead as I assumed I was, as I looked at the rest of the file.

Although Tewels never gave interviews, McMahon had enough contacts in Seattle to find out that he lived in a large house on Capitol Hill, had a ranch in the Sierras west of Tahoe, a midtown Manhattan apartment, and a seventy-five-foot yacht. He was a large contributor to Seattle social and artistic organizations. He had three children—a daughter who was an off-Broadway set designer, another who was an anesthesiologist in Santa Barbara, and a younger son from a second marriage who was a tight end for Stanford. At fifty-nine, Tewels was still a nationally ranked seniors squash player.

After I went through the notes one more time, I handed them back to McMahon, then told him to get out his tape recorder. When I finished telling him everything that had happened and everything that I suspected, he whistled, then stood up. "I sure as hell hope I don't have to defend you, man," he said.

"It'll never come to that," I said. "They've covered it too neatly. I just wanted somebody to have a record, if—ah, worst comes to worst . . ."

"Sure. What about your friend in the waiting room?"

"I'm going to try to fire him," I said, "and I want you to draw me a will."

"Are you serious?"

"Damn right," I said. "There's an old woman I owe, seriously."

While he got the forms, I went out to talk to Simmons. He lounged in a chair beside a stack of tattered *Field and Stream*s, thumbing through one carefully as if he planned a long fishing trip to some distant exotic land.

"Okay, Bob," I said, "you're fired. It's over. I'm paying you off, and you're walking."

"You can pick your nose, boss, but you can't pick your friends," he said quietly. "No more of this thirteen-month-tour crap, man. I've signed up for the duration."

"You got any family?"

"A litle brother in a foster home in Denver," he said, "and two little girls living with my ex-wife down in Casper."

"Give me their names and addresses," I said.

After I noted them down, I went back into McMahon's office, where we wrote a new will that split my father's estate, half going to my son, half to the Rausche children and Simmons' little brother and his daughters.

"How about witnesses?" McMahon said, and I followed him down the hallway, where we found a legal secretary working late and a janitor. "I'll file it in the morning," he said as we went back to his office, "first thing. Now what are you planning to do?"

"You know I can't tell you."

"Right," he said. "Good luck, Mr. Milodragovitch."

"You can read about it in the papers," I said, "the funny papers."

Even though, and melodramatic as it sounded, we seemed to be on a suicide mission, I wanted to do some reconnaissance work on Tewels to see where to hit them. I had some vague notion that I could trade Tewels for Sarah and Gail if they were still alive, or use him to hurt the bad guys if they weren't. And I had to tell Simmons what was going on. He didn't say much, just "Sure, boss," and hit the cocaine a little harder. He wasn't alone. I tried to interest him in a couple of really high-priced hookers, one last touch of flesh before we went under, but like me, he seemed embarrassed by the idea.

For the next three days and nights Simmons and I put a twenty-four tag on Tewels, and he kept us busier than a one-legged man at an ass-kicking contest. The second day, I bought a couple of portable CB units and a base station and rented a camper so we would have a place to sleep and shower. I lost count of how many times we changed rental cars, how many hours of sleep we lost. And all for nothing. While we were standing tired in the constant rain or trying to stay awake as it softly drummed on the tops of the cars, Tewels maintained a busy work schedule and an even busier social life—a Broadway roadshow, a dinner party, a cocktail fund raiser for a local film society, which I crashed in my rich man's suit. I managed to stand three feet away from Tewels, sipping sparkling French water and lime and listening to him discuss the New Wave directors, whatever they might be. He was a tall, lean man, bald except for a silver fringe, and moved like an athlete.

Even as my vague notion of kidnapping Tewels evolved into a real idea, he had so many people around him that it looked as if we would have to mount a military operation to snatch him. A young man, who looked as if he had a steel lump under his arm, drove Tewels around in his Bentley. The driver lived in an apartment over the garage, but a butler, a cook, and a housekeeper lived in the house. Even the housekeeper looked as if she could climb off her broom and chop down a tree with her hard, angular face.

But about eight o'clock on the third night as I was sitting down the street from his house in an anonymous dog-turd-brown Champ, the driver came down the stairs in a gray three-quarter-length parka with a fur-trimmed hood. He opened the garage and backed out a Toyota Land Cruiser station wagon. Tewels, wearing a shearling coat, a watch cap, and heavy gloves, and carrying a briefcase, met him in the driveway, and they drove away like men with business in mind.

As I followed, I stuck the portable CB's antenna out the window and tried to wake up Simmons. "Break two-seven for Spider Man," I said several times. "You got a copy on the Russian Bear?"

"You got the Spider Man," he answered sleepily. "Over."

"Spider Man, Spider Man," I said into the mike, shaking because this felt like the right time to take them down—they weren't dressed like that and driving the Land Cruiser to take in a show, "the Garbage Man is on his way to the dump. I want the pickup, winter duds, and all the rest. Over."

"The rest? Over."

"Pineapples and them little things that play bush-time rock 'n' roll," I said, "Over."

"That's a big ten-four," he answered, laughing, "from the Viet-Vet Spider Man. Over."

"Heading east on I-Ninety," I said, "pedal to the metal, so shake it, bo. Russian Bear eastbound and down."

"Spider Man back door and down."

Simmons must have flown, because he came up behind me before we made Issaquah, flashed his lights once, then dropped back.

The traffic wasn't too heavy, and the Land Cruiser was easy to tag. We went on up Snoqualmie Pass into a light, blowing snow, then past the ski areas, which hadn't had time to groom the slopes and open the lifts yet; just before we reached Cle Elum they turned north on 903, heading toward Cle Elum Lake. I jammed the Champ into a snowbank at the exit, then dashed over and jumped into the cab of the pickup.

"Cut your headlights," I said, "and stay after that rig."

"You're the boss!"

We could have used a real snowstorm, but the light flurries mixed with the blowing snow were enough to keep the pickup invisible. "Watch his taillights," I said, "and stay off the brakes."

Then I changed into my snow pacs, checked the loads in the Browning and the M-11, stuffed two grenades into the pockets of the Kevlar-lined vest, and two extra clips for the Ingram in my hip pockets.

"Jesus, boss, what's happening?"

"I don't know, son," I admitted, "but they're going out here where it's dark and cold." Already so excited that my breathing had shifted to rapid-fire, I added, "This is it, lad."

"It?"

"Showdown city."

"Oh shit," Simmons sighed as he fumbled for the cocaine vial, which we snorted sloppily off our fists.

Beyond Roslyn, the Toyota's brake lights flared, then disappeared as the rig turned left. Simmons down-shifted and slowed, coasted up to the place they had turned. I could see a sign by the road but couldn't read it. I climbed out, ran over to the sign. VARNER AND ASSOCIATES, it said, REAL ESTATE. A number of four-wheel-drive vehicles had been up the snowy track recently. Through a gap in the storm, the brake lights blazed again about fifty yards up the hillside, and the headlight beams swung around a switchback behind the thick evergreen screen, and another fifty yards above that, I thought I could see the dim glow of house lights.

While Simmons put on his pacs, I drove the pickup on up the road until I found a place to pull off, then parked, dug through the parkas for woolen ear bands and sliced gaps in the palms of our mittens so we could get our trigger fingers out. Simmons' fingers were trembling so badly that when he checked the loads in the .357, he nearly dropped it in the snow.

"Easy," I said. "Let's see if we can't do this without blowing anybody's shit away, okay?"

"It's cold," he said.

"You can still back out, son, stay with the pickup."

"I'm scared of dying, you're scared of killing somebody," he said. "We make a great team—but we're a team, Milo."

"Okay."

We blackened our faces with muddy slush from the wheel wells, tried to grin in the freezing wind, then trotted back to the uphill track. Halfway there, we saw headlights and dove into the snowy ditch. A four-wheel-drive camper van turned up the road. We gave it a few minutes, then ran on.

After a short rest at the track while the storm seemed to intensify, we started up the frozen ruts of the road. At first we rested every twenty-five steps, trying to hold down the clouds of our breath, then every ten as we eased up the road. When the glow of the building showed up the last switchback, we stopped, walked more slowly, pushing our pacs into the snow before we shifted our weight forward. The tree trunks rubbed each other, moaning in the wind, and the branches rattled brittle and icy. When we reached the switchback, we went around it uphill, flat on our bellies, buried in the shadows of the snow-plowed berm. After another twenty-five yards we could see the front of the real estate office at the dead end of the road.

It was a wide, low log building with a parking lot cut into the slope on the side nearest us. Tewels' Land Cruiser, the camper, and a jeep station wagon were parked there. A porch with floodlights at either end stretched across the front of the building. In spite of his large, fluffy down parka, the man on the porch looked very cold as he walked back and forth, stamping his feet and slapping his gloved hands together. When he paused under the far flood, I could see his face. It was the dude in the Porsche who had wanted to get Western when I took his keys on the ferry dock. I was glad to see him again. Now we could have all the horse shit and gun smoke he wanted.

Simmons followed me as I bellied in a long loop until we were in the shadows of the parked rigs and had a clear shot at the guy's feet and legs on the porch. I extended the wire stock of the Ingram, switched it to single fire, then handed it to Simmons.

"Cover me," I whispered, "but don't switch this little bastard to rock 'n' roll."

"Gotcha, boss," he said. Even in the darkness, I could see his lips, blue and trembling.

I slithered around the side of the parking lot to the building, stood up slowly and peeked through the corner of the window in the narrow gap that wasn't covered by frost. A long office took up the front half of the building, with three desks that looked little used spaced out along its length. Tewels' driver and the partner of the guy on the porch sat at the far desk, smoking and flipping the pages of a property album. Three doors were set into the back wall, but only one of them had light underneath it. The guy on the porch came in, complaining about the weather, and the driver cursed, zipped up his parka, flipped up the hood, and went outside.

I went on around to the back of the building, struggling in the deep, drifted snow, the Browning automatic freezing to my hand. The drapes were shut in the lighted office, but they didn't quite reach the bottom of the sill. I couldn't see much—two sets of hands smoothing out a map, another set counting bundles of money—and couldn't hear anything but the rumble of their voices.

The odds didn't look good, but I heaved on through the drift to the far corner and peered around. The driver had stepped off the porch out of the wind to take a leak. From the wavering pattern of his smoking stream, it looked as if he were trying to write his name in the snowbank. That made the odds better. These guys might be tough in town, but this was my frozen turf. He was too busy melting snow and chuckling like a little boy in the wind to hear me as I crept up behind him. I jerked his hood back and laid the barrel of the Browning against the side of his head as hard as I could. His ear burst like a rotten plum and he fell into a snowbank, where I clubbed him again.

He had an S&W 9mm automatic on him, which I unloaded and pitched into the storm, then I took his parka, ripped out the drawstring, tied his wrists to his ankles, gagged him with his handkerchief, then buried him in the snow. I crawled around the porch and back to Simmons.

"Okay," I whispered, putting on the driver's parka and tucking the fur-lined hood around my face. "Are you ready to hit it?"

"One more toot, boss, okay?" he said. It was windy and imprecise, but we did the best we could. I couldn't tell if the tears in his eyes were from the cold or the fear. "I'll be fine," he said.

"It's not your war," I whispered as I took the grenades out of my vest pockets.

"It's never anybody's war, boss," he muttered through chattering teeth.

"Okay," I said, trading him the grenades for the submachine gun, "I'm going through the front door. You stand to the side, and if I shout 'Bob,' you pitch the grenades in on the right-hand side of the room."

"What about you?"

"I'll get behind a desk," I said as he straightened the pins. "Let's do it."

We crawled around the rigs onto the porch and across it under the front window to the door, where we stood up, Simmons with his back to the wall. He lifted one snow-covered eyebrow, and I turned the doorknob, stepped inside.

They let me get three steps into the office before the big guy raised his head to tell me to shut the door, but three steps was all I needed to get to the center of the narrow room. I thought they might give it up when they saw the ugly shape of the Ingram, but they didn't. They leapt to their feet, reaching for iron instead of the sky, and I chopped them down with two soft, sputtering bursts.

I tried to hold low, to wound instead of kill, and it worked for the smaller man—his right leg crumpled under him and he flopped to the floor—but I held the burst too long and the Ingram kicked up and away and stitched the big guy right up the middle, blood and goose feathers exploding up his chest. He would never get Western again. The silenced, subsonic .380 rounds hadn't made much noise at all, but the big guy crashed into a file cabinet and a large metal ashtray as he fell. I knelt to get the small wounded man's piece as the door to the rear office opened. I put a short burst under the chin of a man I had never seen before, blew him backward into the room. I was in the office before his body hit the floor, the blood-lust growl tickling my chest.

Four men sat on the far side of a long table, their faces and clothes splattered with blood and brain tissue, sat very still, their hands poised, their heads cocked, as if listening for something, perhaps the muffled drumming of the dead man's heels on the carpet. It was all I could do to keep from emptying the clip at them.

I stepped past the rattling heels—that soft, final sound that had echoed in my head since the night of my father's suicide—and got my back against the wall. The little guy in the front office still had a piece on him. "Mr. Rodgers," I shouted out the door. "I want you to count to ten, and if you don't see two pieces on top of the desk, I want you to pitch the grenade in."

"Holy shit," he grunted, "gimme a minute!"

"One," Simmons said loudly, "two . . ."

"There," the wounded man said as he clunked his piece loudly on the desk top.

"Now the other guy's," I said.

"Right, right!" He groaned with the effort, and I heard another clunk before Simmons got to seven.

"Mr. Rodgers," I said, "unload them and pitch them outside. And when you're done, drag the little guy in here where I can see him."

After a moment Simmons backed through the doorway, dragging the man by his collar. He clutched his thigh tightly above his bloody knee, and his right foot dangled off at an impossible angle. Simmons propped him against the wall of bookshelves in the back of the room.

"Now let's see what we've got," I said.

Tewels sat at the far left, a scrap of gore stuck to his forehead, sweat and blood leaking between his eyebrows and down the side of his nose, where it dripped off his neat mustache and splattered on a Forest Service map. The man next to him looked like a Hollywood actor who once had hopes of playing leads but who had drunk himself into character roles that featured close-ups of his corrupt, bloated face, his mean, frightened eyes, and his silver thatch of hair. Beside him sat a very scared Oriental man, his slim frame draped in a silk suit, not a Japanese or a Chinese, but perhaps a Malaysian.

On the far right sat a pale blond man in his thirties with the weak chin and beady eyes of a bureaucrat, but except for a flicker of his pale eyelashes, he didn't look impressed. "You were supposed to be dead, you fucking clown," he said calmly, "and now you are."

"I've got a family," the character actor said, his oddly high voice full of tremor, the whiskey sweat rolling off him.

"We can work something out," Tewels offered quietly.

I put a short burst into the bookcase over the blond man's head, said, "Shut up, gentlemen," then watched the paper fragments drift down in the silence. "Over here, Mr. Rodgers," I said as I moved to the other side of the doorway, tripping over the feet of the dead man, just a brief stumble, but the blond man looked extremely amused. "Get this piece of shit out of here," I said to Simmons.

When Simmons got hold of his feet and tugged, the bloody back of his head popped softly loose from the carpet, like the sound of a top-feeding trout sucking down a May fly. The actor looked as if he was going to faint at the sound, and I had to struggle to hold my dinner down.

"You stupid drunken jerk," the blond man said. "Your nerves just aren't up to it anymore, Milodragovitch."

"Would you please shut up," Tewels said. He looked worried.

"Cover them," I said to Simmons as I moved the Ingram to my left hand and drew the automatic with my right and handed it to him. "If anybody moves," I added, "gut-shoot the albino."

"Ain't got the heart for it, old man," Blondie said as I put a fresh magazine in the submachine gun.

"Please," Tewels pleaded, and the actor mouthed the word silently.

As I traded guns with Simmons again, Blondie said, "You clowns juggle too?"

"Us old cowboys just don't seem to scare anybody anymore," I said to Simmons, then shot a brass ashtray off the table beside the blond man. After all the stuttering pops of the Ingram, the roar of the 9mm automatic sounded like a major explosion in the office. And it was true—we didn't—except for the actor, whose eyes rolled back into his head as he buckled out of the chair in a dead faint.

Everybody wants to be a hero these days. When I glanced at the actor's fainting fit, the blond man's hand snaked under his coat while he dove for the corner. It was so easy it wasn't even funny—I shot him twice in the ribs in mid-dive, then once in the head when he hit the floor. But the little wounded guy, he was a pro; he came up with a hideout gun, a dinky .25 automatic, two tiny pops that bounced Simmons off the wall. God love him, though, he pulled his weight. Like good old Roy, he shot the gun out of the wounded man's hand, but unlike the movies, the fragments tore his gun hand to shreds and blew his face off. Simmons fell to his knees, lifted the Ingram, and took out the Oriental with a burst as closely spaced as a close-range shotgun blast, throwing him out of his chair and into the wall. Tewels had stood up, his hands raised as high as they would go, but Simmons started to pull down on him, too.

"Please, Bob, no," I said as he pitched forward onto his face.

I did what I had to do, business as usual in my crappy line of work, made Tewels kneel, his fingers laced behind his head, his forehead leaning against the bookcase, then I made sure the dead were really dead. Nobody at home in Blondie's head, the little guy had swallowed his tongue, choked on his own blood, and the actor's buttocks jiggled like jelly when I shook them with my foot, unconscious. Then I went to check on Simmons.

The first round had flattened against his vest, but the second had caught him in the face, a black hole the size of a bee beside his nose, the flattened slug lodged somewhere beyond his brain pan. As I lifted him off the carpet and held him on my knees, the dark, echoing rattle had already begun. I said those empty words you give the dying—I'm sorry, I am a jerk, a fucking clown—but he didn't hear me, heard only that windy rush down the last highway. When he got there, I closed his eyes, covered his face with his useless vest. Then went back to work.

Just so we got off on the right foot, I put a round two inches above his bald head. "Just so we know where we stand," I said, "you're one nerve twitch from dead."

"Yes, sir," he said.

"Get up and take your clothes off, slow and easy," I said, and he did. He might have looked athletic in his expensive clothes, but naked he was just another skinny old man. "Tie Captain Faintheart's hands behind him with your belt." When he finished that, I ordered, "Outside." Then we went out into the storm.

After I let him sit cross-legged in the snow with his hands behind his head for a few minutes, I lit a cigarette, and said, "Answer quick, answer right. Maybe I won't blow your fucking head off, maybe we'll get through before you freeze to death."

"Yes, sir," he said, shivering, "anything you want. We can work something out. I promise.

"Maybe," I said. "Who's Captain Faintheart?"

"An EPA official from Denver, Sikes."

"And the blond guy with the big mouth?"

"Head of security," he said, "an ex-CIA cowboy, Logan."

"The Oriental gentleman?"

"A representative of the holding company that owns EQCS."

"And what was supposed to go down up here tonight?"

"We give the EPA official twenty-five grand and a list of dump sites where we can't stand the heat," he said, "and he makes sure we don't get any."

"Nice business," I said, "garbage. Who's John Rideout or Rausche?"

"Nobody. A driver. He picked up waste material on the East Coast, the Midwest, the South, hauled it out here."

"Cassandra Bogardus?"

"She applied for a secretary's job at our downtown office, and when Logan's men checked her out, we discovered she wasn't who she said she was."

"A reporter, huh?"

"Not even that," he said, "just a nosy rich girl who sometimes billed herself as a wildlife photographer, but when Logan found out her employment application was a fake, and that I had . . . ah—"

"—been taken in by a pretty face and big tits?" I said, and he nodded. Scared as he was, he wasn't generating enough body heat to melt the snow on his bald head. "You're not the first," I assured him. "Why plant all the arms and drugs on Rideout before you killed him?"

"Logan killed him," he said quickly, "Logan. To discredit anything he might have told the Bogardus broad. 'Disinformation,' he called it."

"And why try me?"

"Nobody knew who you were at first, and Logan said he was just being tidy, but when we found out you were a security guard, I think he wanted to kill you out of contempt."

"Nice people you have working for you."

"They used to work for me," he said sadly, "but somewhere along the way I discovered that I really worked for them."

"An innocent bystander?"

"Sort of . . ."

"You didn't mind killing people at long range with your goddamned toxic dumps," I said, "but when it got down to gunfire, you didn't like it?"

"Something like that," he said, then added, "I don't know how much more cold I can take."

"I'll let you know," I said. "Where's Sarah Weddington?"

"Who?' he said, so confused and afraid that I knew he was telling the truth. As much as I hated it: the truth. "Who?" he asked again, pleading.

"Nobody," I said. "Help me get your driver and let's go back inside."

"I can't move," he said, shaking so hard that the tiny drifts of snow scattered off his head and shoulders.

"You better figure out a way to make it," I said, then went around the corner and dug the driver out of the snowbank. By the time I had dragged him onto the porch and up to the front door, Tewels had made the first step. I dumped the driver inside the door, then went back out for Tewels and carried him into the back office. As he struggled into his clothes, I collected all the weapons I could find, even the grenades out of the pockets of Simmons' vest, and made a sloppy pack out of the driver's parka.

"Any whiskey around?" I asked Tewels when he had his coat on. He reached behind the second shelf of books, ran his hand down it until he came up with a half-pint of vodka. He had a quick snort, then offered it to me. I shook my head, and he hit it again.

"Guy that runs this place drinks," Tewels explained.

"Do they actually sell real estate?" I asked, and he nodded, sucking on the bottle. "They keep a camera in the office?"

"Probably," he said.

I followed him as he checked the desks in the front office—he walked like a man who had played his last game of squash—where he found a Polaroid and three packs of film and a flash attachment. I took several pictures of Tewels and each of the dead bodies, with the maps and the lists and the money, with the sleeping face of the EPA official, used all the film. Then I cleaned up the table, rolling up the maps and the papers, checking the briefcase full of money. Tewels had fallen into a chair behind the table, still shivering, still sipping at the vodka.

"Can you get this place cleaned up and dispose of the bodies?" I asked, adding, "Mister garbage man."

"I've never done it before," he said, "but I know the drill."

"Listen," I said as I unholstered the Browning, "I think you've been in the business from the beginning."

"The business?" he said, looking at the pistol.

"Chop shops, stolen cars, the whole number, and when you

saw a way to run drugs and arms and dump poison illegally, I think you jumped at the chance. The greed business. And if you try to pull this innocent-bystander shit on me again, I'm going to spend the next hour blowing chunks of you all over the room. Do you understand?"

"Whatever you say."

"Let's go back to 'Yes, sir,' " I said. "I sort of like that."

"Yes, sir," he said, but didn't mean it. I should have left him in the snow a bit longer. "Whatever you say."

"Can you clean up this mess without involving the law?"

"No problem—sir."

"You better hope there's no problem," I said, "because this is how it's going to be. These maps, these photos—they're my get-out-of-jail free card, okay? As long as I'm alive and healthy, untroubled by people on my tail, and as long as all my friends are, too, you guys can go on with business as usual ..." Tewels looked surprised. "What you do in your business, that's the government's problem, not mine. I got into this mess by accident, and tried to work it out to save my ass. We could have made a cheaper trade a long time ago, but you bastards were too busy trying to be tidy by blowing me away—"

"Logan," he said.

"Logan's ass," I said. "And there's one other thing—I'm taking the twenty-five grand and buying a contract on one of your children ..."

"Leave my children out of this," he said, alcohol-warm now, "they don't know anything about this—ah, side of the business."

"I'm buying a contract, and you better hope I live a long time Tewels, and die in bed of natural causes because if I don't, your business life is over, and one of your kids turns to mincemeat," I said. "Understand?"

"Yes, sir."

"Don't try to get in touch with me," I said. "I'll see you at the Stanford–Washington State game in Pullman a week from Saturday—wait by the main gate for me, alone—and let me know if you're having any trouble arranging the details."

"Of course," he said. "Pullman. A week from Saturday."

"Now I'm going to fix the telephones, and the transportation—I'll leave the rotor of your rig by the sign post at the bottom of the hill—if I were you, I'd wait for at least an hour, warm up, before I went down for it. Okay?"

"Yes, sir," he said, but his eyes were as cold as his heart.

After I jerked the phone lines out of the wall and threw the sets into the snow, I loaded up the weapons and the briefcase. Tewels and I didn't bother to say goodbye. After I went out the front door, I paused long enough to give myself some insurance against insincerity. I pulled the pin from one of the grenades and left it leaning against the front door, planning to take ten or fifteen minutes of his hour buried in a snowbank across the road. If he stayed put—fine, I would put the pin back in. If he didn't—fine, too. After I lifted the distributor caps out of the rigs, I tucked myself into the snow across the parking lot.

He only waited five minutes and came out carrying a scoped hunting rifle—I should have checked the other office; I shouldn't have threatened his children—came out in such a hurry that he didn't even hear the handle pop off the grenade. Maybe I had seen too many dead people lately, maybe I didn't want it to end like this—whatever, I rose without thinking out of the snow, screaming "Get down!" into the wind. But he made his choice, turned and fired from the hip, plowing snow at my feet, and he was working the rifle bolt when the grenade blew him off the porch. Even lying sodden and bloody in the snow, his hands searched for the rifle as I ran the twenty yards to him.

"No deal," he whispered as I knelt beside him, "no deal."

"That's the trouble with your business," I said, "there's always somebody ready to make a deal." But I don't think he heard me.

Chapter 13

There is this little lake down in Wyoming, outside of Pinedale, Fremont Lake, and it is supposed to be nine hundred and some odd feet deep. After I called the night emergency number for EQCS and finally got hold of the assistant director of security and told him he'd better get a cleaning crew for a blood bath up to the real estate office, I headed home by way of Fremont Lake.

Two nights later, by the light of the waxing moon, I sat in the dark center of the lake in a small rubber raft dropping firearms over the side, dropped them all, then the ammo and the grenades, the rest of the cocaine, and a half-full pint of schnapps into the cold black water.

I had heard once that a colleague of mine down in the Southwest, a private investigator by the name of Shepard, who, when asked by a journalist if he carried a gun in his work, replied, "Hell, no. If somebody wants to shoot old Shepsy, they're gonna have to bring their own gun."

Me too, Shepsy, me too.

Then I went back to the motel in Pinedale where I had been lying low watching television, the newspapers and an unopened half-gallon of vodka sitting on the dresser. Some of us had made the news, right, but only after the cleaning crew had dealt with the garbage. Tewels' yacht had been found floundered in the Juan de Fuca Strait, his body missing, supposedly lost at sea, along with the director of security and a distinguished Oriental businessman.

I waited a day, then called Sarah's number in Meriwether, but when Gail answered, I hung up. I didn't want to talk to them yet.

A few days later I saw the EPA official's picture in the Denver *Post* above his obituary. His heart had failed him, it seemed. None of the other deaths had been reported, the bodies probably run through an automobile crusher, then ground into pellets and shipped to Japan. Or gone to sea in a floating incinerator. Simmons, God rest his soul, deserved better than that, to be treated like junk, then built into a Toyota or something. But I was going to have to live with that, and wonder if he might have lived if I hadn't been so far behind the cocaine.

Washington State and Stanford played their football game while I was in Pinedale, but it wasn't on television, so I didn't see it. According to the newspapers, though, my son had five tackles, sacked the quarterback twice, and blocked an extra point. The Tewels boy had caught three passes and scored the winning touchdown on a reverse. I wished the boys a better world than their fathers had made.

For another week or so, I wandered around Wyoming, Colorado, and Utah, leaving copies of the maps and papers, a few of the Polaroid prints, and detailed tapes in safe-deposit boxes and with small-town lawyers. Occasionally I called Goodpasture down in New Mexico to see if he knew where the fat lady sang, but she hadn't called. And I didn't open the vodka.

I found myself beginning to like motel rooms too much, spending too much time staring at my stubby gray beard in crooked mirrors. It was time to come out of the cold. When I called the new director of security at EQCS, I congratulated him on his promotion, then we made our deal, slightly different from the one I had made with Tewels, now that I had seen the dump sites marked on the maps, but business as usual. My untimely death wouldn't close them down, but it would cut into their profit margin.

A Mexican stand-off, as Charlie Two Moons had said.

Finally, the fourth or fifth time I called Goodpasture he had a number for me, an all too familiar number, so I headed north home with Mexico on my mind.

Back in town, I waited a few days until I could catch all of them at Sarah's at once. It was one of those gray, still afternoons when the light seemed filtered through old glacial ice, but I could see their shadows moving against the sheer drapes of the solarium. I slipped the front-door lock and eased up the stairs. Pausing at the top, I could smell the sweet stink of marijuana, herbal tea, and freshly baked cake, and could hear their laughter, that stoned laughter I knew too well myself, laughter without cause or purpose, and I guessed that on an afternoon much like this one, the ladies had gathered and come up with their insane plan. Somehow they would save America from toxic waste and corruption, and I would be their stooge, dance to their lies, dream of love in their arms. I didn't have the heart to be angry.

Without sunlight, the large room seemed adrift on some Arctic sea as I stood in the doorway. Carolyn saw me first, rose from the wicker couch, moved two steps toward me, then turned, her face in her hands, and went to the far corner of the room to stare at the weak light. Cassie suddenly became very interested in the pattern of the Oriental rug at her feet, and Gail busied herself picking up cake crumbs with her fingers and lifting them carefully to her mouth. Only Sarah Weddington had the guts to look at me, and even her eyes kept slipping away.

"Hello, Bud," she said quietly. "Would you like a drink?"

"No, ma'am," I said.

"An explanation, darling?" Cassie asked lightly as she lifted her lovely face, one eyebrow arched.

"It's not necessary," I said.

"Take off your coat and stay awhile," Gail offered with false hospitality.

"I won't be here that long," I said. "I just came by to tell you ladies how it's going to be." I walked over and tossed a list of names and addresses on the coffee table between Sarah and Cassie.

"What's this?" Cassie said. "I don't know any of these people."

"They're the innocent bystanders," I said, "the children. And you and Sarah have twenty-four hours to set up trust funds—don't be stingy—monthly payments until they're twenty-five, then the rest of the money goes to them. Okay?"

"Of course, Bud," Sarah said, looking at the names.

"Now just a minute, darling," Cassie said to Sarah. "Who are these people, anyway?"

"A teen-ager in a foster home in Denver," I said, "two little girls in Casper, two little boys, and a little girl with a cancer behind her eye on Vashon Island . . ."

"Rideout's," Cassie murmured. "What is this—blackmail?"

"Let's just call it conscience money, okay?" I said. "I've seen your Dun and Bradstreet rating, love—you can afford it."

"Not if you don't explain, darling," she said softly.

"If I do that," I said, "then you'll either have to go to the police or become an accessory after the fact to half-a-dozen assorted felonies."

"Leave Cassie out of it," Sarah said, almost weeping. "I'll take care of it, Bud, for the memory of your father . . ."

"Just leave my father out of it," I said more harshly than I meant. "Please."

"My conscience is clear," Cassie said, almost laughing as she touched her smooth, lovely throat.

"I'll help however I can," Carolyn said from the window. "I wasn't in at the beginning, but I could have stopped it—should have stopped it."

"Can you forgive us, Bud?" Sarah said weakly, her fingers kneading at her temples.

"I don't think so," I said. "You dug up my father's memory, old woman—"

"Oh, to goddamned hell with your father's precious memory!" Gail shouted as she stood up and kicked the corner of the coffee table, splashing tea out of the china cups. "My father's dying . . . everybody dies, eventually. That's not the point."

"What is?" I asked.

"Those bastards," she said, "they poison the air, pollute the ground water systems—thousands of children will die needlessly, horribly. Have you seen pictures of them? Their skin rots, their blood fails, they're born dying. Don't you care?"

"I guess so," I said, "but I do know that because of this dumb stunt you pulled, eight people died in front of me. Maybe a few of them deserved it. I don't know. That's not my decision to make. Or yours. You people made a terrible mess and now you have to clean it up."

"Eight?" Cassie said thoughtfully, smiling. "And how many did you personally blow away, Mr. Milodragovitch?" At the window, Carolyn turned as if to say something, but kept her mouth tightly shut. "How many?" Cassie demanded sweetly.

"Enough to last me a lifetime," I said.

"Eight!" Gail shouted, storming around the room, pounding floorboards with her boots. "Eight? What's eight against eight hundred thousand? Eight million? The whole goddamned planet earth, huh?"

"You sound like an officer I knew in Korea," I said.

"Well, by God, it is a war."

"Right now," I said, "I'm having trouble choosing sides."

"We chose you, darling," Cassie said, "because it's your war too, because—"

"Bullshit," I said, "you chose me because I was convenient, because you knew I could be manipulated. With your kind of money, you could have hired a battalion of lawyers and private detectives."

"They did try," Carolyn said from the far side of the room, "but nobody was very interested in taking on a multinational corporation."

"And how did you do, darling?" Cassie asked.

"Not very well," I said. "I got out alive. You people are still alive. Call it a draw."

"A draw?" she said. "Didn't you find out anything?"

I lied to keep from laughing. "Hell, lady, I'm still not real sure what this was all about."

"You want to know what it was all about?" she said. "Well, let me get my coat and I'll show you what it was all about."

"In a minute," I said. "I've got two other things to settle first." I took out an envelope and tossed it into Sarah's lap. "There's your credit cards, ma'am, my expense sheet, and your bill."

"Her bill?" Cassie protested as she stood up. "For what?"

"I did what I was hired to do," I said. "You're the bitch in the rented car, which is all she needs to know, and the guy in the yellow Toyota, his name is, or was, John Rausche. A long-haul trucker. An ex-con. He got blown to pieces over in Elk City, Idaho, then fried." I turned to Cassandra Bogardus. "And, sweetheart, you killed him with your little dumb-ass number in Seattle, you killed him the first time you let him touch that great body of yours . . ."

"Oh, for Christ's sake," she murmured, "that little worm."

"You should be more careful where you put your mouth, lady," I said, and Cassie shuddered. "By the way, Mrs. Weddington, you'll also be getting a rather large bill from Haliburton Security. They spent some time looking for you after you and Gail pulled your cute little disappearing act."

"I'll take care of it, Bud," she said, her face so gray I hoped she'd live long enough to get it done. "I'll take care of everything."

"Well, are you quite through?" Cassie asked.

"One more thing," I said. "I want my bearskin back."

"It's still in my trunk," Carolyn said.

She came across the room, still not looking at me, and Cassie and I followed her to the door. Behind me I heard Sarah moan my name, the clatter of Gail's boots as she went to comfort the old lady. This foolishness had claimed enough victims, so I went back.

"It's okay, Sarah," I said as I touched her wet cheek. Gail tried to shoulder me out of the way, but I didn't move. "It's okay," I repeated. "What's done is done. In a couple of weeks, I'll call. We'll have tea and crumpets. Okay?"

"Please try to forgive me, Bud."

"Ah, there's nothing to forgive," I said. "Your heart was in the right place. I just wish you hadn't chosen me."

"Me too," Gail complained. "Nothing got done."

"Hush," Sarah said, her finger lifted, "hush, child."

When I got ouside, Carolyn and Cassie were struggling angrily with the grizzly hide. I gave them a hand. We got it out and into the bed of my pickup.

"Well, are you ready now?" Cassie said sharply. "To see what this is all about." I nodded sadly. "We'll need snowshoes," she said.

"Nope."

"Nope?" she said, her hand to her cheek.

"The illegal dump in the old mine above Camas Meadows," I said, "has been cleaned out."

"Cleaned out? How do you know?"

"I went up yesterday," I said.

"But why, what . . ."

"I had a list of their illegal dumps in seven Western states," I said, "and I made a deal."

"A deal?"

"Right," I said. "I traded that list for cleaning up that one dump . . ."

"It wasn't yours to trade," she said, her face pinched with anger.

"Sure as hell was," I said, "and I traded it for my life, Sarah's life, Gail's, even your piss-ant, rich-girl ass."

"But why—"

"I had some notion I might like to see your goddamned face, lady, when you saw the empty mine galleries, but the truth is, it's not worth it."

"What's not worth it?"

"Spending two hours in the same pickup with a piece of trash like you."

"You son of a bitch!" She drew back and slapped me as hard as she could. I let her. It felt all right, washed the last bit of her out of me, the memory of her touch.

Carolyn turned around, pivoted neatly from the hips, and dropped Cassandra Bogardus in the snow with a perfect right cross. We laughed as we watched her scramble to her feet, moving backward, frightened by the small violence and the tiny trickle of blood out of the corner of her mouth, her green eyes gone gray, no glitter left.

"And you know, Cassie," Carolyn huffed, "if you don't do what Milo said about the children, I'm going to follow your ass around and knock you down every day for the rest of your stinking life." Cassie nodded dumbly, then fled into the safety of the mansion. "God, that felt good," Carolyn said, her flat cheeks flushed. "If only I had done that when I first found out what sort of crazy crap she had in mind."

"I knew I was being taken for a ride," I said, "but I hoped she would be at the end of it."

"Men," she snorted. "Ah, but what the hell, I was a fool too. Once you wouldn't turn loose of your—that is, your grandfather's—timberland, she convinced me that whatever happened to you was your fault. I'm sorry."

"Not as sorry as I am, love."

"What about it?" she said suddenly.

"What about what?"

"The deal I offered you the last time I saw you."

"I've made my last deal," I said, "but I appreciate your persistence."

"We'll get it eventually, you know," she said. "You can't get a draw with the government."

"Over my dead body," I said.

"God, I should have broken the rules," she said, "stayed at your house all night that night, fucked you to a frazzle, then gotten you to give your word at a weak moment. Isn't that the way it works out West? You can take a man's word to the bank?"

"Trigger's stuffed, love, and Gene Autry owns a baseball team," I said. "Now that the dump is gone, you people shouldn't have any trouble making a trade for the C, C&K sections, but you have my word on this—you'll never get my grandfather's land."

"You're going to be bitter about all this, aren't you?" she said, reaching for my cheek with her cold hand. "I like the beard."

"You bet your sweet ass, lady, I'm going to be bitter."

"How long?"

"As long as it takes."

"So what now?"

"Chores," I said, brushing her hand away, "then I'm heading south, down to Mexico, try to grow old peacefully in the sunshine."

"So it's all been for nothing?"

"Almost nothing," I said. "An EPA official down in Denver recently died, a fellow named Sikes. Get some of your hot-shot environmental lawyer buddies to check into his estate and his recent decisions. That should keep them busy for a few years, maybe even clean up some garbage in the process."

"Sikes," she said. "Thanks."

"For nothing, babe."

"However you want it, Milo."

"And, babe . . ."

"Yes?" she said, pulling the hood of her jacket up against the cold.

"Nothing," I said, and we left it like that, went our separate ways, either because of or against our better judgment. You always hate to lose a good woman, one you might love for a long time, but she wanted to save the wilderness to look at it, and I wanted ... well, I wasn't sure anymore what I wanted, maybe just an end to confusion.

When I knocked on Tante Marie's door in the fading, ashen dusk, she answered it wearing a long woolen robe with curlers in her hair. Over her shoulder, I could see the television set. A *Hawaii Five-O* rerun. She recognized me, saw me glance at the program, then said, "One must study corruption to defeat it."

"And take the occasional rest from the crusade," I said.

She nodded without smiling. "Can I help you?"

"You already have," I said, handing her the deed to my grandfather's three thousand acres, "and this is my end of the bargain."

"What is it?"

"Camas Meadows," I said, "where the bears used to dance."

"What?"

"That was the deal," I said, "Camas Meadows for Charlie Two Moons' name."

"I'll be damned," she said, digging her glasses out of her pocket.

"Sometimes even coyote tongue speaks without joking," I said, "and there's no need to thank me."

"I hadn't planned on it," she said, her eyes like wet black stones.

"Goddamn," I said, "you knew about the mine, didn't you?"

"The mine?" she said blandly.

"Jesus Christ, lady," I said, amazed, "when the gunfire starts, I want to be on your side." But her small smile told me I hadn't bought a thing.

"Let me tell you a story," she said. "Once upon—"

"Lady," I interrupted, "I've heard enough stories lately to last me a lifetime."

She was too busy rechecking the deed to pay much attention to my departure, but as I turned the pickup up the South Fork Road to spend one last night among my grandfather's ashes, I saw Tante Marie in my rear-view mirror. She still stood on the front porch, and at a distance it seemed as if she was dancing.

The road had been plowed over the divide and down to the old mine, but it was still hairy. I liked the idea of the crooked bastards out in the snow, putting tire chains on garbage trucks, but I suddenly realized that it was just some working stiffs out wrestling in the cold while the real bastards sat in warm offices on leather chairs. They hadn't done a great job at the mine, but at least the leaking drums had been removed and some of the toxic puddles shoveled up. Not a victory, not even a draw. God knows how much poison had already seeped into the ground water.

I parked at the mine and got out my snowshoes and pack. I set the grizzly hide on a pair of plastic saucers, then hiked like a coolie down the unplowed road to the edge of the meadow. There, I dug a great circular pit in the blue, glowing snow, then built as big a fire as I could find deadfall wood. I sat for several hours as the fire burned down, listening to the wilderness. The nearest wolf was probably in Canada, and the coyotes snuggled warm in their dens, so that night was silent except for the crackle of the fire. When it had burned down to embers, I shoveled them aside, then dug a shallow hole in the thawed earth and rolled the bearskin into it, then built another fire on top. When I had coals again, I baked a couple of potatoes in aluminum foil and grilled a large T-bone steak I had picked up in town. I didn't have much appetite, though, and threw most of the meal back into the fire, an American offering, a backyard barbecue.

I don't know what I planned to dream wrapped in my sleeping bag—sweet dancing, perhaps—but if I dreamed, I didn't remember the visions. When I woke, I felt as purified as I was ever going to feel, so I loaded up and hiked back to the truck.

The next week I finished my chores, sold my lot to the first cash buyer, and used some of Tewels' money to hire the best criminal lawyer in the Northwest for Billy Buffaloshoe and to take Abner and Yvonne out to dinner. They wanted to get married, but some goddamned Social Security regulation kept them from the altar, so they took up living in sin. I had a dull, sleepy tea with Sarah and a sullen Gail. Sarah showed me the trust-fund papers. They seemed fine. And she said Cassie was coming around, but as far as I knew she never did. Gail told me that next year there would be a government regulation to prevent the dumping of liquid toxic waste in landfills, but I just laughed at her, tried to explain that they would fight it in the courts until the government backed off. Then it was her turn to laugh, an unpleasant, naïve sound that brought tears to Sarah's eyes.

After that I put Meriwether in my rear-view mirror, heading south with something over forty thousand dollars in my kitty, planning to measure it out slowly in Mexico until I came into my father's estate.

I detoured through Seattle, though, with five thousand in an envelope for the former Mrs. Rausche. When I parked in front of her house on a dingy Sunday afternoon, John Paul, Jr., in a bright red parka that looked new, and Sally, with a white patch over her eye, were playing some game with rules only they knew, running from one edge of the sagging porch to the other, then freezing in place.

When he saw my pickup, the boy ran out to the driveway and gave me a crisp salute. Then he recognized me, even behind the beard. "You're a private," he said shyly, "you're supposed to salute me."

"Sorry," I said and complied. "Is your mother home?"

"She's gone to the store with Baby Luke," he said as Sally crashed into his back.

"Will you give this to her?" I asked, and Sally peeked under his arm. "It's from Captain Rausche's friends."

He took the heavy envelope out of my hand, weighed it in his. "Will you tell them 'Thank you'?" he asked.

"I will," I said, and we exchanged salutes again.

I went south like a gut-shot deer, breathing hard.

My intentions were the best, my reasons endless. My hometown had died inside me, and I craved sunshine and simplicity. I made it as far as Red Bluff, California, where I gave up, turned around, headed home, back into the heart of one of the worst Montana winters in years. Some things you can change, some you can't. A few months after the government put the regulation against liquid toxic waste in landfill into effect, they suspended it. For further study, or something.

I still have my beard, though, and haven't had a drink since the night Simmons died. When I see myself in a barroom mirror, I look like a ghost of my former self, and I see myself a lot as I tend bar at Arnie's across the street from the Deuce, work the day shift and swamp out the bar at night. Sometimes old Abner comes in for a short beer, but not too often because Yvonne gives him hell about it. Sometimes Raoul comes in for a laugh, sometimes the colonel to offer work, which I refuse. Carolyn even dropped by once. Her offer was harder to refuse, but I managed it. The poor postman, who somehow started all this, comes in occasionally, but he has lost his job and his wife, and doesn't have much to say after the third or fourth drink I turn down. I am not tempted. I live close to the grain, avoid even the appearance of evil, forgive all things, live alone in the tiny swamper's cubicle beside the alley, keep my nose clean.

I have learned some things. Modern life is warfare without end: take no prisoners, leave no wounded, eat the dead—that's environmentally sound.

Fifty-two draws closer every day, and with it, my father's ton of money. So I wait, survive the winters, and when the money comes, let the final dance begin.

James Crumley was born in Three Rivers, Texas, and
spent most of his childhood in South Texas. He currently
teaches creative writing at the University of Texas at
El Paso and summers in Missoula, Montana. His earlier
works include a novel of Vietnam, *One to Count Cadence*,
and three detective novels: *The Wrong Case, The Last
Good Kiss,* and *Dancing Bear*. Mr. Crumley is at work
on a novel about Texas.